Dear Reader,

Thanks so much for coming back to the world of Glory. This book isn't so much about small-town life as it is the things we learn from the family of community. How it makes us stronger than we know, holds us up even when we let them and ourselves down. This book is about learning to forgive ourselves and finding one's true place in the world, and best of all, being able to give and receive love knowing you're worthy of it. That seems like such a simple thing, an obvious thing, but for a lot of us, it's not. It's something we have to learn, something that has to be proven to us time and again, as our hero and heroine learn.

I enjoyed making this journey with Damara and Byron, and I hope you do, too.

Much love,

Sara Arden

Also available from
Sara Arden
and HQN Books

Return to Glory
Unfaded Glory

SARA ARDEN

UNFADED GLORY

Recycling programs
for this product may
not exist in your area.

HQN™

ISBN-13: 978-0-373-77932-1

Unfaded Glory

This edition published by arrangement with Harlequin Books S.A.

For questions and comments about the quality of this book, please contact us at CustomerService@Harlequin.com.

Printed in U.S.A.

For Nicolase Mallat
and things both spoken and unspoken.

CHAPTER ONE

BYRON HAWKINS HAD an earworm.

Most people got them at one point or another—a Top 40 hit they couldn't escape, a catchy ad jingle, a children's song heard one time too often. A bit of auditory flotsam that's busywork for the brain, a refrain that plays over and over.

Byron had such a loop, but he wasn't lucky enough to have anything as innocuous as the last song he'd heard on the radio. He had the screams of his team as they died.

Their terror and pain was always with him whether it was a damning whisper or a roar that sounded like the army of hell.

He knew it was no less than he deserved for his failure. If he hadn't given the order to pursue the guerrillas, they'd have all made it back to camp. They'd have gone home to their families at the end of the mission.

Instead, they were ambushed and tortured.

Instead, he was the only one who went home.

And Hawkins knew it was his fault no matter what the incident review board had to say about it.

It had been a mistake from the beginning to believe that he could be a good man, that he could redeem himself by sacrificing for his country. Byron Hawkins had always been better at taking life than saving it.

He'd been a fuckup for as long as he could remember; nothing was ever good enough. So he'd stopped trying, and life was easier when he didn't care—when he didn't bother to try to fit himself into a box that was labeled "supposed to" or "should have."

When he didn't give a damn, he didn't have responsibilities he couldn't handle. No one trusted him, and no one paid for his inevitable mistakes.

It was a mercenary's life for him. No attachments. No responsibilities. A way for him to channel all the destruction that roiled inside him like a hurricane.

The voices were especially loud tonight—the screams—they always were before a mission, but here in the darkness, he could silence them. He could shut off the outside world and hone all his highly trained senses on one target—the mission. As an "independent contractor" for the Department of Defense, he never had to be responsible for another life again.

Unless he was ending it.

He silenced the howls of his fallen brothers. He drowned out that song in his head as he moved through the darkness toward his target—the Jewel of Castallegna.

The Jewel was being kept in the Carthage National Museum in Tunisia. It would be no easy feat to get in and out with a national treasure, but breaking and entering was a skill he'd acquired during his delinquent youth.

He didn't ask his betters how a gemstone could serve the DOD. That wasn't his job. His job was to acquire the item and bring it home. He didn't give a damn what they were going to do with it.

Byron entered through the front door. Security

rolled in staggered shifts and there were only three officers since the museum was closed to the public. He'd tranqued an officer in his car before he'd come on duty, and taken his keys. Easy as his granny's pecan pie.

Until he heard voices coming from the first chamber. He flattened himself against the wall and peered through the door.

Two men had cornered one of the most beautiful women he'd ever seen. She was petite, but he could tell from her stance that she could hold her own. She'd been trained. Krav Maga, perhaps. She was poised for a fight. Her eyes were a most curious shade of blue, and her skin was dusky and golden. It was too bad so much of it was covered by her black fatigues. She looked ready to do battle, and Hawkins had to admit it didn't get much hotter than a gorgeous woman with a thigh holster and a utility belt.

"You know the Jewel should never leave Castallegna," one of the men said.

He swore under his breath. There would be bodies to dispose of. Byron wouldn't be much of a ghost if he couldn't get in and out without a trail of blood a mile wide in his wake, and he could tell this guy wasn't going to let the Jewel go without a fight.

He hoped he wouldn't have to dispose of the woman, but he would if she stood between him and his mission. He wasn't just a trained killer; he was a born killer.

"The Jewel *isn't* going back," the woman answered defiantly.

"I can't kill you yet," the man said, sadistic glee lighting his cruel face. "But I can hurt you."

Byron knew he had to act. The woman had the Jewel or she knew where it was. He launched himself from his hiding place and snapped the big man's neck with a single fluid motion. He dropped like a stone, and the other would-be jewel thief sprang to action. He hurled himself toward the woman. Hawkins would've saved her, but she saved herself. As he watched her seamless movements taking the other man down, he realized he'd been right in his assessment: Krav Maga.

Hawkins was impressed.

Even though she'd subdued the other man instead of killing him, he wouldn't make the mistake of underestimating her.

She didn't seem afraid of him. In fact, she looked almost happy to see him.

That didn't bode well, not at all. It was almost as if she were expecting him, but if that were the case, that would mean his cover had been blown. If she thought he was someone else, maybe he could use that to get her to hand over the stone.

"Thanks for the assist," she said.

Her voice was melodic and sweet with an accent he couldn't place. She wasn't Tunisian—it was almost Greek. The dossier said the culture and the people of Castallegna were a blend of the two. He wondered if she was a rebel or a patriot. He could tell from the fire in her eyes that she burned with one cause or another.

It would be easier if she was just a jewel thief, an unscrupulous antiquities dealer. Those could be bought off—not so much when it was a cause.

"Don't thank me yet, sweetheart. I'm here for the Jewel." He flashed a slow, lazy grin that belied the urgency of the operation.

She smiled, baring all of her straight white teeth at him. "You're looking at it."

"You're shitting me." There was no way, no way that this woman was the Jewel of Castallegna. His eyes narrowed, and he assessed her with a particular intensity.

"No, Mr. Hawkins. I would never do that. I'm Princess Damara Petrakis, also known as the Jewel of Castallegna. We better get moving. The last thing we need is to get caught with a dead body on our hands."

She knew his name. She had been expecting him. *Damn it.* This screwed all of his plans. "That's going to be a problem. I only made provisions for one."

"They didn't tell you the Jewel wasn't a stone?" She arched a dark brow.

"No." And Hawkins knew why. As a private contractor, he could decline an assignment. His handler, Daniel Renner, knew that Byron would decline this one if he had all the information. He wouldn't—couldn't—be responsible for another person's life. Renner didn't seem to understand that anyone under his care was more likely to die than be rescued.

Damn him. Damn him straight to hell. Renner knew what he'd been through in Uganda. Knew why he'd left the army. He knew it, and he hadn't cared. The DOD wanted this woman on American soil whatever it took, whatever the cost to Byron.

He swallowed hard. Hawkins was a soldier to the marrow. He knew how this worked. The sacrifice of the few for the many, but this wasn't what he'd signed up for. He was willing to give his own life, and some nights when the screaming in his head wouldn't stop, he prayed it would be his turn to give it. He owed his team that.

But he couldn't be responsible for someone else's safety. Not again. Not after Uganda. If Renner had dispatched him to kill the two men on the floor in front of him, he would've accepted that gladly, but this… He couldn't do it.

The petite woman seemed to know his inner turmoil. "Whatever is going through your mind, you can't leave me here."

Her hand was so small, so delicate on his arm, but he knew she was fierce.

"You don't understand. I planned a water exit in a small fishing boat that's only big enough for one. It's hours from Tunis to Marsala by water. How long before there are others looking for you? Before they start watching the airports in this region? I only have papers for one."

"Your Mr. Renner already provided me with documents. I won't complain about the accommodations." She looked down for a moment. "Please. My country—"

"I can't be responsible for you. That's how people die," he confessed. He didn't want to lay himself bare like that to someone he didn't know, but he'd never see her again. And, for some reason, he needed her to know that he wasn't leaving her behind to be cruel. It was the only kind thing he could do for her.

"I'll die or worse if you don't take me with you." She cocked her head to the side and one lock of her hair came free from her long braid. "And of course you're not responsible for me. I'm not a child. But you can help me. That's what you do, isn't it?"

"What I do is kill people," he said, as if that wasn't clear.

"And for that, I am grateful." She nodded, wearing an earnest expression.

He scrubbed his hands over his face. She wasn't giving up; she wasn't afraid. So why was he? He'd only ever failed one mission before. His last one—and he'd failed because no one came home. Not even their bodies for their families to mourn.

Byron couldn't help but insert her face into the macabre tableau. The burning, the screaming… Or even her pretty face made stark in death, framed by the black wings of a body bag. God, he was sick. So sick and rotten inside. He couldn't help her. Help from him was no kind of help at all.

If he left her behind, this fearless princess, it would be Uganda all over again. He kept seeing her beautiful face bloody and beaten…. He'd heard her attacker: *I can't kill you yet, but I can hurt you.*

Byron Hawkins supposed there was some decency left in him yet, some goodness that had hidden itself away from the shadow that lurked inside him. The tactician part of his brain said he had to leave her. Their probability of survival was cut in half without a clean escape. But he knew with a certainty that if he left her, there would nothing clean about his escape. His hands would be covered in one more person's blood.

Only logic told him they might be anyway. By taking her with him, he was accepting responsibility for her. She'd said she wasn't a child, but she was an innocent, no matter how fast or hard she could punch. He was the one with combat experience; he was the one who'd be making the calls. And he was the one who had to live with her voice in his head if he failed.

Even as he debated with himself, he knew what his answer would be. Dread curled like a poisonous snake in his gut, ready to strike.

FOR ONE HORRIBLE MOMENT, Damara thought her savior was going to leave her behind. She could see his eyes harden with what must have been resolve; then they were filled with so much pain. Something awful had happened to this man and sliced him so deep there was nothing to cauterize the wound. It was obvious in his every movement, but most especially in the darkness in his eyes. It struck Damara as strangely beautiful.

Yes, he was definitely a killer. He'd snapped Sergio's neck with the swift and easy brutality of a predator. She hadn't been lying when she'd said she was grateful—Sergio was her brother's head security adviser. A pretty title for what amounted to head torturer. She needed this Byron Hawkins to make her escape, and, in doing so, to save her country from Abele.

And she knew there was more to Hawkins than this machine he'd made of himself.

Damara found herself intrigued by him, by his pain. It didn't hurt that he was handsome and strong. He dwarfed her, a giant, deadly wall of lethal power. What woman wouldn't find that attractive?

Damara had to remember she wasn't just a woman. She was a princess. In her heart, there was only room for her people—her country. She understood what it was to live a life in service. She also understood that she'd do whatever was required to get herself out of Tunis.

"It's ten minutes to the port of La Goulette, but I plan to make it in five. Let's go."

Relief flooded her. He would help. She followed him outside and he led her through some well-groomed shrubbery to where he'd hidden a Ducati.

He handed her the single helmet, and she took it gratefully.

"It's a 1199 Panigale R. Wish I could take it with me," he said, a certain amount of wistfulness in his voice.

"Did you steal this?" She eyed him.

"What do you think?" He mounted the bike, swinging one long, powerful leg over the side.

She supposed that didn't matter. Damara had more pressing problems. The seat was tiny, and he dwarfed the machine the same way he dwarfed her. She didn't think there was any way she was going to fit on the thing, but Damara had said she wasn't going to complain about accommodations and she wouldn't break her promise.

Especially not when he could still change his mind and leave her behind.

If she didn't fly off the back end of the bike. She was very certain that on this bike lay the path to some horrible maiming.

"Don't be shy now, Princess."

She'd never heard anyone say *princess* in that way before. It made her shiver. It wasn't reverent or at all proper. In fact, it was rather intimate. As if she was his princess to do with as he pleased rather than a head of state he'd been contracted to escort. She wasn't sure if she liked it or not.

His arm snaked out and wrapped around her waist as he hauled her onto the front of the bike. As he revved the engine, he said, "Hold on."

She was barely aware of the speed or even the scenery as it melted into swirling colors at the edges of her vision.

The man holding her dominated all her senses.

He was a solid wall against her back—his body was immovable like a marble statue, but he exuded heat like a bonfire. Even when she'd been surrounded by bodyguards in the royal palace, she'd never felt as safe as she did right at that moment. It was insanity. They were tearing through the streets, barreling toward even more danger. Damara was about as far from safe as she could be.

Only she was almost out of Abele's reach, and that felt amazing, too. It made her giddy, a false sense of freedom. She knew she'd never be truly free—she had a duty—but it would be a gift to be able to serve without being under his cruel thumb.

When she tried to stop thinking about the strong man who held her, she couldn't help but focus on how fast they hurtled through the air. She'd swear that the bike wasn't even touching the road. It was either the bike or him.

She breathed deeply, centering herself and pushing down her fear. Damara could smell the salt and the sea, something that never failed to ground her. Strangely enough, it seemed to be coming from him more than the air around them.

Their bodies swayed and twisted with the bike as it

shot through the streets and alleyways, and for a moment, Damara could swear she was riding the wind. That thought somehow made it better. The wind was her friend, or so she'd thought as a child. It reminded her of the time she'd launched herself off the small cliff at the summerhouse, leaping into the wind so it could carry her safely to the lagoon with the bright blue fish below. Her nanny had almost had a stroke, but Damara had been so confident that her friend the wind would cradle her gently until she slipped into the clear waters. And she supposed she was lucky that it sort of had.

The colors and scenery slowly untangled into recognizable things as Hawkins decelerated the machine. They emerged on a small hidden beach that stank of fish guts and gasoline. Damara had been to Tunis and La Goulette numerous times, but she'd never known anything like this was here.

Well, what had she expected? To leave a secured international port from a monitored dock?

She saw the boat that would be their mode of transport. He wasn't kidding—it was going to be a tight fit. She bit her lip. It was true that she'd trained hard for the skills that she had, but she wasn't used to hardship or discomfort.

You can do this.

She would do anything she had to do to stop Abele and save Castallegna, she reminded herself.

"Get in and lie down. I'll cover you with the tarp until we're clear."

Damara did as she was told. The boat stank like old fish and must, and she pulled her shirt up over her nose. The roar of a small motor soon rattled the hull, and Damara didn't know how long she lay there under the tarp as still and quiet as she knew how to be until he pulled it back from her face.

The first thing she noticed was the sky. The stars were big and bright, like glittering holes burned out of the pitch—breathtakingly beautiful. She could smell the salt in the air again, and the ocean around them seemed so black and fathomless, except for the pale ribbon of moonlight the shone down like a winding road over the inky waves.

"There's no way we can make it together to Marsala in this. There's a cargo ship anchored just over there that's headed to Marseille. It'll be close quarters, dirty and dank for about twenty hours, but I think it'll do the job."

Twenty hours? She could do this. Damara was used to sitting in on political dinners, parties and other things where she had to be still and quiet. This was just more princess training. She turned her attention from the sky to where he gestured. "How are we going to get aboard?"

"Captain is a friend. I got in touch with him before I dumped my cell. You're not carrying any electronics, are you? Phone, iPod..."

She shook her head. "No, I knew they'd be able to track me."

"Smart girl."

Pride swelled and bloomed at his praise. She didn't even know him, and after this she'd never see him again. It didn't matter what he thought of her as long as he got her to the States.

"He's going to linger there for the next twenty minutes, and we have to get aboard and down in the cargo hold before any of his crew sees us. So I need you to do exactly as I say when I say it. Can you do that for me?"

"Yes," she agreed easily.

He maneuvered the boat up next to the cargo ship, and the sound of the small motor was drowned out by the idling growl of the giant engines of the ship. A rope ladder had been left hanging down the side for them.

She grabbed hold of the ladder, the rope abrasive on her palms. For all of her training, she still had the hands of a princess. Damara wouldn't complain; instead she would just do as he instructed. She tried to be as quiet as she could, remembering her ballet lessons and balancing her weight so she didn't flail and clang against the side like some alarm alerting everyone to their presence.

When she pulled herself to the top, she heard voices and she ducked her head, still clinging to the rope ladder. She looked down at Hawkins.

What's wrong? he mouthed.

She made a talking motion with her hand, and then held up three fingers to indicate the number of voices she'd heard.

He put his head down for a moment, and then he began to climb. She would have shimmied back down the ladder and into the boat, but she saw it had already been set adrift. They were well and truly stuck.

Damara made herself as narrow as possible while still holding herself steady, and he started moving up the ladder behind her, his feet and hands on the outside of hers.

Even though Damara was used to warm temperatures and to heat, she wasn't used to *his* heat. His body was so hard and hot—even with the layers of clothes between them, his skin seemed to burn her.

She tried not to think about it—the way she fit against him, the way the hard planes of muscle pressed against her, how small and safe she felt, even dangling off a rope ladder hanging over dangerous waters.

As he moved higher, she became very aware of another part of his body that was just as hot, hard and insistent as the rest of him. Her cheeks ignited, and she knew that even in the dark, her face would be scarlet.

He didn't stop to apologize or make excuses or even acknowledge all the intimacies that were now between them. This was just a job to him and his arousal was just another bodily function.

Damara didn't know him, but she knew his kind. He may be there to help her, but he was still a mercenary. Still a man paid to kill. She rather imagined a man like him would have to be cut off from attachment to anything. Even himself.

She exhaled heavily and pushed all of those thoughts out of her head. She didn't have the time or the luxury to think about anything but escape, if the muffled sounds of a struggle were any indication.

Damara bit her lip to keep from calling out to him.

Every second dragged on for what felt like hours as doubt and fear filled her until he reached over the side and grabbed her arm to help her up. His knuckles were bloody, but he was otherwise unharmed.

The image of his hands, though—it burned itself into her brain like a brand. They were broad and strong, scarred, purposeful. They were the hands of a man who'd had to fight for everything he had. The way he moved, helping her, still using those hands even though he'd split his knuckles open, it was as if he didn't even notice the pain, if there was any. It was as if he'd simply chosen not to feel it.

Damara found that impossibly noble.

And it made her blush hotter.

She had to stop thinking of him as a man and think of him as what he was—a means to an end.

Another echo of voices spurred him to action, and he lifted the cover off a lifeboat so they could crawl inside.

She could barely see him in the darkness, but the moon was bright enough overhead that a tiny bit of light shone through the canvas tarp. He held a finger up to his lips to indicate she should stay quiet.

Something sharp needled her back and hip. Damara wanted to stay still and silent, but it quickly became agony. Hawkins seemed to know and he pulled her tight against his body.

Time stopped again, just as it had on the ladder. She was stiff and frozen, but this time his fingers pushed her hair out of her face.

Those same bloody, damaged hands touched her gently, soothed her. This man said so much without saying anything at all. It was all there in that one simple gesture.

You're safe.

I'll protect you.

And she believed he would.

There was a part of her that didn't want him to protect her. Part of her that wanted him to be a bastard. She didn't want to get caught, but she couldn't stop thinking about his hands. What they'd feel like on the rest of her body, what they'd look like on her skin.

Her face was so hot now she was sure that her cheeks would explode. She was embarrassed by the direction of her thoughts. It was all just fantasy anyway. She'd read too many forbidden books and been denied reasonable human contact for too long all in the name of purity. Her body might be untried, but her mind certainly wasn't.

Damara shifted carefully to make herself more comfortable, but she was at a loss for what to do with her arm. If this was a lover's embrace, she'd have clung to him, but he was a stranger. It was as if her own arm was this awkward part of her that didn't belong on her body.

"It's okay." His breath tickled against the shell of her ear. "You can touch me. There's nowhere else to go." His voice was so low, she could barely hear it.

Heart hammering against her chest, she did as he suggested and wrapped herself around him.

The hard length was still there and it occurred to her that it might be a gun instead of— She was such a silly girl. She'd been so caught up in the fairy tale of being a princess he had to save, she'd imagined this whole attraction between them like some stupid movie. She'd even romanticized his indifference. Another reason why she had to get her head back in the game. She couldn't afford to be a princess now. She had to be a leader. Damara had learned there was a big difference.

Except, he went through the motions of pushing her hair out of her face again. It was a caress, a touch for the sake of touch.

"Sleep, Princess. It's a long ride to Marseille."

She didn't bother to tell him that there was no way she'd be able to sleep. Not with his nearness, his heat, the adrenaline still coursing through her veins from the events of the day. Or the possibility of being discovered.

Damara tried not to notice how strong he was, tried not to think about how good he felt under her hands, his strength wrapped around her. No, she was certain she'd never sleep. Especially when he'd said, *It's okay, you can touch me.* It made her think about touching him. A lot. Being touched by him.

What if his hand strayed just a bit, and what if she arched into his touch. What if— No, there was to be no sleep for her.

But she was wrong, because it was some time later that she was startled awake by gunfire.

CHAPTER TWO

THE SOUND OF SEMIAUTOMATIC gunfire launched Byron into high alert. He'd been enjoying the feeling of holding Damara in the dark and the quiet. It was as if there were no other people in the world but them. She'd been pliant and warm, and she smelled of things like hope, things he dared not name. She'd quieted that buzz of guilt that played almost constantly in his head.

He heard yelling now but no return fire. They were being boarded.

They'd been at sea for several hours and piracy was more common in the waters to the east of them. The shipping lane they were on was largely unmolested. He'd made sure of that.

Stomping, banging on the side of the ship and loud voices echoed through the tiny space. He recognized the language as Russian. Byron only had a rudimentary knowledge of the language. But there was a heavy presence of Russian mob on Cyprus and in Greece, so he'd encountered several factions in his work for the DOD.

But as of yet, he didn't have any intel that they were involved in piracy—at least not outright. They were subsidizing some of the Somali crews but not Russian crews. Shit, this was about to get dicey. The imagery of her face peering out from the body bag haunted him.

Just let me keep her safe. Just let her live through this.

When she started awake, he pressed his palm over her mouth gently to keep her from shrieking. "We've been boarded, but everything is going to be fine. Just remember to keep quiet and do as I say," he reassured her.

Her eyes were wide and luminous, still so trusting.

He started processing their situation from every angle—each scenario that was within the immediate realm of possibility. He strategically moved them around the chessboard, trying to figure out the safest and most expedient course of action.

Until he heard *Castallegna.*

Renner had told him there were international and unsavory buyers for the Jewel.

For Damara.

He'd kill them before he'd let them touch her.

A calm came over him. His heartbeat slowed and the peace he'd been seeking filled him. Because this was his purpose; this was what he'd been born to do. And in this, he could keep her safe.

"Don't leave me," she whispered. It was the second time she'd sensed what his actions would be before he took them.

"I'll be back." He shifted carefully, hoping to make his exit from the lifeboat unseen.

"What if you're not?" Damara asked.

"Then stay here. And when you dock, get to the American Consulate. Ask them to get in touch with Renner."

She grabbed his hand.

He smiled in the darkness. "This is what I'm for, remember?"

"There's too many of them to kill them all," she pleaded.

"I like a challenge." He didn't say "trust me" because that was the last thing she should ever do, but this, this he could handle. Byron slid out onto the deck and crouched behind the boat, watching. No matter what he decided to do, he had to do some recon to see what exactly they were dealing with.

He saw the captain of the ship—his contact Miklos Sanna speaking with one of the boarders.

"Ah, Grisha! You should have told me you were coming. There was no need for the display of firepower," Miklos said as he clasped the man's shoulders.

The man he'd called Grisha, a hulking beast with narrow eyes, grinned. "I need to let my dogs run free now and then. Or they will get soft." He shrugged. "But I don't have time for pleasantries. Do you have the Jewel?"

Miklos nodded to the stairs that led to the hold—where they would've been hiding had the deck been clear when they'd boarded. "They should be below."

That bastard, Byron thought, even though he wasn't surprised.

"They?" Grisha arched a simian brow.

"You didn't think the princess escaped Tunisia alone, did you? A hardcase mercenary helped her. American."

"A cowboy?" Grisha said the word as if his mouth were full of marbles, as if his tongue couldn't wrap around the syllables.

"A real John Wayne motherfucker," Miklos agreed genially. "He won't be bought. You'll have to kill him."

Again, Byron wasn't surprised at the betrayal—that's what people did. The only person that could be counted on was oneself. And even that was sometimes sketchy. He thought about their options again.

Damara was right. He couldn't kill them all—at least not while he still had to keep her safe, and that was his number one priority. It would be a dangerous game of cat and mouse to hide until they made port. It was possible Miklos would weigh anchor until they were found.

The Russians had several smaller boats that were unmanned while the crew was aboard the *Circe's Storm.*

He had enough C-4 he could create a diversion and disable the cargo ship, but that wouldn't stop the other boats from pursuit. From the position of the stars, Byron judged that they were about ten hours away from Marseille.

There was one other option.

He could let Grisha take Damara.

As soon as the thought entered his head, everything in him screamed in protest—except for his logic.

Grisha wanted her to control Castallegna. She was a princess schooled in diplomacy. She could keep herself safe for however long it was until they made port and they could escape. Byron didn't see any other way that didn't put her life at risk. Grisha wouldn't kill her.

That's not to say it wouldn't be uncomfortable for Damara. But they were outgunned and outnumbered here. A firefight on open water could lead to her injury or her death. It was like when an animal had locked its jaws on you, you didn't pull away because the animal would just bite harder. You pushed yourself into its mouth to force its jaws wider until you could break them.

He didn't like his options, but they were all they had.

Byron had to make decisions with his head, not his feelings. His rage had gotten his men killed in Uganda, and he hoped that this would save her.

If not, he'd die trying.

Byron crept back to the lifeboat and found Damara gone.

A string of profanity hovered on his tongue, but he didn't dare speak for fear of raising alarm and alerting them to his presence.

Where was she? Had they caught her already?

What if she was afraid?

But what he really meant was what if he had to add the sounds of her screams to the loop in his head.

"You don't have to kill anyone," he heard her say. Pride and anger swept through him. He was so proud of her for being strong and brave, but he was angry that she'd revealed herself to protect him.

Byron knew he was completely at odds with himself. That it was okay somehow for her to face Grisha only if he told her to, but the fact that she'd done it on her own made it foolhardy.

He watched her. Even in dirty fatigues, she had a regal bearing.

"I think I do. You belong to me, you see." Grisha grinned.

She flashed him a look that made the temperature

around them drop several degrees. "No, I don't. You haven't paid my brother for the privilege. Until you do, anything that you do to me could be considered an act of war on Castallegna."

"A tiny country with no allies." Grisha shrugged.

She smiled. "Perhaps. Or perhaps my brother has had other offers for my hand from stronger, more powerful men than you. There are sheiks and princes who would marry me for Castallegna's diamond mines."

Grisha was still smug. "Then why are you not with them?"

"Don't underestimate what I will do if you make me angry." Damara may have been small, but she'd positioned herself in such a way that she appeared to be squaring off with the big Russian.

"Where is your guard dog? The American?" Grisha demanded.

"How should I know? I paid him to get me passage out of Tunisia. I don't need a keeper."

"If he comes for you, I'll kill him."

Miklos scanned the area. He seemed to sense Byron's presence. "I think you should stay aboard the *Circe* until Marseille."

"Why is that?" Grisha asked.

"I know the American is still on board. I feel it in my bones. Here, we control the situation. There would be a lot of, shall we say, *opportunities* for him between here and Italy on a smaller craft."

"I see your wisdom. If the princess is dead, I can't very well marry her. We'll take your cabin, Miklos."

DAMARA HADN'T SEEN any possible way out of the situation that didn't involve revealing herself. Maybe it was naive of her to trust Hawkins as she did, but she knew in her gut that he'd come for her.

She could stand a few hours of Grisha's company—she'd had to endure it at home all the time. Of course, she'd always had her bodyguards and her brother and it had always been in a formal environment. But she was sure she could maneuver him to treat her gently at least until Hawkins could get to her.

Damara followed behind Grisha, wondering exactly how hard she'd have to hit him in the back of the head and with what to slow him down—if such action became necessary. She was thankful she'd asked her bodyguards to train her and even more thankful they'd agreed.

Abele would've had them put to death if he'd known. He'd thought it unfeminine and a sin for a woman to know such things. Of course, it had suited his purposes when hiring a contingent of female bodyguards to keep her secluded from men.

The captain's berth was small, but it had been outfitted with every luxury. Damara knew immediately that the cargoes transported on this ship weren't always on the manifest. If the Russians knew Miklos well, then he must have been transporting people, as well.

One of her objections to Grisha was that he'd been linked to sex-trafficking rings and she found that repulsive. How long before the young women of Castallegna began to disappear with him as their crown prince? No one would ever be safe.

It was times like this she wished she had more power. She wished she was more than a princess.

"Plotting my death?" Grisha asked conversationally.

She studied him for a moment. "Of course not. It's no secret I don't want to marry you, but I don't wish you dead."

"Why *don't* you want to marry me, Damara? I have money and power. I can trace my lineage back to Catherine the Great."

She doubted his royal lineage, but she wasn't going to say so. "You're a bad man, Grisha."

"All great men are."

She shook her head. "I must marry for my people. You know that. What would you bring to Castallegna? Convince me." If she could keep him talking, maybe she could buy some time.

He grabbed her and pushed her up against the wall, but she shoved at his shoulders. "I said convince me for Castallegna. My body may come as a gift with the responsibilities of my people, but it has nothing to do with the decision of who will lead them."

She prayed he heard her. His hands were just as strong and just as damaged as Byron's, but they were not noble and they turned her stomach. Damara held her body stiff and immobile. She didn't close her eyes, and she didn't look away from him. Not even when he dipped his head to kiss her.

Grisha paused when they were eye to eye. Damara didn't flinch, didn't hide from what was about to happen. Something he saw there caused him to pull back. "Perhaps you are not as useless as your brother says."

"Perhaps not," she agreed.

"How is it that you make even your acquiescence sound like a challenge?"

"I assure you, it's not. You're obviously the one with the power. You've caught me. I have nowhere to go and no one to turn to for help," Damara said calmly.

"But you're not afraid of me."

"Should I be? Would you like me to be?"

"You said I was a bad man." He studied her.

"Just because you're bad doesn't mean I should fear you. Fear is a waste of imagination. You will do what you must and I will do as I must."

He eyed her, hard. "I meant what I said about the mercenary. I will kill him." As if she'd somehow said otherwise.

"I've no doubt. Which is another reason I can't marry you. You kill someone because they disagree with you? My father had a dream for Castallegna."

Grisha snorted. "A dream of democracy?"

"Yes. Being born into a family doesn't make a person any more fit to lead than any other."

"I did not expect to drag you to the captain's quarters to talk politics." Grisha scrubbed a hand over his face.

"No? What did you expect? To haul me down here, make me cower in fear and then force yourself on me so I'd be so humiliated that I would have no choice but to marry you? If my brother told you that would work, you are sadly mistaken."

"And yet if we were on Castallegna, we would be legally married if I did."

"That's another thing that's gotta go." Tendrils of fear unfurled in her belly, but she ignored them. It didn't matter what he did to her. She was still the Jewel of Castallegna. But her brother and men like him were convinced that her only worth lay between her legs. No man would want her if she wasn't a virgin.

"What if I agreed to all these things you wanted?" Grisha surprised her.

"In writing? A contract that would be for all the world to see?"

"No, not in writing." He unbuttoned his shirt and she gritted her teeth, fear blooming like a rancid flower. But he didn't pounce on her. Instead, he showed her the tattoos on his chest, his belly. His arms. His shoulders. "I already have a contract in writing, you see. *Bratva.* If I am ever found unworthy of the ink on my skin, it will be removed for me."

She found herself looking at the art on his skin. The stars on his chest. The church with the spires on his belly. "I don't understand."

"These are what mark me as a bad man." He pointed to a marking in Cyrillic she didn't understand. "The first man I killed for The Brotherhood."

"And you want to sit on the throne?" She was incredulous as to why he would think she'd choose him to lead her people. To be her husband. He'd admitted to killing a man. Not just one, but the first of many.

"It could be good for both of us, Damara. When you lead men, you must make choices, hard choices, and sometimes people die. If you order your army to war or you set your people against me, you're sentencing them to death."

"You can't offer me peace with one hand and threats with another." Why didn't anyone understand that?

"It's how things are done."

"No." It would not be how things were done. She'd

never agree to marry him. Never. No matter what he did to her.

"I don't want to hurt you, but I will." His voice was a growl, low in his throat.

"As I said," she said, her mouth dry as the desert, "do as you must." Damara tried to focus her mind, find her center and remember her training. He was bigger than she was, but she had speed and strategy on her side.

She studied her surroundings surreptitiously looking for a possible exit and weapons.

He lunged for her, and she grabbed the lamp on the nightstand, but it had been secured to the table in case of rough waters. So she used the table and the desk as leverage to deliver a roundhouse kick to his head.

It stunned him long enough for her to do it again, but he still didn't fall. The man's head must have been fashioned from concrete.

The door to the room swung open, and a flower of blood bloomed on his chest where Byron shot him with a .38.

Grisha clutched at his chest and staggered forward, but Damara didn't stay to watch him fall. Byron grabbed her hand and pulled her out into the hall.

"This was not how this was supposed to go down." His hand was warm and strong; his very presence made her feel as though everything was going to be okay. "But next time I tell you to stay put, stay put."

"It was the only way."

"I know that. But I had a plan." He yanked her up the stairs toward the deck.

"What's the plan now?" she asked as she hurried up the stairs behind him.

"Run like hell."

She didn't like that plan very much, but it seemed that it was all they were left with. An explosion rattled the ship and she screamed, but alarms drowned out the sound.

"Don't worry. It's forward aft. We'll be exiting toward the rear."

"What did you do?"

"Answers later. Running *now,*" he commanded.

The sun was overhead by this point, and the crewmen who saw them were too busy responding to the emergency and keeping the ship afloat to bother with them.

When they got to the side, he started to climb over. "I'm going to jump and then you're going to jump, okay? I'll catch you."

Damara froze.

"Don't bail on me now, Princess. You've faced down ruthless thugs like you were at a cotillion. A little leap is nothing."

He landed on the deck of one of the Russian's boats. Then he emptied the .38 into the rear of the boat ahead of him, damaging the rudder. Hawkins held out his arms for her. "Hurry. They can still use the lifeboats, and they might catch us. You have to jump *now.*"

Damara's brain screamed at her to keep moving, but her feet were rooted to the spot.

Castallegna. She had to do this for Castallegna. If she was caught… She couldn't finish the thought. They'd blame her for Grisha's death. They'd punish her for it, and she knew from what her bodyguards had told her that Abele's head torturer had nothing on the Russians.

She remembered again from when she was little—the wind would carry her safely. Like it had then, like it had on the bike…and it was Hawkins. He'd kept her safe before. If he said he'd catch her, he'd catch her.

She jumped. Time stopped, and for Damara, it was as if she'd flung herself out into nothingness rather than over the side of a boat down to waiting arms on the deck of the small yacht. Terror froze her limbs, but he caught her easily and deposited her on the deck. She didn't want to let go of him; her arms stayed around his neck even as Byron started the boat. Soon, *Circe's Storm* grew smaller in the distance behind them, as did the smoke billowing up from her. So far, no one was in pursuit, but the captain knew where they were headed and a radio or a satphone would be much faster than a boat.

"You know we'll still have to be on our guard. It'll be best if we choose another port. Maybe Barcelona. It's closer. If the fuel doesn't hold, the wind will."

She leaned against his shoulder, knowing she should release him but unwilling to just yet. "Thank you for everything that you've done."

"You're not safe yet."

"Safer than I was."

"You did good in there, Princess. You're going to be okay." He pulled her closer for a minute. When he released her, she finally let him go.

Again, his praise shouldn't have been so warm, like basking in the sun, but it was. She'd never been good for anything but getting her brother what he wanted. Pride swelled at the notion that a man like him thought she could handle herself.

But she remembered the look of surprise on Grisha's face. The sound of the gun as the bullet exploded out of the barrel and into the man. She knew it had to be done, but that didn't make it any less horrific.

Damara shivered.

"Are you cold?" he asked, wrapping his arm around her again.

How quickly this physicality came to be normal between them, this touching. She leaned into his warmth and let him shelter her there for just a moment. Perhaps it was the stress of the situation, but she liked how easily he touched her, how he allowed her to touch him. This sort of intimacy was unheard of for her.

But as much as she enjoyed it, guilt swarmed her. "A man died. Because of me."

"Are you sorry he's dead?" He didn't look at her, but out at the water as he guided the craft.

"Of course. He was a living being. I don't want anyone to die because of me, but he was going to hurt me. And if he had the chance, he'd hurt Castallegna. He told me he was *Bratva.*"

Byron nodded. "Russian mob. They have a heavy presence in the Mediterranean. With the state of geopolitics, it makes sense."

"I can't believe my brother would align himself with these kinds of people." No, she supposed that wasn't true. She could believe it, but she didn't want to. Abele had loved her once, when she was very young. Before he'd gone power mad when their father had died.

Before the Council of Lords had tried to have him declared illegitimate.

She tightened her arms around Hawkins's waist

and just buried her face in his chest. It was safe there. The outside world didn't exist, only his warmth and strength.

Why couldn't a man like him want her?

He was fierce and strong as all good leaders must be, but he was noble, too, self-sacrificing.

"Castallegna is small. This seems like much trouble to go to simply to have a base and consulate on Castallegnian soil." She sighed.

"It would be good to have a government that was receptive to our operatives. Safe houses, if you will. Priceless, really. The Russians are trafficking in people, arms, munitions, and a lot of it is filtering through Greece, Cyprus and Italy."

"Won't that make Barcelona too dangerous because of the proximity to the Mediterranean?"

"No, I have contacts in Barcelona. We may have to lie low for a few days, but we'll get you on U.S. soil soon."

"I don't mean to look a gift horse, Hawkins, but wasn't Miklos a contact?"

"He was an associate." Hawkins laughed. "Contacts. U.S. government. They'll get us stateside safely. I promise you."

"Then what will happen to me?"

"I'll turn you over to Renner, the guy you spoke with. Then he'll take it from there."

"What will you do?" She didn't want to be handed over to anyone else. But she had to remember that to him, she was just a job. A package that had to be delivered. Something he hadn't wanted to take to start with.

"I'll have to go back to Italy. I'm still on assignment there."

"I hope I didn't blow your cover."

"No, it'll be fine. Miklos doesn't run with the same people. We've never had any transactions anywhere that was well lit, and I have a different name. Different social circles. They think I'm in finance. It's not a bad gig, really."

"So if I asked you how the yen was doing in comparison to the dollar, you'd be able to tell me?"

"Yes. Do you want to hear it?"

"Not really." She laughed. "I've acquired many skills, but finance and global trends all turn to gibberish when I try to make sense of them. I understand spending money, and I understand budgets and taxes. But crude investments versus pork bellies because of the rise in gold? Nothing." She'd always felt as if she should know more about international finance, but her brain just didn't work that way.

"Whenever anything else was going wrong in my life, numbers always made sense. They're irrefutable. Math is a universal language. Even though people say money is cold, hard and unfeeling, it's not. It's a tool. The stock market is attuned to feelings. When people don't feel safe, the numbers drop. When they do, they rise." He shrugged.

She liked that view of things. It made sense to her.

"I wish you could come with me after we're stateside. I don't know Renner. I know you." It was the closest she could come to asking him without actually saying she wanted him.

"You don't. Not really. I'm not a good guy, Princess. It's nice that you see me that way now. But it's like I said, I'm not really good at this protection gig. Killing is more my speed."

"Then why do I feel so safe?" She was still tucked against his body, shielded by his heat and his strength.

"Because you haven't learned any better." His tone wasn't quite condescension, but it was close.

"I've learned what you've taught me." She looked up at his hard profile. "And what you've taught me is that I'm safe with you. That you'll protect me. Even at the cost of your own life."

"I work for the good guys, but don't let that fool you into thinking *I'm* a good guy." He turned away from the controls and stared down at her, his gaze focusing on her mouth.

For one second, she hoped he'd be what he thought was a bad guy and kiss her. He probably thought she was some sheltered girl with no experience. She supposed that was true, but it didn't mean that she didn't know what she wanted or wasn't capable of making her own choices. She trembled and wanted to ask him if he was going to kiss her, but she knew that would shatter the moment. She wanted him to slam his mouth into hers and kiss her with no thought of where they were, who she was or what it meant.

His eyes were even more intense, his pupils dilated and his breathing was rough and hard, as if he exerted some superhuman effort just standing there. Maybe he wanted to kiss her, too. Her eyes fluttered closed, and she tilted her head up slowly.

"This can't happen," he said, his voice as low and guttural as Grisha's had been when he'd demanded to know why she didn't want him.

It occurred to her then that she wanted Byron Hawkins with the same intensity with which she'd despised Grisha.

CHAPTER THREE

SOME PEOPLE WOULD think that because Damara was a princess, she didn't understand the word *no.* She understood it plenty. She heard it so often that *yes* was more of a surprise. So rather than be upset, she asked, "Why not? Am I not pretty?"

"You know you're beautiful."

"Am I?" She lifted her chin, wondering if that's actually what he thought of her or if he was just being polite.

"Now you're fishing for compliments and you're not going to get them. You know how you look."

"I don't. Not really. My suitors all tell me I'm beautiful, but all they want is the power that comes with being married to me. I have maids. I have servants. They all tell me I'm beautiful, but they all must. What is it you don't like?"

She dared to ask the question, but she was actually afraid of the answer. She didn't want to be told that she wasn't enough—that she had nothing to offer him since he didn't want a crown.

"Your innocence."

"I see." Damara didn't. Not really. "Because you're a bad man?" She turned the conversation back to familiar territory.

"A very bad man."

"A bad man wouldn't care. Had I offered myself to Grisha, he wouldn't have waited." She shivered, both with fear and anticipation.

"You deserve better than a man like Grisha."

"I know that. That's why I picked you. But you're not cooperating."

Damara Petrakis wasn't sure who was more surprised by what came out of her mouth. The expression on his face looked like she'd kicked him somewhere unforgivable. She wasn't sure what strange maggot had burrowed into her brain, but she suddenly realized that this was the answer to half of her problems. Not only would it eliminate many of Abele's contenders for her hand; on a more selfish note, it was something she wanted to experience. She wanted to know what it was like to be wanted for herself, not her position. She had a feeling that Hawkins didn't care if she was a princess or a beggar.

His eyes widened. "You have lost your mind."

She scowled. "That's *not* what a lady expects to hear from her chosen beau."

"This ain't a cotillion, Princess." He sneered.

This wasn't the reaction she'd expected. "No, it certainly isn't." She pursed her lips and decided to appeal to his logic. "But my brother is going to have a hard time marrying me off if I'm not a virgin, isn't he?"

"That's still a thing?" He wrinkled his nose.

Still a thing. Damara closed her eyes for a second as the emotion threatened to overwhelm her. The whole of her self-worth had been wrapped up in the slight veil of flesh. It had been drilled into her head that it belonged to her country and she owed it to her people to keep herself chaste until she was married. But now, getting rid of it seemed like only way to give them and herself some measure of protection until Abele was captured and tried for treason.

Of course, this soldier wouldn't understand. She knew that. It was part of why she'd chosen him. So she couldn't be angry at him or hurt that he didn't understand. His culture was different.

She took a deep breath. "It's very much still a thing in Castallegna and in many parts of the world. I was under armed guard for most of my life. If I'm worthless to him, maybe he'll stop killing people to get to me."

"Sweetheart, I don't know if anyone told you, but he could lie."

She swallowed. "He could, but the kind of men he wants an alliance with would demand an examination before we were married."

"How about I just kill him for you?" Hawkins said as if he were asking her permission to do something as mundane as trimming the hedges below her window. Hope surged in her chest for all of a single millisecond. Life would be so much easier. So many people would be saved. One life for many—one of the founding principles on which she was raised. His death would mean she'd be free to dissolve the monarchy, to bring true democracy to Castallegna, just as her father had always dreamed.

But she couldn't do it on the back of an assassination.

"I can't ask you to do that." She swallowed the hope that had turned to bile in her throat.

"You're not asking. I offered. See, like I said, killing is what I'm good at."

She wet her lips, as if that would help ease her next words into the world. Damara may not have been experienced in the ways of the flesh, but she did know people. Politics and manipulation had been part of her extensive education, as well. "So are you saying that you're not good at making love?"

"*Fucking,* little girl. It's called fucking," he snarled.

Damara found it so telling that he could speak of killing—of death—without blinking an eye, but when the discussion turned toward softer things, it made him angry and defensive. At first she'd thought intimacy was the problem, but it didn't get much more intimate than taking a life.

A million retorts came to mind. She wanted to tell him she was no little girl, she was a grown woman, but she didn't need his validation to know that. It didn't matter if he wanted to use those words to push her away, to keep her from whatever it was he didn't want her to see.

"You still didn't answer the question." Damara was proud of how steady her voice was, how she met his regard with unflinching resolve.

"I'm warning you, Princess. Steer clear of this and me." His eyes raked over her with an intensity that made her feel exposed, naked.

He didn't have to answer the question. She sensed that if he touched her, she'd never be the same.

But she supposed that would be true of experiencing this with anyone. Maybe it was because he seemed reluctant that she wanted it to be him so very badly. Men always wanted something from her, and this one didn't want anything. How perverse of her.

She responded before she had time to think it

through. "Steer clear of you or what? You'll do what I've asked? What exactly do you think is going to happen to me? Do you have some hideous disease? Are you malformed?"

"I am formed very well, and clean, thank you," he growled. "How do you propose we do this, Highness? Hmm? Here in the boat? With no condom?"

She blushed.

"Oh, for— You demand I service you, but you blush when I mention *condoms?* If you can't say the word, you shouldn't be using them. And if you're not using them, you definitely shouldn't be having sex."

"I can say the word." Damara brushed some imaginary bit of something from her pants so she could get away from his scrutiny. "I just…I hadn't thought about the geography of where. Obviously, this boat isn't very practical for such things." She couldn't fight the heat that suffused her cheeks.

She was very aware of his proximity. Of his scent, of his strength.

Of her reaction to him.

And how what she'd said couldn't be unsaid. He didn't want her. Her tutors and trainers all made sure to tell her that any man who got her alone would try to "ruin" her. As if all men were ravaging beasts who couldn't control their baser urges. Even without a crown she did nothing to inspire his "baser urges." If her tutors had been wrong about that, what else were they wrong about?

She shook her head as if the action would rattle those thoughts out of her brain. Damara always said she wanted to be just a girl. Now he treated her like one and it rocked her worldview. Damara wanted to be strong; she wanted to be fierce and brave. Only she was alone and on unsteady ground. She felt incredibly weak and small.

At the core of that, what cut her the most was that she felt useless. She was a princess who'd escaped from her tower but didn't know how to do anything to care for herself.

She couldn't even seduce a man.

"Are you *crying?*" he asked her in a low voice, but with the same inflection as if he'd asked her if she had the plague.

"No." She wasn't. She wouldn't. But she wanted to.

"You think I don't want you," he stated in a monotone.

"You don't." If he did, why wouldn't he take what she offered?

He turned off the motor and dragged her against him. She went willingly, pliant in his arms. That was when she realized that he did want her. His erection was pressed against her intimately, which both thrilled and terrified her.

"I— Oh. I thought that was your gun."

He'd wanted her the whole time. Her whole body tingled.

Byron glanced heavenward as if she were the very definition of a cross to bear.

"As a princess, aren't there things that you want but can't have? Aren't there things that you know better than to reach for because you might lose the hand doing the reaching?"

His shoulders were so wide and hard. She found her hands wandering of their own volition down his broad back, his biceps. He was like one of the statues at the museum.

She understood what he meant, but Damara was much too distracted by his physicality.

"Oh," she said again breathlessly.

His fingers tightened and released around her hips before tightening again, finally drawing her even closer against him.

Damara burned in a way that she didn't know was possible. Every nerve ending was awake and wanting—this was desire.

She rose up on her tiptoes slowly—this was madness. He said he couldn't—they couldn't—but she needed his lips. She had to know what it was like to kiss him. She might never have another chance.

Hawkins didn't turn away from her, and he could have. He was bigger than she was, stronger. He was the one who'd hauled her against him, who kept touching her. One hand slid up her spine to cradle her neck and angle her for his pleasure.

His mouth crashed into hers with all the intensity she'd expected. It was a furious heat, but there was a need there, too. He gave as much as he took. His mouth was so hard but soft at the same time. Her blood turned to molten lava, and Damara was sure she'd burn up from the inside out. Just when she thought she'd incinerate to ash, he broke the kiss. But he didn't release her.

"Please," she whispered.

He touched his forehead to hers; their breath mingled in the aftermath of the kiss. He said with a ragged exhale, "If you still want this when we reach the safe house in Barcelona, God help you."

THAT MOMENT WAS everything that kissing a beautiful woman should be, Byron realized.

In a word, it was *awful.* The expectation, the hope—and the difficult truth that he could never fulfill any of those higher needs.

Her kiss made him want, made him remember what it was like to need something he couldn't have. She tasted of all things sweet and pure, and it roused something animal in him—something primal that wanted to claim her and mark her as his own. Hawkins wanted to touch all that lovely honey skin that he knew would taste just as good as her kiss.

But she was a princess, a regular damsel in distress.

And he was no knight, no prince and certainly no champion. He was Byron Hawkins, fuckup extraordinaire.

There'd been a time when he would've tried to seduce her just to see if he could get away with it. Part of him was tempted, sorely tempted, to see just how far the lovely princess would take this. He couldn't believe the way she pressed herself against him, so innocent but so wanton at the same time.

He tore himself away from her and concentrated on the task at hand. Where to stay once they got to Barcelona and the fastest way to get her on United States soil. Just as he'd promised.

But instead of focusing on those issues, his thoughts kept wandering back to how good she felt pressed up against him and the jasmine scent of her hair.

The things he wanted to do to her.

Her innocence should've been a mood killer—he broke fragile things and dirtied the pristine. Instead, it only stoked the flames hotter. He wondered what she'd look like writhing beneath him, what sounds she'd make from those luscious lips while he tasted her—pleasured her.

Hawkins steeled his mind to chill the heat of his arousal and shut down his imagination.

"You keep telling me that you're a bad man, but you're a better man than you think."

Perhaps she was the one who was dangerous. The sooner he could get away from her and that fragile hope he saw in her eyes, the better. "And sometimes, people who believe they're good have tunnel vision and can't see the destruction they leave in their wake," he answered.

"A bad person wouldn't care."

"Are we really having a philosophical discussion in the middle of the Mediterranean?" He tried to change the subject before he proved to her just what kind of man he was.

"Why not? What else is there to do?" She arched a brow and put a hand on her hip.

Hawkins wondered if she meant to dare him to take what she'd offered. If she meant to tease him. The expectant look on her face told him that she actually wanted an answer. She wasn't just taunting him—and he was a twisted bastard to think that she was.

"I'm not here to entertain you, Princess," he said more sharply than he meant.

She was contrite. "I'm sorry to pry. I won't do it again, but don't shut me out. I've never had anyone who talks to me like you do. Like I'm a real person rather than a dress-up doll." Damara put her hand on his forearm. "Please?"

It took everything in him to walk the line between

jerking away from her as if he'd been burned or crushing her against him and drowning in her sweetness.

It was the *please* that was his undoing. He supposed that he'd be able to say it was Damara herself that was his undoing. He knew if she didn't get away from him, all his noble intentions would be shot to shit.

All it would take was a glance, a touch, and he'd do anything she asked—even ruin her. It wasn't that he thought a woman was ruined after she lost her virginity, but she'd be ruined if she lost it to him.

"You're not a doll, but you *are* a princess."

"That doesn't make me any better or any worse than anyone else. All it means is that I was born into a certain family."

"Don't be so quick to shed the protection that affords you, Highness."

"Don't call me that. Just Damara."

But he had to call her "Highness," because it reminded him of all the reasons—no matter her words—why she wasn't for him. He flexed his fingers around the controls, wanting to reach out for her, but he knew better.

When he got ahold of Renner, he was going to punch him in the dick. Maybe until he couldn't raise his arms. That would only be half of what this felt like for him. There were any number of operatives who would've been a better choice for this gig.

Part of him was ready to hand the man his resignation the next time he saw him, but then where would he be? A killing machine with no purpose. What would he do? Where would he go? And what would happen to him once he had no outlet for the darkness inside of him?

No, Byron had no other options. This was where he belonged; this was what he was for. He had to believe that.

She sat quietly for a long time. It could have been hours, or it could've been minutes. Time lost its meaning when he was around her. He hated that. It made him ineffectual.

"Will you talk to me now?" she finally asked.

"What do you want to talk about?"

"Anything. Where are you from?" She looked down at her hands. "I wasn't going to pry. Right. Seems I can't help myself."

He cocked his head to the side. It wouldn't hurt to tell her where he was from. That was nothing. It was in his jacket. He could share those things. They weren't intimate; they weren't where his demons had hidden themselves.

"We lived in Virginia Beach when I was a kid and we had a boat. My dad would take us out at night and we chased what he called the Moonlight Road. He always said Blackbeard's treasure was at the end."

"That's how you know your way around the sea. I bet you could tell me all about the stars, too." She smiled. "Don't the stars inspire wonder and curiosity?" Her eyes were bright, and there was a kind of excitement on her face.

Hawkins hadn't thought about it in a long time. Not since he was a kid chasing moonlight ribbons across the water. They were maps and signposts for navigation, burning masses so far away that the light they were looking at was from something long dead and dark. They weren't hopeful or inspiring. They were pale remnants of what had once been.

"Not so much anymore, Princess. I see constellations and stories made up to make sense of a world a primitive people didn't understand. Andromeda, Perseus—myths that, like starlight, aren't real."

She laughed. "What do you mean it's not real? I can see them. The shapes they take, the stories behind them."

"Wishing on stars is like pinning your hope on the past and expecting it to change."

"I didn't say anything about wishing, although it's a nice thought. I used to wish all the time that I was just a girl instead of a princess. I know how far wishing gets you. That doesn't mean that they're not awe inspiring."

For the first time, it hit Byron that she had her own pain. He supposed that was a stupid thing to think. Of course she had her own pain, her own demons. Everyone did.

The wonder on her face was suddenly snuffed, like turning off a light. "Where do you live now?"

"Everywhere, really. I don't have a home base. I haven't since my parents shipped me off to a military boarding school my junior year in high school."

"But surely you're from somewhere? Virginia Beach, then?"

"No, we lived there until I was seven. Then we moved to Glory, Kansas. What about you, Princess? Did you spend your whole life on an island?" He turned the conversation back to her, shutting down all the memories, all the emotion that flooded over him whenever he thought of Glory.

She smiled and looked down at her hands. "I did. I'm the Jewel of Castallegna. I'm never supposed to leave the island. Going to Tunis was the farthest I've ever been from my home."

"Do you miss it?"

"Like missing part of myself."

They were dangerously close to touching things he'd buried deep and dark. Like wanting to belong, knowing that there was place that was always his—always part of him.

"Do you miss Kansas?" She interrupted his thoughts.

"Not hardly. The last view I had of that place was from the back of a police car." He hadn't been back since then and never would, if he had his way. He hated the faux piety of small-town life, the shiny picture they painted on the town's facade to outsiders who didn't understand there were no opportunities for anything better and there was definitely no forgiveness for your sins. Everyone in a small town lived in a glass house, but they all threw rocks.

"You were really a little hoodlum, weren't you?" She laughed, the sound light and happy. If she was anyone else, he'd have thought she was laughing at him. But he could see that she found delight in his delinquency. "All the better for me, I suppose. You wouldn't have the skills to do your job without it, I imagine."

Again they veered too close to things he'd rather not disturb. Hawkins didn't know what it was about her that dredged every unholy thing to the surface, but she was like a magnet.

A wise man would decide that it was time to face those things, but Hawkins had never been accused of being a wise man.

She seemed to sense his discomfort. "I've never been to Barcelona. What's it like?"

He shrugged. One port was much the same to him as any other. He tried to think of the city with the unabashed awe that the princess would feel. From her questions when they were first at sea to now, she seemed to find joy in the smallest details, fascination with the most banal of things.

"It's a major economic center. My cover takes me there often." He flashed her a grin, thinking of how much she would enjoy a particular hotel. "I know exactly where we can lie low until we can get a flight. I stay at the ABaC sometimes when I'm in town. I have a safety deposit box in the hotel and the staff are discreet."

She grinned. "See? My questions were helpful. I'm not just a nuisance."

He wanted to tell her that she wasn't a nuisance, that it wasn't that at all. But he knew once he started talking, he wouldn't be able to stop—it would be a tidal wave of confessional bile and she didn't need to hear all of that. There were things that once they were seen, once they were heard, they lived. They breathed. And they were eternal.

Like screaming.

Like blood.

Like death.

"I'm sorry we won't be able to sightsee."

"Maybe someday, I'll be able to travel and see the world. When my people are free, I'll be free."

"My offer still stands." That would take care of everything. The threat would be neutralized and Damara would be safe.

"To kill my brother?"

"Yes."

"I can't. He's my brother."

"Even though he hates you? Even though he'd do any number of things that could be worse than dying to get what he wants from you?"

She looked up at him, her eyes bright. "Even so."

He vowed at that moment that if her plans failed, that was just what he would do. She deserved to be safe. If she hated him for what he'd done, well, so be it. It occurred to him again that was what he was for. He did the jobs that no one else would—or no one else could. And bearing her hate, he could do that, too.

Resolve hard as stone, he changed the subject again. The port was in sight. "Look over there. It's Barcelona."

She perked up like a tiny wren who'd spotted a succulent worm. The closer they got, the wider her eyes were. "It's so beautiful, even from here. Are we just going to dock and walk into the city like we didn't just escape pirates?"

"Yeah. Why not?" He shrugged and flashed a smirk. "Half of my job requires balls." There was a slim chance there'd be some of Grisha's men stationed at the port to watch for them, but he'd have to take that chance. He'd burn that bridge when he had to cross it.

"Excuse me?" She arched a brow.

"Balls. You know…guts? Half of it is fake it until I make it. I fake a lot of things a lot of the time. Most of the time, if I act like I know I belong, I'm not questioned."

"Even dressed like a guerilla from hell?"

"Even then. We'll get a taxi and have him drop us

off a few blocks from the hotel. I'll check in to the penthouse, if it's available. You need a special key to get on to that floor and that will help with our security."

"From a stinky fisherman's boat to a penthouse suite. This has been an adventure."

Her smile didn't meet her eyes. He could see that she was scared. She'd have to be stupid not to be. Everything was uncertain, and it was likely the Russians were still after them. Even when she got to the States that was possible—even likely.

"That's the way to look at it, Princess. An adventure."

He maneuvered the boat through the port, dodging larger ships and other crafts until he found an abandoned slip and docked.

"You ready to go?"

She bit her lip and nodded.

"Just think about the room service. It's exquisite."

"I am hungry. I could eat a goat."

"I don't think they have any goat."

"Lamb?" she asked hopefully.

"Most definitely." He thought of the garlic-roasted lamb he'd had on his last trip. It had been so good his mouth watered even now. "But it'll make your mouth stink like a dead—well, it will give you bad breath." His comparison to a dead body wasn't exactly fodder for royal ears.

"Good to know. I'll brush my teeth before I kiss anyone."

The idea of her kissing anyone but him didn't sit well. Not at all. But it wasn't his place to say anything about it.

Things happened just as he'd said they would.

They disembarked from the small boat and walked up the dock and through the marina and no one said a word to them. It was as if people did such things all the time. It wouldn't be too long, though, before they found the boat and discovered its owners were nowhere near Barcelona. The boat would be impounded and dusted for prints; there would be an investigation.

Although by then, Byron hoped they'd be long gone.

He had no trouble getting a taxi, and it dropped them at the hotel. He always kept a variety of monies on him, and he had just enough euros to tip well without being overly generous.

As soon as he walked into the hotel, the staff recognized him.

"Mr. Hale. What brings you back to Barcelona? Business or pleasure?" the desk clerk asked him in unaccented English.

"Pleasure. Most definitely." When he noticed she was examining his attire, he said, "Cave exploration. Been wanting to do it since my first visit."

"I would have been happy to set that up for you." She made a show of wetting her lips. "And anything else you need, Mr. Hale."

"I'll keep that in mind for my next trip." He gave her an easy smile. Part of him wanted to take her up on it now. He could just bend her over the couch in the office and slake his lust. Something, anything, to ease his body before more hours of confinement with the beautiful but innocent princess.

Except he wasn't actually interested in anything this woman had to offer him. She was beautiful, accomplished and he was sure from the way she moved she'd be great in bed.

But she wasn't Damara Petrakis.

He had to get those thoughts out of his head—he didn't know how, but it would be so much easier once he'd put some distance between them.

"The penthouse suite is available. Shall I charge it to the card you have on file?"

"Yes, thank you. Double the room service order from my last visit, please. And I'd like to access my box while I'm here, as well."

"I'll let security and the kitchen know. Is there anything else I can help you with, Mr. Hale? Anything at all?" She smiled and leaned over the desk, emphasizing her ample and lovely cleavage.

"Not at the moment." He accepted the key and winked at her.

"Is there anything else I can do for you, Mr. Hale?" Damara said in a sickly sweet voice as he took her up to the penthouse.

Byron laughed. "Are you jealous?"

"No, of course not. But that was just pathetic." She rolled her eyes. "Even I know that a man won't buy the cow if he can get the milk for free."

"I don't want to buy the cow." He snorted.

"Glad you see it my way." She harrumphed.

He laughed again. "Call me Brian while we're here. It'll most likely be for only a few hours, but just in case, okay?"

"Yes, Brian."

"And what's your name?"

"I get to play, too?" Her pique seemed forgotten.

"I want to be Holly Golightly, like *Breakfast at Tiffany's*."

"You know she was a prostitute, right?" He raised a brow.

"It's not a bad profession. It's not unlike being royalty."

"How's that?" He couldn't wait to hear how she'd managed to work that out in her head. Byron opened the door to the suite.

"Pay to play, right? I have to trade myself to my husband for his resources. It's basically the same thing. He gets to sleep with me, but he has to pay for it."

"I think that's just being married."

"So she gets to be married to a lot of men, doesn't have to stay with any one of them and still gets to utilize their resources. I like this idea. Maybe instead of freeing my country, I should just go home and have a harem?"

"I'm not calling you Holly Golightly."

"I'm surprised you even know who I was talking about. My brother said it was a movie for women to make themselves feel better about being powerless."

"We've established that your brother is an asshole." He studied her for a moment and tried to imagine any scenario where he'd ever think of Damara as powerless. There wasn't one.

"Did you order food?"

"Yes, Highness."

"Don't call me that." She bristled.

"Why not?"

"I already told you why not. I'm a woman, the same as any other."

"Who talks about having harems of men to do her bidding." He could admit, the thought was like rubbing sandpaper on his face. Byron didn't want anyone to touch her but him. It was good that he needled her. Maybe she'd get tired of him and stop engaging. Maybe she'd want to get away from him as much as he needed to get away from her.

He had a burner phone in the deposit box, and he hoped he could make contact with Renner and work out an end to this soon.

If he had to spend more than one more night with her, and she offered herself to him, he didn't think he'd be able to turn her away.

CHAPTER FOUR

TREPIDATION AND EXCITEMENT were tangled up like vines in Damara's belly.

This wasn't what she'd expected at all. It was definitely better than a lifeboat or being chased by men with guns.

When he left to access his security box, Damara took stock of the room. It was a master suite with every luxury, from a wet bar to a king-size bed. She sat on the bed, running her fingers over the purple duvet.

For a brief moment, she wondered if she was being selfish. Maybe she should look for another royal to marry, someone strong enough to defeat Abele— No. *No.* Her father had wanted to bring democracy to Castallegna and if she married another royal, he wouldn't want to give up a crown for her father's dream.

Even though it was the right thing, it still felt wrong and strange to go against what she'd been told was her duty her whole life.

Damara told herself that her duty was to protect her people, to do what was best for them. And this was it. A monarch was a law unto himself, and Abele took that to the extreme. She was the only one who could stop him.

She exhaled heavily. She couldn't wait to get into the shower. Maybe it could wash away the dirt and that feeling of guilt.

Probably not, because she'd decided.

Even after everything, Byron Hawkins would be the one. She wanted to experience him, and what did it matter anyway? They'd never see each other again after this.

Sometime later, when he reentered the room, their eyes met and it was as if they'd both been caught in some high-voltage current they were helpless to stop. She moved toward him, unable to direct her steps anywhere else.

He welcomed her into his arms but did nothing more. The tension between them was thick and heavy, like a weight pressing them down.

Her breath caught in her throat. "Are you going to kiss me?"

"No." Only his head dipped toward her anyway.

"Oh." She was disappointed. "Then I guess *I'll* have to kiss *you.*" Damara arched her back, twined her arm around his neck and mashed her lips against his.

He wrapped one arm around her, his palm splayed on her waist, and he became the aggressor. She held her lips stiff and rigid, but gradually, under his guidance, she opened for him.

He tore his mouth from hers and pushed her away. "This can't happen," Hawkins said raggedly.

"Why not? You already said that if I still wanted this when we got to Barcelona, then God help me. So maybe he is." His parted lips were swollen and even more inviting. "After you hand me over to your Mr. Renner, we'll never see each other again."

"What is it you want from me?" He met her regard, but his eyes seemed so tired, a deep well of sadness.

She almost lost her nerve. "I thought that would be obvious, Mr. Hawkins. I want you to make love to me."

For the briefest moment, Damara thought he was going to deny her. Especially when his expression became guarded and closed, his mouth a tight line. "Then take off your clothes."

This wasn't what she'd expected, either, but she wasn't turning back now.

SHE TOOK OFF her utility belt and hung it on the bedpost.

"That's where I put mine." He smirked.

With shaking hands, she undid the clasp on his utility belt and hung it over her own. She wet her lips, and she couldn't quite bring herself to look up at his face. Her heart pounded against her ribs like a thousand butterflies looking for an escape.

He took her hands in his own, and the weight of his stare drew her gaze upward like a magnet.

"You can still change your mind."

"No, this is the path I've chosen and I'll see it through to the end." She searched his eyes. "It's what I want."

"Don't say I didn't warn you."

The softness of his voice was at odds with the fury of his kiss. Heat incinerated her and she melted against him. His hands were everywhere—rough and calloused, but sparks burst in their wake.

"Can I touch you?" she asked against his mouth.

"Anywhere you want."

For some reason, his words made her feel powerful. She pushed her hands under the soft cotton of his shirt, and she marveled at the way he felt. His skin was smooth, but it was like velvet wrapped around steel. She supposed that was a stupid comparison, but she had nothing else to liken it to.

Damara loved the way his muscles rippled under her caress, the way he held her tighter when she touched him in a way he liked. It was hard to concentrate on what she was doing, though, because he'd filled his hand with her breast.

It was a decadent sensation, his thumb stroking over the peak of her nipple. It was no wonder people did such things to have more of this.

"Boots," he whispered in her ear. "They have to go before we can take this any further." He released her, and she felt his absence acutely. All the places on her body that had been hot were now cold.

He sat down on the bed and began unlacing his boots.

Damara blinked at the sudden change. It was like a light switch for him, it seemed.

"Do you need help?" he asked her.

"Uh, no. I got it." But she didn't want to have it. She'd imagined when this happened, it would be some great unveiling, that he'd undress her tenderly— Enough of that. Dreaming and reality were two different things. He was the one who knew what he was doing, and if he said to take off her boots, she'd take them off.

"Hey." He lifted her chin so she'd look at him. "There is no way to take off combat boots that's sexy." Hawkins winked at her.

And suddenly all the cold fled and she was hot again. She wondered how he did that, how he could change the barometer of a situation with almost no effort.

Damara kicked her boots off and started on her shirt.

"Ah, no. Don't take away all my fun." He pushed her back on the bed and pulled her shirt up just over her rib cage before pressing his mouth to the dip of her belly.

She shivered at the contact—the warmth of his mouth a contrast to the cool temperature of the room. His hands made short work of her bra, and he tugged off her shirt, divesting her of both garments.

He didn't give her a chance to feel vulnerable or self-conscious.

"You're so damn beautiful." Hawkins dipped his head to her breast, taking her nipple in his mouth, and whirled his tongue over the tight bud. Then he kneaded both breasts in his strong hands as his mouth traveled south down toward her belly, down farther still to the waist of her fatigues.

He pulled them down her hips, taking her knickers with them.

And his mouth continued its descent.

The proper girl who'd been raised as a princess and cut her teeth on propriety wanted her to stop him, to tell him that people didn't do such things. But the newly awakened woman in her wanted more. And it was the woman who was in charge. Damara trembled when he peeled the last of her clothing down her legs, but she wouldn't tell him to stop. Not now. Want and need had become indiscernible from one another.

"No one has ever touched you here? Not even yourself?"

She bit her lip.

"Tell me, Princess. I want to know. I want to picture your pretty little fingers right here." He touched his mouth to her womanhood.

His taboo words—for they were indeed taboo as no one had ever spoken to her in such a way—stoked her fire so hot she thought she'd erupt with it.

Once his mouth was on her, his lips, his tongue delving into places she'd never imagined a tongue should go—all rational thought fled. There were no more questions of what she should do, of what a princess would do, of what was proper. Only what she could do to get more of this sensation.

She arched her back and pushed herself toward the source of her pleasure.

He was committed to his task, a devotee of ecstasy. He knew exactly what he was doing, what she needed as he pushed her ever higher toward some unknown peak—and then her senses all narrowed to one small pinpoint until it exploded outward, thrusting her into the stratosphere.

Damara had never felt anything like it.

He pulled away from her, and she watched in a bliss-shrouded haze as he removed his shirt and fatigues. She'd wanted to do that, unwrap him like a gift she was giving herself.

"Nightstand drawer. Open it."

She didn't want to look away from him, but she did as he demanded and saw the box of condoms inside. She supposed the hotel concierge had thought of everything. Damara pulled one out and held it up for him.

"Oh, no, Princess. You're putting it on me."

The idea of touching him so intimately intimidated her, which was completely stupid given what they were about to do.

"How?" she asked.

He tore open the package and rose above her. Hawkins took her hand in his and drew it between them down to his erection.

"Roll it down the shaft, like this."

She followed his lead and pushed the condom down the length of him. But he moved her hand back up and back down again, acclimating her to the feel of him.

Trepidation was dominant as her excitement quelled. She knew this was going to be uncomfortable.

He braced himself on his elbows and kissed her softly. "It'll hurt at first, but the pain will pass."

She didn't care if it hurt; she wanted this. Damara locked her legs around his hips. "Just do it."

"As you wish, Princess."

She steeled herself for pain, but it was his tenderness that was her undoing. He pushed inside her slowly, giving her time to adjust to his girth. He cupped one cheek, and his thumb stroked her face as he filled her.

When she opened her eyes to look into his, Damara thought that action spoke of something more intimate than the act itself. She knew she'd never forget him, but this had been an act between strangers who had to remain just that. Only this small thing, this tenderness, it bound them together.

Byron pushed past her veil, and her nose prickled

the way it did before she was about to cry. Not because of the pain—it was fleeting—but because it had only taken a second to rid herself of what made her the Jewel of Castallegna. In a single instant, she'd rendered herself worthless.

She refused to cry. This was what had to be done and it was good.

Damara shut out the doubts, the fears, everything, and flung herself into the moment. She clung to him with the kind of abandon that could only be felt when an ending loomed above like a storm cloud. This was a memory that would have to last her a lifetime, because, after today, she'd never see Byron Hawkins again.

She was frantic to feel everything. "More."

He increased his speed and drove himself deeper into her, but it still wasn't enough. She wanted him closer, tried to memorize the way his body felt working in tempo with hers. The scent of him, the way his lips tasted.

Damara wanted everything.

Even if she fell in love, even if she married, no one could ever be first, and she was determined to make this a good memory.

"If we had more time, I'd do this to you for hours. I'd stop and bring you off with my mouth again, my fingers. I'd taste and touch every inch of you, Damara."

She shivered and clung tighter, dug her nails into his back as if that could anchor him there and keep the outside world from ever intruding.

A strange sensation fluttered inside her when she clenched herself around him. He stilled, his muscles tense and taut. With a groan, he started moving again, pushing deep.

"Is that right?" she asked shyly. She wanted to make him feel as good as he made her feel.

"It's more than right."

Damara did it again, and he buried his face in her neck, clung to her as she clung to him and rocked them both toward another culmination.

This one was different; rather than an explosion it was a fluttering that originated deep in her core and radiated outward. Not like fireworks—more like the concentric circles of a stone dropped in a pond.

Hawkins reached his completion after her, hips jerking and tensing before his whole body stiffened and then he went still. For a moment, she wondered if she'd killed him. He was so still and the look on his face had been so intense she couldn't tell if it was pleasure or pain.

Then he rolled off her and lay on his back, staring up at the ceiling.

She felt as though she should say something, but she didn't know what. So she lay in silence until the blurry aftermath of pleasure faded. Damara was torn between thanking him and asking if they could do it again.

She didn't know what she expected from him, but it was as if he'd never touched her. Never kissed her.

Never made love to her.

She didn't care what he said. What they'd done together wasn't fucking. He'd been so gentle, so reverent. Damara didn't think all men were that way with every partner. It meant something to him. Not love, they barely knew each other, but there was a connection.

"You can have the shower first."

So it wasn't at all like the novels she'd read. They wouldn't lie together, holding each other. She'd go shower as if it was just another day, another thing that had happened.

Okay. She could do this.

When she got out of the bed, she saw the tiny stain of blood on the sheets. Wars had been fought over something so insignificant. It seemed incredibly stupid. Not that the experience wasn't magnificent—it was. But a little splash of blood for king and countries?

Damara walked gingerly toward the door and was reminded of her activities with every step. She was incredibly sore, but each twinge of discomfort brought back a memory of a touch, a caress. It made her sigh. She wished she could linger and they could do it again.

But her father had a saying about wishing in one hand and holding goat crap in the other. The wishing hand was always empty.

She stepped under the spray of the hot water, and, just like she'd wanted it to wash away the guilt, she let it wash away any possible regret. This was what she'd wanted, and she'd gotten it. Damara wouldn't complain now.

She'd focus on the next step of their journey. He'd done everything she'd asked of him and more.

Damara relaxed into the water, letting it pour over her. An array of little bottles were lined up for her to try, and she sniffed each one until she found one that smelled vaguely of home. Jasmine.

When she was done, she bundled herself up in a fluffy towel and wondered what she should put on. She didn't have any other clothes. The thought of putting her dirty fatigues back on was less than appealing.

She should've known Byron would take care of it.

A brand-new T-shirt lay folded on her side of the bed. The sheets had been changed as well, and he lay sprawled on one of the chaise couches at the end of the bed, eyes closed.

She couldn't tell if he was sleeping, but she knew he hadn't slept at all in the past twenty-four hours. If he was, she didn't want to disturb him.

Their food had arrived, too.

Damara shimmied into the T-shirt and panties that were folded discreetly beneath it and attacked her food with gusto.

She didn't know if it was because of the adrenaline or everything else that had happened to her, but the lamb was the best she'd ever tasted. It melted on her tongue. She didn't realize how decadent it really was until Byron spoke. His eyes were still closed.

"Woman, if you keep making those sounds, I'm going to have you flat on your back again in about five seconds."

Damara shivered, delighted at the thought. "With lamb breath and all?"

"Lamb breath, dog breath, I don't care." He'd flung an arm over his head; his eyes were still closed.

"You don't look like you'll be doing much of anything to me," she teased.

"I've been up for thirty-six hours."

Of course he hadn't said anything. As if it was unmanly to sleep or something. "So go to sleep."

"I'm trying, but you're having mouthgasms with your lamb," he said drily.

"I'm sorry." Her apology was sincere.

"It's all right—I was only teasing. I never sleep well anyway. Insomnia."

"After thirty-six hours, I imagine you'd have to pass out sometime." She thought about the pain she'd seen in his eyes. Damara would bet anything he had nightmares and that was why he didn't want to sleep. She thought about the way he'd watched over her while she'd slept on the *Circe's Storm.* He'd stayed awake to make sure she was safe. She could do the same for him.

"Now that I'm full, I'm tired, too." She got up from the table and made sure the door was locked, all the shades were closed and the lights were off. "Come to bed with me, Hawkins."

She made sure to use his last name so it wasn't too intimate. So he didn't think she expected or was trying to give anything more than what he wanted.

"I'll feel safer knowing you're in bed with me," she prodded.

"I'm dirty."

"And I have lamb breath." She grabbed his hand, and he hauled himself up from the chaise and followed her the short distance to the bed.

He flopped down on the bed, shirtless, his fatigues half-unbuttoned and his feet hanging off the side. A gun had somehow managed to make its way to the nightstand.

She studied him in the dimly lit room. His chiseled body, his scarred hands, the enticing way his fatigues looked like a half-wrapped present. Then back up to his face.

"Are you going to stare or get in bed? Thought you were tired," he grumbled.

"You really don't ever sleep, do you?"

"Certainly not when I'm being stared at. I feel like a hare being stalked by a wolf."

She blushed. Her comportment tutor would probably have apoplexy if she could see her now. Damara wondered if there was even protocol for this. "You're pretty to look at. What do you want from me?"

"Pretty?" He cracked an eye open. "How's that?"

"Never mind. Go to sleep. I am." She slipped under the covers and curled against him and pretended to sleep.

"No, you're not, but I'll let you get away with it this time." He wrapped an arm around her and held her close.

With his arm around her, Damara felt as if she'd been hidden away from the world at large. Nothing could find her and nothing bad could touch her.

BYRON HAWKINS HAD fallen asleep breathing in the scent of jasmine with a soft woman in his arms.

He awoke with a strangled scream in his throat and a cacophony of suffering in his head.

His team.

His whole team.

Christ, the way they screamed.

And it was his fault. His fault they screamed. His fault they never came home. Barnes with his easy smile and the dog-eared picture of his three-year-old daughter. Foxworth and his dreams for a life after his service.

"There's more to life than this, hoss." Foxworth's Texas twang thudded behind the noise of death.

But there wasn't. If Hawkins could go back and exchange himself for them, he'd do it. He never wondered what it would be like if he'd never given the order, because if it hadn't been this, it would have been something else. He knew that.

No matter what Renner told him. All his talk about PTSD, and therapy… He didn't have PTSD. He was just born bad, and he knew it.

Gentle fingers cupped his cheek. "Are you okay?" she murmured.

He looked down at her, eyes half-lidded and sleepy but concern plain on her face. "Fine. Go back to sleep."

Somehow it was more horrible because she was awake. She'd become a witness to his shame. He had to get away from her, away from the forgiveness on her face, especially when it wasn't hers to give.

He untangled himself as quickly and gently as he could and went outside to stand on the giant balcony.

They'd slept for the remainder of the day, and dusk had fallen. The city lights of Barcelona lit up the landscape like thousands of twinkling stars, and he thought of their conversation about starlight and stories to soothe children.

That's what she'd give him if he let her—a story to soothe everything that ached in him. But he deserved to suffer, deserved his pain.

He scrubbed his hand over his face, sat down and dipped his feet into the Jacuzzi tub that was on the balcony. The hot water gurgled around his ankles and over his toes, giving him another sensation to concentrate on besides the buzzing in his head.

The princess sat down next to him and dipped her feet in, as well. He didn't want to look at her, talk to her, but his eyes were drawn to her dainty ankles.

They were a gateway drug, because from there, he appraised her slim legs up to where the T-shirt brushed the tops of her thighs. Her nutmeg skin looked warm and smooth, so perfect. He remembered what it was like, running his hands all over her. The soft cries from her full lips.

Fucking and killing—all he was good for.

"Did you have a nightmare?" she asked.

"Don't want to talk about it."

He thought she'd pick at the scab, but she didn't. "I didn't even know this was out here. I've always wanted to try a Jacuzzi tub."

He arched a brow. "Seriously? You're a princess. You didn't have six or seven of these?"

She laughed, the sound light. "No, my brother thought they were immodest and invited sin."

"They do." Yes, they most certainly did, he thought, as his eyes raked over her.

"You seem to be doing fine. I'm sitting here with my legs exposed all harlotlike, and yet you're controlling yourself," she teased.

"It wouldn't take much to push me over the edge." He kept his tone light.

"Oh, really? What do you define as 'much'?" She slid one leg deeper into the water, watching him as she did so.

Now she taunted him, dared him.

He liked it.

"You're just about there." He gave her a half grin.

She slid all the way into the water, heedless of her T-shirt and panties, and moved to stand between his legs. Damara braced her hands on his thighs and leaned in close to his mouth. "Am I there yet?"

He laughed, not because he thought she was funny but because she delighted him.

In that moment, with his hands on her hips and her mouth only a breath away from his, she wasn't a princess and he wasn't a fuckup extraordinaire. They were just Byron and Damara.

"Do you wanna be?"

"Most definitely."

"Aren't you sore?"

"Sure, but I can be sore later, too. You and I won't get later." She brushed her lips against his carefully. "I don't get to explore any of the new places I've been, the things I've seen. But I can explore you."

It was official. She was killing him.

And it was a glorious death. He'd drown in her, be lost in her, anything she wanted from him so long as she kept touching him. He forgot everything when he wrapped himself in her.

Damara ran her hands up his thighs and hooked her thumbs around the belt loops in his fatigues.

"You don't need these."

He obliged her and let her peel them off him. Then he sank down into the Jacuzzi tub and pulled her into his lap so she was astride him.

The wet T-shirt was even sexier than if she was naked. Her dark skin was a contrast beneath the white of the shirt and her nipples were hard dusky peaks that begged for his attention.

Byron loved the way she felt against him in the water, soft, wet and slick. She braced her palms on his shoulders and bit her lip as she rolled her hips experimentally against him.

The moonlight was a slash of light that knifed through the darkness and fell like a fey ribbon on her hair. Just like it would on the open dark sea. He wanted to bury himself in it, and her. It would be so easy to push her panties aside and drive home deep into her heat.

Byron liked teasing them both a bit, too, dragging it out, making the sensation last. It had been a while since he'd been with a woman, and he'd never been with a woman like Damara Petrakis.

He let her grind on him, work her hips and cleft against him and crank herself higher. Byron liked the way her lips parted and her intake of breath, the way the soft material of the tee clung to her. He liked everything about this.

"Tell me what you like. Tell me how to make this good for you," she whispered against his ear.

He thought of every deviant thing he'd imagined doing to her, every fantasy he'd had in the past twenty-four hours, and none of them compared with what was happening to him right now.

"It's already good for me. Like you said, you don't get to tour the cities we've been to, but you can tour me."

Her hands slid over his shoulders, his biceps, her fingers pausing to explore the muscle there. Testing his bulk, his strength. Damara scored her nails lightly down his chest, and his eyes fluttered closed at the sensation. So she did it again.

Down his pecs, his abdominals and down lower still until she wrapped her hand around him.

"What about this? Do you like it?" She moved her hand slowly.

He curled his fingers around hers and applied more pressure, just a bit more speed. "Like this."

"I like how powerful your body is. How strong."

Her words were as intoxicating as her touch.

His hips moved up to meet her caress and when he would have told her to stop, to slow down, she kissed him.

"It makes *me* feel powerful to do this to you," she said against his mouth before kissing him again.

Her kisses were sweet and had been almost chaste at first, but she learned quickly—tasting him, darting her tongue against the edge of his lip, making the same motions with her tongue against his in time to the strokes of her hand.

She was almost too good to be true.

Any minute he'd wake up and find it had all been a dream and he'd be spilling into his hand thinking about a woman who wasn't real.

Wave after wave of pleasure rolled over him in great swells until he was swept out to a sea of bliss.

She was still kissing him even though her hand had stilled and he found he didn't want to stop. When he did, he'd have to fall back to earth, be slammed back into a reality where he knew being with her was wrong.

Damara felt so good in his arms—so right. The thought kept playing over in his head, as if that would make it all okay.

It didn't.

He finally broke the kiss. "There's a car coming for us in a few hours. We should be ready."

"Okay." She seemed so fragile now, so breakable.

Her lips were swollen and raw from his kisses and it made him want to kiss her more. Byron had to find the line again and remember that he couldn't cross it.

Yes, in just a few hours, he'd hand her over to another operative and she'd go stateside. He'd go back to his house and manufactured life in Marsala. Even though he'd never see her again, he'd think about tonight and the princess for a long time.

"What should I put on?"

She turned away from him and trudged up out of the Jacuzzi tub.

"There are clothes in the closet."

Her shoulders were squared, back straight, and she walked dripping, but regal, back inside their room.

He looked up at the sky and then to Damara's profile as she dressed. Byron couldn't believe that she didn't know how beautiful she was. Maybe he should've told her. He'd already complicated things enough as it was.

Byron grabbed his fatigues and walked naked into the bathroom, where he showered quickly, rinsing the chlorine from the Jacuzzi tub from his skin and hair. He noticed an open bottle on the ledge, and he brought it close so he could smell it.

Jasmine, just like Damara. He inhaled the scent and closed his eyes, committing the scent along with the memory of her to stone in his mind.

After he'd dressed in the slacks and shirt he'd had the concierge purchase along with Damara's clothes, he saw she'd curled up on the chaise.

After all her talk of being powerful and strong, and after how fierce she'd been fleeing both Tunis and the pirates, she seemed so vulnerable now and very much in need of protection.

In need of him.

It wouldn't hurt to comfort her now, to hold her for a few more hours. He'd trespassed already by being with her. He owed it to Damara to keep her safe, even from himself.

He sat next to her and put his arm around her slim shoulders.

She melted into him as if they were two pieces of the same whole.

Byron couldn't let himself make that comparison—not now, not ever. He pushed it out of his head.

"Everything is going to be fine, Damara."

"Do you swear?"

It seemed like such a little-girl thing for her to ask him. So full of trust and promise, brimming with hope. Byron knew it would be kinder to be honest, but he found he couldn't. He'd have promised her the moon would taste like peaches if that was what would make her happy.

"I swear."

She sighed and leaned her head against his chest, wrinkling his shirt.

Byron didn't care about wrinkles. He just wanted her to feel safe.

"I wish you were going with me."

"I have to stay here. I'll make sure you get on the plane safely. Then another operative will get you to Renner."

“I don’t know the other operative,” she said, her voice small.

“You don’t know me, either.”

“I know enough.”

The part of him that was infected with guilt wanted to confess to her why she was wrong. It wanted to tell her every bad thing he’d ever done, and it wanted her to hate him for it.

“Don’t trust anyone but yourself, Princess.”

CHAPTER FIVE

DAMARA MANAGED TO KEEP herself poised and collected until she stood with Byron on the tarmac in front of the steps up to the plane that would take her so many miles away. She knew he had his reasons for maintaining his distance.

Damara was embarrassed to admit that she wanted him to try to find some way to stay in touch, to write letters, emails, something to acknowledge this thing that had happened between them. If she were being wholly honest, she'd say that she wanted him to decide to stay with her because he needed her, he wanted her.

She knew it was stupid and childish. She knew that neither of them had fallen in love just because they'd spent the night together. Although she wondered if it hadn't been the same for him as it had for her. He had no problem saying goodbye, walking away from her. Damara was already reliving the way he'd touched her, how good it felt to be in his arms.

Looking at him and knowing she'd never see him again did something strange to her insides. It was almost a physical pain. Except, even if he did feel the same way she did, what future could there be for them? She didn't have to marry royalty, but someday she would return to Castallegna, someday soon, and her place was there, working for democracy and freedom. Fulfilling her duties to her people. The same as Byron Hawkins. His duty was to his country. She tried to imagine him in Castallegna. No matter how she spun it, how outlandish her fantasies were, she just couldn't see him there. He belonged in this other world of blood, danger and intrigue. Not pretty manners, state affairs or even sneaking off to lie naked in the sun on their own private beach—as much as she wished it could be otherwise.

She flung her arms around him and pressed a kiss to his cheek. Damara wanted to stay in the circle of his arms, but this was time for goodbye. She wouldn't shame him or herself by making a big deal out of it. He'd been silent in the car on the way to the airport for a reason.

"Thank you for everything, Mr. Hawkins." She disengaged from the embrace and, without looking at him, started up the stairs.

"Take care of Her Highness, Gregson," she heard him say.

"You can do it yourself. Renner wants you on this plane. You're taking her home to Glory, via D.C.," the pilot said with a laugh.

She turned on the stairs to watch his reaction.

The absolute fury on his face stung. After hearing the pilot's words, she'd been ecstatic. Damara hadn't expected Byron to be pleased, but she'd thought maybe he might see it as an opportunity to spend more time with her.

She could see from his expression that was the furthest thing from his mind.

"What the actual fuck?" She flinched at the profanity, but not because of the word itself. It was the anger behind it.

"I don't know. Those are your orders. We're taking off in ten, five if I can swing it, so if you're coming, I suggest you board. There's some Russian diplomat trying to ground the flight."

He grunted, and Damara didn't know if it was supposed to be a word, a phrase or a curse. "Let's get her in the air."

Hawkins stomped up the stairs behind her.

She was ushered into a luxurious cabin. Damara was sure the cost of this flight would be taken out of the Castallegnian treasury. She supposed if she had to be a refugee, it was better to do it in comfort.

The ship hadn't been comfortable at all, and yet she'd felt the safest she had in her whole life under a tarp in a lifeboat curled into Byron Hawkins. Now, though, everything had changed between them. In getting closer, she was somehow further away from him.

Byron sat down with a heavy thud in the chair across from hers and strapped in.

"Looks like you got what you wanted." His voice was a growl.

She kept her expression neutral and drew on all her training to keep her voice steady so it wouldn't betray how she felt.

"Am I safe yet? Are my people free? The answer to those questions is no. So I didn't get what I wanted." She lifted her chin and fixed him with a regal stare.

"And you never will if Renner sticks you with me. You should do your level best, Princess, to convince him you don't want me on your detail."

Princess was back to being a dirty word that

seemed to taste foul on his tongue rather than the endearment it had been last night. “I will.”

She leaned back in the seat and picked up the nearest book. Damara didn’t know what it was about or who it was by because instead of reading it, she used it as a shield. Something for her to focus on instead of him, something to physically cut the space between them.

The words ran together on the page.

“Damara,” he said, his voice suddenly soft.

The engines revved and the plane moved forward on the tarmac toward the queue for takeoff.

She didn’t want to look up at him, but his regard was palpable on her skin. She thought about ignoring him. She’d learned to do that with Abele, whenever he’d stare so hard she was sure she’d burst into flame from his hatred.

The part of herself she’d shared with him last night, the part that no one ever saw, it cringed away from him.

On the outside, though, Damara Petrakis was always a princess.

Damara flipped the switch on her feelings. She liked to tell herself they were off, but rather they’d been stuffed down so deep inside of her that no one could get to them without a scalpel.

She closed the book, folded her hands over it in her lap and fixed him with a direct stare.

“What is it, Mr. Hawkins?”

“It’s not you.”

A wealth of retorts rose on her tongue, but none of them were what she really wanted to say. So instead, she exhaled slowly and inhaled, using the action to gird herself. Breath could be like armor when one had nothing else. It made her hold her back straight; it squared her shoulders and forced her to lift her chin. "Of course it isn't."

It was Byron who looked away first, glancing out the window. Then he unbuckled his belt. "I'm going to check with Gregson."

He headed toward the cockpit.

Damara swallowed hard.

She chided herself again for being upset.

"The diplomat's name is Vladimir Kulokav," Hawkins said when he sat back down. "He's saying that you're wanted for questioning in relation to his brother's attempted murder."

"Attempted murder? Grisha's not dead?" She closed her eyes. He wouldn't forgive this. He and Abele would both make her pay if they caught her.

"It *was* only a .38. That would probably only make me angry, too." He offered her a half smile.

She'd had enough body language courses to know that this was his peace offering. Damara hated that she knew that. She wanted to be angry. If she was angry, she wouldn't have to be hurt. And Damara knew better. She'd known he didn't want any kind of commitment. He'd been wary of giving her what she wanted even for a night. He'd been tricked into helping her the first time and forced into helping her yet again. He had to be feeling betrayed.

Damara exhaled heavily and tried to think of a neutral response.

The plane reached optimum speed, and they were launched into the air.

"This is only my second time flying."

"When was your first?" He seemed glad to talk about something else.

"When I was smuggled off Castallegna. But it was in the cargo hold—this is much nicer."

"The cargo hold?" He growled again. "You could have been killed."

"It was the only way to get off Castallegna. My brother's men 'inventory' every ship leaving and entering port. So they get their cut."

"Why didn't they search the hold?"

"It was my brother's plane. He had a shipment going to Tunis." She bit her lip.

"No wonder he's so pissed." He gave her a genuine smile this time.

"I've been planning this for a long time. It took almost a year to get everyone into place." She looked out the window and down at the landscape below. "It's amazing, you know."

"What is?"

"Flying. That we launch ourselves into the air and simply trust that this unseen force will hold us aloft."

"Rather than the unseen force that holds us down?" He raised a brow.

"Yes. Exactly." She studied the patches of land, cityscape and countryside as they soared higher. "I think that people who rule often feel like this. Except they forget that they're actually one of the ones down there, the tiny ants going on about their survival."

"I don't know. I think men like Grisha know they're ants."

"Perhaps." She looked back at him. "Is it horrible that I'm sorry he's *not* dead?" When Byron didn't speak, she rushed to add, "He's a bad man. He did bad things. Hurt people."

"No, that's not horrible."

"His brother," she began, unsure how to articulate what she wanted to say.

"Is probably a bad man, too."

"No. I mean, yes, but…Grisha had a brother. A mother. People who loved him. Cherished him."

"You could say that about all the people I've killed, Princess."

She had to fight to keep from flinching at his words.

"Or did you forget that's what I do?" When she didn't answer, he continued, "Just because someone is loved doesn't mean they have a place in the world. What about all of the people he's hurt? The women he's bought and sold? The children?"

She nodded slowly.

"That's how I justify *my* place in the world."

In one sentence, he'd laid himself bare. All his hurts, if not the reasons for them, were suddenly on display just like the artifacts at Carthage.

He didn't think he belonged in the world. He didn't think he deserved to breathe.

Her heart ached for him.

She knew anything she said to him he'd take as pity or the babbling of a naive girl who hadn't seen anything of reality.

HOME TO GLORY? Had Renner lost his fucking mind?

Number one, there was nothing in Glory. It was a pissant roadside stop on the way to hell. It was nothing but gossipy old biddies and antiquing military wives.

Or local townies looking to marry a military man to get themselves out of there. Why on earth would he stash a princess there?

If he managed to keep her face out of the news, it was possible it could work. But nothing could stay hidden in Glory for long. Everyone knew everyone's business. Within five seconds of he and Damara crossing the county line, everyone in town would know he was back, that he had a princess in tow and that his combat boots were a size thirteen.

And then she'd have a whole town to change her mind, to wipe that look of perfect trust and faith right off her beautiful face. A whole town to tell her what a loser he used to be, and still was. For all his talk about wanting her to know he was a bad man, he'd liked that adoration on her face.

When he'd thought they were parting on the tarmac, a part of him had been thankful that he hadn't sullied it or broken her belief in him. It was okay because it was a pretty fantasy—hers and his. He could let himself believe in the quietest, darkest part of the night that he wasn't all bad. Glory would change that for them both.

She said she'd liked his bad-boy history, but how much would she like it when it was in her face?

How much would she like it when he finally failed her? Because he would. He didn't want to, of course not. If he had his way, he'd wrap a bubble around the princess. He wanted to keep the light in her eyes, the hope, the innocence. He didn't want to see it flicker to dust and ash, and he definitely didn't want to be the cause.

Just being this close to her now with nowhere to

run set his teeth on edge, made him itch to be anywhere else. Her very presence was a sword of Damocles hanging over his head and he either wanted to escape or needed it to drop. Something definitive in the next moments to slice through this awful expectation of pain. Sometimes the expectation was more torture than the sensation itself. This twelve hours was going to be the longest of his life.

What the hell was Renner thinking?

He'd be sure to ask him when he got to D.C. Byron thought about quitting again. It was insane to keep putting Damara's life in his hands. Only an idiot would trust him with her, and Byron didn't want to work for an idiot.

Byron looked out the window at the clouds, the horizon line where the pale blue sky became darker as the atmosphere thinned. Memory after memory of Glory washed over him.

Stomping down those cobbled brick streets in boots not unlike the ones he wore now, buying cigarettes off the old man who ran the bait shop and being a constant, ever-present disappointment to his father. His grandmother dying of a stroke after he'd been arrested—his dad had made sure he knew that it was Byron's fault when he'd signed the papers to send him to Mauer Hill Military Academy.

Death followed his failures as if they held some particular enticing perfume.

He couldn't go back. More important, there was no need for him to go back. Picking open his scars wouldn't help the princess and it wouldn't help him.

The best that Byron Hawkins could hope for was one more night in her arms and dying a good death in defense of his country—maybe sooner rather than later.

Byron chewed over his thoughts for most of the flight. It was all he could do to keep from staring at her—or worse. Dragging her into his lap and burying himself inside her where she took all the pain away, where there was only jasmine and pleasure. Only peace and her sweetness.

All things wasted on a man like him.

He never should have touched her. She was like a drug, and he needed another hit.

He took a deep breath and centered himself. He turned off his emotions because that's what had to be done. It was the only way he'd complete the mission. At least until he could figure out what Renner's plans were and how to change them.

He steeled himself and finally stole a glance at her when Gregson announced they were landing at Dulles Airport outside D.C. She'd tried to hide how his words had made her feel, but the more proper and royal she became, the more he knew he'd hurt her.

Hawkins decided as soon as he saw Renner, he'd tell him he was going back to finish Grisha. A one-two pop to the back of the head with a 9 mm would handle what the .38 to the chest couldn't.

She shifted, trying to get comfortable in her seat, but she didn't complain.

He knew she wouldn't. It would be beneath her to complain. Uncouth.

"After Dulles it will be about three more hours to Kansas City, and then another hour home."

Home. Not that Glory was really his home.

And not that he'd even accepted he was going.

"What's Glory like?"

Hell?

The look on her face was hopeful, earnest, so he tried to think of something good to say. "It's not flat. Everyone thinks that all of Kansas is flat, but it's rather hilly in some places. Where I lived, we're only a few hours from the Ozarks, so there are glacial hills. Glory and Fort Glory were strategic points on the Missouri River, a gateway to the West."

"Like cowboys and gunfights?" She perked.

"Yes. There's a small town close to Glory where Jesse James was born."

"So much history in one place. We were always taught that America is new, so everything must be new. But you revere your history as much as Castallegna."

Not my history, he wanted to say. Never his own. Maybe his country's, but Glory had nothing for him now.

"If you like ghosts, we're close to Atchison, Kansas, and they have a restaurant that used to be a whorehouse. Legend has it, the ghosts of the women will sit at your table with you."

She laughed. "Now you're teasing me."

"No, I'm dead serious."

"Can we go eat there?"

"We'll take the whole ghost-hunting tour if you want." Christ, what was he promising her? He wasn't going to be around long enough to take her on a tour. She shouldn't even be going to Glory. What was he thinking?

"Were you the class quarterback who dated all the cheerleaders?" she asked, interrupting his thoughts.

"I never dated them." Taking them for a ride in his dad's Bimmer and banging them under a slide in the park couldn't be considered dating.

"Did you play sports?"

"Nah, that wasn't me. I was the guy in the leather jacket under the bleachers with the cheerleaders. I was the guy they took home to piss off their daddies. I was the kid with an ADHD diagnosis and I sold my pills for cigarette money until my parents shipped me off to a school for 'behavior modification.' My rap sheet was as long as my arm before I joined the rangers."

She tightened her seat belt as they descended to land. "Special Forces? I'd love to hear more about that."

"Didn't last very long." He hoped the way he clipped his words would keep her from digging any deeper.

She seemed to be content to let the conversation die, and neither of them spoke again until they disembarked and were taken to a private part of the airport used for maintenance.

They were surrounded by men in suits, with Bluetooth earpieces, leather gloves and guns. Yeah, that was subtle.

Renner was a tall man with a thick gray handlebar mustache and hair cropped close to his head. He reminded Byron of Sam Elliott in more than just his appearance.

He didn't bother with introductions. "Our plans have changed."

"That's not surprising." Byron arched a brow, daring Renner to take him to task for anything.

Renner returned the expression and the dare. "By

leaving Grisha Kulokav alive, you've stirred the crap pot to a full boil."

"Come on," he drawled. "She's a princess. There was going to be an international incident no matter what happened. Save your spin for the oversight committee." He already knew that Daniel Renner wasn't about to change his mind concerning whatever he'd concocted. He could tell by the tone of voice, the set to his jaw and the look in his eyes. Made Byron want to cuss all over again.

Renner gave him a lazy smirk. "Glad you brought up spin because this is how we're going to play it. We can't deny what happened on *Circe's Storm.* I really would've thought Kulokav wouldn't have admitted to trying to kidnap the princess, but he says they're engaged. Abele Petrakis had the engagement ratified by the Council while Grisha was sent to retrieve her."

Byron didn't see any discernible difference in Damara. Her expression was one of serenity, but he just knew. He could feel her fear as if it were his own.

He didn't care for that.

Not at all.

Not her fear or the man who put it there. Yet again, he'd failed. And, yet again, someone was in danger because of him.

"I'm going to kill him." He growled low in his throat like a wild animal and Damara put her hand on his arm like a mistress holding back a mastiff.

"I'm sure you will, but it's going to be a while unless you can find a way to kill him from Glory."

"I'm not going to Glory," Byron said with surety.

"Yes, you are. Otherwise the spin won't work. And this has been approved at the highest levels. Do you understand what that means? This is a matter of national security."

What Renner was actually saying was that the plan was the plan, and if Hawkins didn't get his ducks in line, he'd go to prison as an unperson. They'd shove him in a hole so deep no one would ever find him.

Damara was attuned to the doublespeak. "Whatever your plan is, I'd rather have a protector who is willing. Mr. Hawkins kept me safe and got me here. I don't think I, or Castallegna, could ask any more of him."

"Good thing you're not asking and I'm telling, then, right?" Renner grinned.

And Byron was reminded of Foxworth's grinning rictus. *More to life than this, hoss.*

Byron gritted his teeth. What the hell did that even mean now? More to life than war? Yeah, he knew that for some men there was. But not for Byron.

"Listen to me. We've already released a statement. Byron, you're a ranger. You never resigned. You were sent to aid the princess, but you fell in love. It's going to be just like the Bahrain princess and the marine. People will understand wanting freedom for your country, but the world at large has a thing for star-crossed lovers." Renner focused his attention on Damara. "People will move mountains for love."

"Didn't they get divorced?" Byron drawled, barely able to keep his anger leashed.

"They did. So we will give them something new to believe in. Something new to hope for. This isn't a girl rebelling against her parents. This is a woman running from a brutal man who'd hurt her, who traffics in people, drugs and arms. And she fell in love with the man who saved her. We're going to give the world a hero, Hawkins. And that's you."

Every word was a bullet of higher caliber than the last. "You know why it can't be me."

"Uganda doesn't matter now. For your sake and for hers, you have to put it behind you. Because this is already done. We need that base in Castallegna. What part of *national security* did you miss?"

"National security doesn't mean it has to be me."

"Yes, it does. Kulokav is alive. Your cover is blown. Your picture has been all over the world news networks for the last six hours. There is no one who doesn't know your face. Your work as an operative is done. Do this job and you'll be set for life. Pension, benefits, hazard pay...whatever you want."

Then what would he do with himself? Byron felt as if his whole life, as piss-poor as it was, had just been jerked out from under him.

"You don't know what you've done." With no way to channel his aggression, the dark beast that seemed to live inside him, he didn't know what he would do.

"What I had to." Renner nodded. "Get back on the plane. Go to Glory. I've made arrangements for you there. I'll be in touch."

Byron wanted to roar, to rage, but instead he stood, frozen.

Damara moved her hand on his shoulder, and he jerked away from her. Being near her just made it worse.

He had no outlet for his desire or the need for destruction that filled him. Byron felt as if his skin was nothing more than an organic casing for rage that could erupt at any time.

CHAPTER SIX

THEY HAD TO PLAY at being in love, and he couldn't even stand to touch her.

Damara knew he was angry. Angry at Renner, angry at whatever had happened to him in Uganda, but he was angry at her, as well.

She probably deserved it because she could have complained more loudly, more vociferously. After all, their plan couldn't work without her compliance. But after further consideration, she knew Renner was right. This was the best way.

She remembered the story of the princess and the marine. She'd watched the movie, and, at first, she'd been so grateful she had a father who would let her marry whoever she loved. After his death, she'd thought about how nice it would be to have someone save her from Abele.

Even though Byron had saved her in a sense, her purpose was to save her people. This wasn't about some fantasy. Even though she'd played it that way in her head just a little bit.

They were going to be trapped together on the plane for another three hours. She didn't want to spend it in brooding silence or pretending to read books she didn't care about.

"If I find a way out of this, will you take it?" His voice startled her.

Maybe she did want to spend it in silence, after all. "I don't see any other way, but yes. If you find a reasonable way out of this that will still protect my people, I will take it."

"I'm trying to protect *you.*"

"Don't worry about me. I already told you, you're not responsible for me. I'm responsible for myself."

"If you don't need me to be responsible for you, then why am I here?"

"Because you're bigger, stronger and you might be faster. Oh, and you have more guns. But I'm not helpless, Byron. And, frankly, it's offensive that you think I am. Needing help doesn't mean I'm helpless."

"I didn't say that."

"But you did." She watched his expression. "You do. Every time you say that something is your fault, or I'm going to get hurt because of something you did or didn't do, you're intimating I can't make my own choices and I'm not responsible for them. I am. I'm responsible for a *nation.*" She sounded much more confident than she felt.

"You don't understand. I can't do this. I can't."

"I'm not letting you off here. You talked about your purpose in the world and how you justify it? Walking away from me and this mission would be failure."

He reared forward so his face was inches from hers. "Shut your mouth about things you don't understand, Princess."

The growl was back.

A prickle of awareness skittered down her back. They were being watched. She looked over her shoulder to see a pack of paparazzi watching from the gate area as they headed toward the plane. She hadn't expected to have to face them so soon, but Mr. Renner must have wanted them to get ahead of the buzz before her brother could influence the media.

Rather than be intimidated by his anger, she leaned into him. "We're on." She smashed her lips into his. His fingers dug harshly into her waist, but she didn't care.

She couldn't. It didn't matter what this cost either of them. It was the only way.

Instead, she focused on what it felt like to kiss him. She didn't know his anger could have a taste, but it did. It was like salt, but still it was good. Still lit a fire only he could extinguish.

Damara broke the kiss and waved up at the crowd before reboarding the plane behind him.

If she'd thought their heated kiss would have soothed him, it had only cranked him higher.

"Don't ever do that again," he snarled.

"Then do your job," she volleyed, unaffected by his warning.

"Is that what you want? You want to be just a job to me? What happened to your earlier wish?"

His barb struck home. "Wish in one hand, Hawkins, and goat crap in the other."

"You're going to be sorry for this, Damara. Mark my words."

She narrowed her eyes. She knew in her bones that Byron wasn't threatening her. So she called him on it. "You'd never hurt me," Damara whispered, drawing the sting out of their interaction.

He looked at her, eyes haunted. "Oh, but I will. I won't mean to, but I will."

"Byron." His name was a plea, and she reached out to cup his face, the scruff of his unshaven chin rough on her hands. "You won't." She shook her head. "I won't let you."

"I don't want your pity."

"Of course you don't. Who would? Pity is a form of snobbery and condescension. I won't say I understand *your* pain. I don't know what you've been through because you won't tell me. But I will say I understand pain itself. Loss. Guilt. Those aren't unique to you. You're not alone in your suffering."

"I should be," he answered darkly.

"But you're not. We're in this together, Byron, whether we want to be or not."

"When this blows up in your face, don't say I didn't warn you."

Damara supposed it was wrong on some level that all she wanted to do now was kiss him again. As if that could siphon off his pain and replace it with only good things. She knew she was deluding herself. She couldn't fix whatever was broken in him, but she wanted to shelter him until he could mend himself.

She slid over into the seat next to him, offering him comfort. Damara made him look at her, her fingers on his chin the same as he'd done to her.

"I won't. I promise." She nodded to emphasize her point.

"Don't depend on me." He said it like a warning even as his arm slipped around her shoulders.

"I won't. I'll depend on myself." She already did depend on him. She needed his presence. She felt stronger, more confident just knowing he was near, but she'd never make the mistake of telling him that.

Damara decided that she found this seat next to him much more comfortable than the other one she'd chosen and she stayed there, close to him in the cocoon of quiet acceptance they'd wrought until they landed at Kansas City International.

She wasn't naive enough to think that all his rage and resentment would go away, but for now, in this moment, there was acceptance and peace. Damara had learned that it was those moments she had to choose to live in, whatever happened.

As soon as they walked up the jet bridge, they were met by a woman dressed sharply in white. "I'm Sonja White, and I'm your PR liaison. There is a starving pack of paparazzi waiting to meet you. For now, you are to say you have no comment, but they will be invited to a press junket in Glory. Got it?" She flashed Damara a smile.

Damara decided the woman had too many teeth, like a piranha. That smile wasn't honest and, as her father would say, it wasn't going to launch any ships. Something about her put Damara off, but she nodded.

She knew what she was doing with the press. She'd trained for this all her life.

Sonja wasn't kidding. They were mobbed by cameras and lights, microphones shoved in their faces. When a cameraman got a little too close, Byron immediately placed himself between her and the man, the intent to do violence written plainly on his face.

Sonja had already lost control of the group.

Damara flashed her best princess smile. She crept

out from behind Byron and put a hand on his chest to stay him, and he eased back.

So did the crowd, but she asked for more. "Space please, ladies and gentlemen."

They responded to her calm, cool manner, and she fixed each person on the front lines of the mob with her best princess smile.

When they'd all moved to a distance she was comfortable with, she spoke again. "I'm Princess Damara Petrakis of Castallegna. I know you all have questions, but we've been through quite an ordeal in the past few days. Of which I'd be happy to tell you all about at the press junket in Glory, Kansas. You can get details from our PR liaison, Sonja White."

"Is it true you're fleeing an arranged marriage to a Russian gangster?" a voice asked.

"Please, as I said, we'll take all of your questions after we've had a chance to rest." She leaned back against Byron, and his arms came around her so easily, so naturally, she'd swear it was a habit born of years rather than hours.

They cut a path through the crowd, leaving Sonja to deal with the mess.

"You handled that very well," he told her.

Damara was getting to where she liked praise from him better than chocolate. That simply wasn't to be tolerated because she knew it wouldn't last. This arrangement wasn't permanent, and she had a feeling that before all of this was over, he'd hate her.

"Thank you."

"There's our car." He pointed at a black car.

"How do you know?"

"Government plates." He indicated the tags on the back.

The door opened for them, and Byron made sure she was secured before he got into the car. Just like her other bodyguards.

Exhaustion and relief swept over her. She hadn't realized how tired she was, or that she'd been figuratively holding her breath, until the car was in motion. She sagged against him.

"I wasn't kidding when I said we'd been through a lot in the past few days. I think every bone in my body hurts. Even my face."

"It's about an hour to reach Glory. Then you can sleep for as long you want, Princess. But let me warn you, it's nothing like Barcelona. There won't be any room service."

"I don't even care. The first thing I want to do is eat your McDonald's. Then I want to sleep for a year. Maybe a bath."

"Do you have McDonald's on Castallegna?"

"No. They wanted to put in a few restaurants, but Abele said no when they wouldn't pay him a 'finder's fee.' But they made us their French fries and they were so good."

"The people will like that."

"What?"

"A French-fry-eating princess."

"They will like the hero who saved the princess, too."

"As long as no one forgets this is just a role and I'm not a hero."

She wasn't going to argue with him about it, so she said nothing. Her brain had latched on to the idea of a bath. Of sitting and soaking away the bad parts of the past few days but keeping the good.

Only, thinking of Byron and water… She remembered what it was like when he allowed her to touch him freely. To enjoy him and, in turn, be enjoyed.

She supposed having been intimate with the man she was to pretend to be in love with made it that much easier.

"And in that vein, I think when we're alone, we should keep touching to the minimum."

She realized she'd dropped her head on his shoulder. "I'm sorry." Damara straightened. "But I don't agree. Who knows how long we'll have to use this ruse, and it'll be hard to protect me if you're sitting a mile away from me."

"This is my line in the sand, Damara. Don't push me on this."

"Renner said—"

"Renner is cordially invited to go play a hearty game of hide-and-go-fuck-himself, and he's a quarter behind."

She had no idea what that meant, but she knew it wasn't a good thing. "This isn't going to work."

"No, and I told him that."

She gritted her teeth. "Fine. Maybe we can say that it wasn't you. That you were the guy my fiancé sent to retrieve me. That we were already in love somehow."

He perked. "That might work."

His eagerness to embrace that scenario hurt more than it should have. He was right. Sleeping with him had been a mistake. She might not have done it if she'd known that night in Barcelona wasn't their last. This was too hard. She was supposed to pretend to be intimate with a man she was already intimate with, but also had to pretend that intimacy meant nothing to her. It was too much, too complicated.

"Yeah. It might." She leaned against the car door and watched the scenery go by. Damara didn't want to say anything else to him. She couldn't, not without her throat constricting and all her stupid little-girl ideas getting crushed under his boot.

Damara knew that's what they were, but that didn't stop her from wanting to hold on to them anyway.

SHE DIDN'T UNDERSTAND, but Byron didn't expect her to. He just couldn't have her touching him all the time, clinging to him, pretending to be his when she wasn't.

And never could be.

He knew his rejection stung, but better to sting now than damage later. Because he wouldn't stop with the soft touches, the way she burrowed into him. He'd move his hands up the back of her spine, or down to her hips; he'd cup her perfect breasts, kiss her full lips… And, silly girl that she was, she'd let him.

Byron was already hard with want and she made him feel as if he was a kid again with no idea how to handle his own needs.

There was part of him that had listened to everything she'd said and believed it. It was louder now than it had ever been. She said she was a woman in charge of her own destiny so he should take her up on everything she offered and not look back. Not look forward.

Just look at now.

Byron knew she deserved better than that.

It was all worse now that he was coming back to Glory. He didn't want to be here. The familiar sights as the car passed over the bridge and into Glory didn't bring him the ease it might have brought some people coming home after all these years. Not Byron Hawkins. The last time he'd passed through Kansas City, he hadn't even bothered to make the drive.

Now the familiar sights and smells turned his stomach, knotted it up with knitting needles.

The town had been decorated for Christmas, little wreaths and bells hung off light posts and everything that would stand still long enough to be draped in evergreen. Santa decals adorned a lot of the storefronts, along with fake snow and cozy winter scenes. Sweet Thing advertised a new kind of hot chocolate and "dipping biscuits," whatever the hell those were. The Corner Pharmacy offered a Winter Wonderland Shake, probably some monstrosity of eggnog and cinnamon. The local theater showed scheduled performances of *The Nutcracker* on the old-fashioned marquee.

The car stopped in front of a large Victorian on Broadway. He'd expected they would've decided to house them on base at Fort Glory. It would definitely be safer for Damara. And it would also make press access more difficult.

THE HOUSE HAD BEEN decorated, as well. There was a candle in every window and a large wreath hung on the door.

He didn't want to be here. There were too many ghosts, and his head was already full of them.

A familiar face greeted him when the door of the car opened.

Caleb Lewis. Somehow, he'd become one of Glory's finest. He was in a police uniform.

"What the hell is that, Lewis?" Byron laughed, nodding to the uniform. "It's almost Christmas, not Halloween."

Caleb shrugged. "I don't know, man. It just happened. I could say the same to you. I guess military school did wonders for you. I know it was great for my Friday nights."

"You went, too?" He had a hard time imagining one of Glory's golden boys in military school.

He snorted. "Hell, no. But with you gone, I had more of a chance at getting a girl to say yes to a date with me."

Byron appreciated the easy camaraderie. The meaningless banter that welcomed him home without judgment. Caleb was one of those who'd never judged him, never slunk to his locker needing what he could provide and then talking about him behind his back.

He'll never be anything.

He was just born bad.

"So they put you on princess duty?" he asked, trying to rouse the shades from his mind.

"I requested it. Figured you could use a friendly face." Caleb shrugged it off.

"Where's your partner in crime? You and India were always attached at the hip."

"She's actually my partner. She's getting doughnuts from my sister's shop. She decided the princess had to have doughnuts." At Byron's expression, he added, "Yeah, I don't know. It's a girl thing, I guess."

"We both know India's not really a girl. Brimstone on wheels, maybe. But never just a girl."

Caleb grinned, but he didn't say much else. He realized he hadn't introduced Damara when he felt the weight of her presence at his back.

"This is Princess Damara Petrakis of Castallegna."

"The Jewel of Castallegna." Caleb smiled. "It's a pleasure to welcome you to Glory."

"It is truly an honor. Thank you."

She was every bit the perfect princess, and Caleb was dutifully and predictably charmed.

And Byron was pissed off.

He didn't want her to be so likable and gracious, and he definitely didn't want Caleb to be charmed or charm*ing*. Jealousy he had no right to feel flared like a canker.

"Let's get her inside," he grumbled.

"You've got eyes and ears everywhere, Hawkins. There's a couple of guys posted at various places on the property—it'll be a revolving post. They're camped out above the carriage house in back. Your people chose this house because of the underground tunnel that leads from the main house to the carriage house. Glory P.D. will be doing hourly drive-bys to make sure everything is as it should be. We're not going to let anything happen to either of you."

"The princess has been trained in Krav Maga and can use any weapon you give her."

"That's definitely sexy." Caleb grinned. Just when Hawkins was seriously considering punching him in the face, he said, "India kicks my ass all the time."

"I knew you guys would end up together. She might be the only girl who ever told me no." Hawkins smiled.

"No, we're just friends. But that doesn't mean I don't like it when she's tough." Caleb turned to leave.

"Fair warning. The house has been wired up with surveillance. So no running naked around the garden at night."

He got into his patrol car and drove away.

"Is he a friend of yours?" Damara asked.

"Yeah, I guess he is." Byron had never thought about it before, but he supposed out of anyone in Glory, Caleb was his friend. He hated being back here, hated being home. But Caleb wasn't so bad.

And he guessed the people in Glory weren't all awful, if taken on an individual basis. It was when they started going off in groups and committees that they were a problem.

"No, what I mean is, can we trust him? If something happens, is he someone to seek out or avoid?"

Byron thought about it for a moment. Caleb Lewis was one of those people you definitely wanted on your side. He'd heard that he'd enlisted in the army just so India wouldn't be deployed alone. "Remember what I said? Don't trust anyone but yourself."

"And remember what I said about needing help?"

He did at that. "Yes, Princess. You can trust him."

"I love the house."

"You haven't even been inside."

"No, and I don't need to. I know I'll love it. The architecture is lovely." She looked down. "And the brick sidewalks."

She hurried up the walk.

"Let me go inside first and do a security check before you get all Martha Stewart."

"Thank you for telling Officer Lewis that I could hold my own. I appreciate that."

She picked the strangest times to say the most unexpected things.

"It's the truth."

"Yes, but no one else has ever seen that truth but you. So it's important to me to thank you."

He watched her for a moment longer than necessary before going inside and giving the house a perfunctory scan.

"You can come inside."

Two cell phones sat side by side on the counter. When one rang, Byron answered it.

"You made yourself right with this yet?" Renner asked him.

"No."

"Fine. I'm sending a file to the phone. It's all the other candidates in the area. Choose one."

The line went dead.

The thought of trusting Damara's safety to someone else didn't bring the relief he'd thought it would. He scrubbed his hand over his face.

"What's wrong?"

"Renner said he has some other candidates."

"Oh." She walked up the stairs to explore the second floor.

He supposed it was funny that he'd chosen that word to describe her actions—*exploring.* It was something she liked. Something she was damn good at, he thought, as memories of her "explorations" washed over him.

For shit's sake, it was only one night. Why couldn't he forget it?

He looked down at the phone and the blinking icon that indicated he had a text.

Hawkins downloaded the file and quickly scrolled through every name on the list. None of them met with his approval. None of them could keep Damara safe.

He clicked on Renner's number and called him back.

"Made a choice so quickly?"

"You know damn well I didn't. What the hell is this?" Did Renner want the mission to fail? That list couldn't have been what he meant to send.

"It's what I said it was. It's the list of those operatives available to take your place."

"None of them are good enough."

"I know that, but you wouldn't listen to me."

"Point taken. I'll do it. But this in-love act? How long do we have to keep it up?"

"I don't know. To keep her safe, you're probably going to have to marry her."

"Have you lost your goddamn mind?" Byron meant to sound forceful, but he sounded much higher-pitched and maybe even slightly crazy.

"It's the fastest way to citizenship. Otherwise, we'd have to put it through committees and votes, granting her asylum. It's the only way." Renner sighed. "Is it really such a task to be saddled with a beautiful, accomplished woman?"

"I don't want this, and I don't want her," he reiterated.

"Then you're the only one who doesn't."

He heard a gasp and looked up to see Damara still on the stairs. She'd heard what he said.

"Damara," he began, but he knew there were no words that could soothe the hurt he'd just inflicted.

She shook her head slowly, eyes wide and sorrowful. Her full lips set in a grim line. *No,* she mouthed and trudged slowly up the stairs.

"Heard you, did she? Make your choice now. Either do this with full retirement benefits after this is over or come ride a desk."

"I said I'd do it," he snarled.

"Good. I don't want to hear any more about it."

The line went dead again.

He cursed. Why did he even care if she heard it? Then maybe she'd stop looking at him as if he were some kind of hero. If he was honest with himself, he liked how she looked at him, even though he knew it was fleeting. It wouldn't last. The sword of Damocles had fallen and sliced clean.

Byron saw the other phone on the counter, and he supposed it was as good an excuse as any to follow her upstairs. She should have it on her person at all times.

He picked it up and headed up the stairs.

He found her in the master bedroom, sitting with a book, but he knew she wasn't reading. She stared at the page blankly. It was upside down.

Byron took it gently out of her hands and put it down next to her, then replaced it with the cell.

"You need to keep this on you at all times."

"Thank you."

She didn't look at him. She stared at the phone the same way she'd stared at the book.

"Damara—" he tried again.

"No." She held up her hand. "We will not discuss it again. You will call your Mr. Renner. You will tell him what happened in Barcelona. He will tell Kulokav, and they will not want me any longer. My brother will disown me and force the Council to decree an end to my line of succession. Then I will find another way to help my people." Her gaze flashed up to his face. "And we'll be rid of each other."

"Damara, what's stopping him from doing that anyway?"

"I knew it was a risk when I ran. The original plan ensured that I'd have support in the world theater, and Castallegna is too small to risk trade sanctions. Or so he explained it to me. I didn't know the man who saved me would be the one chosen for this duty. Or that it would be against your will. Go. Call him. I will find another way."

"There isn't another way."

"You told me yourself not to trust anyone but me. So I do. And *I* will find another way."

There was something about the tone of her voice, the way she held herself, it made him cringe away from her like a roach running from the light. Yet it drew him closer, too. Her strength, her surety of self, he'd never known another woman like her. He couldn't trust himself, but he couldn't trust anyone else, either. He'd rather she be with the devil he knew. "You're stuck with me now, anyway. I already told him I'd do it. There's no one else."

"Which he already told you. It's fine. You don't have to change your mind just because I heard you say that you don't want me. You've made it abundantly clear."

"That's not it at all, Damara. Not at all."

"It doesn't matter what it is."

"You were right, okay? I'm not going to abandon you." He realized that must be how she felt, and he wouldn't do that to her.

She didn't say anything else. Instead, she lay down on the bed and turned away from him.

He didn't know what to say to her, what to do to make it better.

Byron picked up the book and sat down in the chair where she'd been. His job was to protect her and watch over her, so that's what he'd do.

No matter what it cost him.

Maybe if he kept her safe, all the lives that she changed, all the lives that she'd save, would be worth Uganda. Or at least grant him a quieter corner of hell.

CHAPTER SEVEN

I DON'T WANT THIS and I don't want her.

Damara didn't need to hear that over and over again in her head for it to make sense. She'd already processed what it meant, but that didn't stop her stupid brain from playing it on a loop. Maybe it was a self-defense mechanism. If she heard it enough times, it would root out whatever silly things she'd thought about she and Byron together. It would help her remember to keep her distance.

But it did more than that. It crushed the air out of her chest.

It hurt.

So what if no one ever wanted her for herself? It wasn't the end of the world. The sky was still blue; the earth still turned.

Her denials rang hollow in her ears. Right now, she was good for something. And that was putting on this show to thwart Abele. It would have to be enough.

Damara had it better than so many. She had wealth. She had privilege. She would always have a roof over her head, food in her belly, and that was a lot more than many.

But that didn't stop the hollow feeling that chilled her insides.

She'd passed the rest of the night without speaking to Byron, and he didn't make any further effort to engage her, so it was startling to hear his voice calling her name.

"Damara?"

"I'll be down."

"Sonja White is here."

The piranha with too many teeth. Before facing her, Damara pulled on her princess armor by brushing her hair, straightening her clothes and doing her breathing exercises. When she descended the stairs, she felt almost like herself again.

Until she saw the way the blonde woman talked to Byron, the way she angled her body toward him, used every opportunity to brush against him.

And who wouldn't? Byron Hawkins was heroic and handsome with his dark hair and sharp eyes. His broad shoulders like Atlas that lifted up the world.

That didn't stop it from irritating Damara to no end.

"Good of you to join us, Princess."

She didn't know if Sonja meant to be condescending, but Damara didn't care for her tone. As if she'd kept them waiting some unreasonable amount of time. She was the Jewel of Castallegna—if she deigned to take hours to prepare herself or decided not to see the woman at all, that was her prerogative. She was royalty. Even on American soil.

"Good of you stop by without invitation," Damara returned with a genuine smile. Genuine because it pleased her to put the woman in her place.

Sonja appeared startled and off her game. Another mark in the win column. Then Damara felt just the slightest twinge of guilt. The woman had been hired to help them. Damara wouldn't be difficult just because she was jealous.

Even though she *really* wanted to be.

She sighed. "I'm sorry. Jet lag makes me cranky, and I'm still tired."

"I completely understand." Sonja nodded. "I'd be more than cranky if I'd been through what you have. You really do have such an amazing story. Everyone wants to hear about it. Have you seen the news?" Sonja handed her a clipping from the *New York Times.*

It was a picture of her and Byron. The moment she'd put her hand on his chest to keep him from doing bodily harm. They both looked every inch the parts they were supposed to play. She was a fairy-tale princess and Byron was Prince Charming, the hero. The way she looked up at him, her emotions were written all over her face.

But so were his. Woe be to anyone who'd dare try and hurt her.

It was such a contrast to what he'd said to Renner on the phone. *I don't want her.*

"That looks like good publicity," Damara agreed. She wanted to take the clipping and fold it up, to keep it to remember what it was like when she still dreamed of fairy tales.

"Every news outlet in the country has picked up the story. There'll be the press junket today, and we need to start thinking about a publicity tour."

"Whoa, hold on. How am I supposed to protect her if we're doing some publicity tour?"

"They'll come to you."

"This hiding her in plain sight stuff is harder than it looks." Byron sighed.

"We'll make her face so recognized and well loved that no one would chance hurting her."

Byron was sacrificing so much to be there, especially by revealing who he really was. He was losing everything. Damara wanted to say something to him that would make it okay, but she knew there was nothing.

"And we need to start planning the wedding."

"Excuse me?" Damara almost choked.

"The wedding. You have to get married. It's the only way to expedite citizenship. I thought Mr. Renner told you."

"He did," Byron said. "Let's just worry about our immediate needs. Press junket. What do you need from us?"

Damara was floored. She hadn't realized that she was actually expected to marry him. And yet the idea wasn't horrible.

Or it wouldn't have been, if he hadn't said he didn't want her.

She didn't have to ask if it would be a marriage of convenience, or inconvenience as the case happened to be. It didn't matter. This would have been her life one way or another. Any man she married would have been doing it for any reason in the world except for loving her.

"Damara?" Byron asked, jerking her from her thoughts.

"I'm sorry. I didn't hear you."

"Do you feel up to be fitted for your wardrobe? If not, we can just do hair and makeup for the junket," Sonja repeated.

Damara gave a wan smile. “That’s fine. I’m a princess. I’m used to it.”

“Better you than me,” Byron replied.

“Oh, no, you’ll be fitted, as well. You need new uniforms, as befits your status and rank.”

Byron paled, but he didn’t say anything.

“Are you sure he needs to be in uniform?” Damara tried to help.

“Ladies love a serviceman in uniform. He’ll fit the archetype. All of the women will want to be you, and all of the men will wish they were Byron. They’ll want you to succeed just because of that.”

Damara nodded.

“The rest of my staff will be here in—” she looked at her watch “—twenty minutes. We’ll order in lunch and we should be done by dinner. Just in time for the junket.”

It occurred to Damara that he knew everything this would entail. It was why he’d wanted to say no. And she’d pushed. She’d pushed so hard with no care for what it did to him. She’d told herself it didn’t matter because she had to save Castallegna, but it did matter.

It mattered a lot.

There was a reason he wasn’t a ranger anymore, a reason for the haunted look in his eyes. It wasn’t her place to make him face anything. He’d already done so much for her.

She wanted to tell him that, but she didn’t know how.

Instead, they were both silent as they were led their separate ways to get ready for the fittings.

Damara endured stoically; this wasn’t a new experience for her, being poked and prodded by strange hands with various materials and designs being shoved in her face.

She still didn't care for Sonja, but she was content to let her do her job. Even when she dragged out a selection of paste tiaras. Damara understood she had to play this a certain way for the camera and for the people.

When the rep would have chosen a larger one, Damara opted for the smaller. "The larger one is too big. When I do a public meet and greet, I like to give them to one of the children."

Sonja blinked. "You're kind of diabolical, aren't you?"

"Why would you say that?" Damara cocked her head to the side.

"That's brilliant PR."

"It's not really about the PR. It's about telling girls that they are all princesses." Damara was determined to give not only the men of her country more power but the women. She shouldn't have to make a marriage just to keep people from hurting her. She should be free to love who and where she would, give of her body as she chose, not for some office. And her countrywomen should be free to do the same. If there was any PR, it was to get that message out.

"Even better." Sonja sighed and directed the staff to leave and finish assembling the princess's wardrobe. "Can I ask you something?" she asked when they were gone.

"Of course," Damara answered. What was she going to say, no?

"I know Renner told me this was a PR thing, but is there actually something between you and Byron?"

Her question was like nails on a chalkboard; it scraped down her back and burrowed into her spine. "Not really."

"Because of him or you?"

"I only said I'd answer one question," Damara demurred.

"Okay. Back off. I get it." Sonja nodded and held up her hands in surrender. "You can't blame a girl for being curious."

"You're more than curious," Damara said.

"You're right—I am."

She regretted adding that last part, but she had to be honest. "I don't have any hold on him, but it wouldn't do for Prince Charming to get caught banging the PR rep, would it? Talk about a fractured fairy tale." It wasn't her place to warn off the other woman—Byron could do as he liked. He didn't belong to her.

Even though she wanted him to.

The thought of him with Sonja cut her deeply, but it was just one more thing to push down deep so she didn't have to feel it. This was stupid; it had only been one night. And maybe he had saved her life, but that didn't mean they needed to spend their lives together.

"No, of course not. I know how important this is. Not only for you. This could make my firm. I'm not going to throw that away for a man."

"Good for you." She meant it sincerely.

Sonja cocked her head to the side. "Now, you really meant that, right? It wasn't a thinly veiled fuck off?"

Damara laughed in spite of herself. "No, really. I think it's wonderful that you're able to prioritize your life so that your value is more than just your ability to breed heirs."

"I can't imagine what that's like." The woman made a face.

No, Damara was sure she couldn't, and she didn't want to talk about it anymore. She had to get control of herself for the junket. "So what should I wear to this junket?"

"The pink skirt and sweater set. It will set off your hair and skin tone. It will also make you look more innocent. I wish you had your engagement ring, but if your first appearance is without it, there will be more buzz when you start wearing one."

Damara nodded, glad that Sonja was back to business. Engagement ring. She supposed if she was a citizen of the United States, she couldn't be queen of Castallegna and qualify for asylum. She didn't want to give up her country, her citizenship. But she supposed if that's what it took to meet the end goal, that's what she'd do.

"I'll get ready then."

"Do you need any more help?"

"No, I can do it. Thank you." She waited for Sonja to leave and dressed. She went toward the master bath to apply the cosmetics that had been left out for her. The makeup artist had wanted to help, but Damara liked to do it herself. It was a sort of ritual that soothed her nerves. She used to watch her mother put on her lipstick before events, and it was something they'd always done together. She missed her so much. It was a way to be close to her and to hear her mother's wisdom when she was frightened or afraid. Unfortunately, Byron was already there. He stood tall and resplendent in his uniform.

He was clean-shaven, his hair clipped and cropped.

His jaw looked harder, his shoulders broader. Yes, there definitely was something about a man in uniform, but this one especially because she suspected it was so very hard for him to put it back on. She was torn between wanting to rip it off him and demand he do salacious things to her, and pulling him softly against her breast and telling him everything would be okay.

At first, she thought he was talking to someone on the phone, but he was talking to himself in the mirror.

"I accept the fact that as a Ranger my country expects me to move further, faster and fight harder than any other soldier. Never shall I fail my—" He broke off, and his fingers curled into a fist as his eyes closed. "Never shall I fail my—" Byron tried again, but instead of finishing the sentence he put his fist through the mirror.

Glass shards exploded everywhere.

He swore.

Damara knew she should leave him with his ghosts, but he was in such obvious pain. She wouldn't leave a dog like that, so she certainly wouldn't do that to a man. And most definitely not to a man who'd done so much for her.

He didn't need her, he didn't want her, but he was getting her. Mindless of the glass crunching beneath her pink heels, she went to him.

Damara turned him carefully away from the remains of the mirror so he'd look at her.

Tears shimmered in his eyes, but she knew he'd never shed them. She of all people understood the futility of tears, the perception of weakness, but sometimes they could wash away the sharpest edge of the pain.

Instead of speaking, she embraced him. It wasn't a soft or kind sort of touch; it was an assault. She dragged him down to her so that he could bury his face in her hair, and she clung to him as if she was the one adrift.

His arms tightened, and he curled his big body around hers.

He was whispering again, and she couldn't understand what he was saying, but that was okay. It wasn't for her—she knew that. She'd hold him like this until he said whatever it was that needed to come out.

"And complete the mission though *I be the lone survivor.* Rangers lead the way."

Byron didn't let go. He just held her hard and tight.

But when it was over, it was as if it had never happened. Just like the night he'd made love to her. It was a moment taken out of context from the rest of existence.

She accepted it for what it was. "Are you ready to go?"

CHAPTER EIGHT

BYRON COULDN'T EVEN recite the Ranger Creed.

He knew he had no business wearing the uniform.

Never shall I fail my comrades.

But he had. He'd failed them.

I will never leave a fallen comrade to fall into the hands of the enemy.

He hadn't even brought their bodies' home. There hadn't been enough left.

He looked over at Damara, serene and pink and perfect. The scent of jasmine was still in his nose. She'd seen him so weak, so lost, and she'd yanked him back to shore with a simple embrace.

The comfort of her body, her warmth, her glow.

Without judgment or any sort of morbid curiosity. She just let him be what he was and that meant more to him than he could—or should—articulate.

It was as if she just knew what he needed. Byron was starting to think it was some kind of supernatural power she had, to see into the hearts of people. To know what they needed when they needed it and to be able to manufacture it somehow on demand. That was Damara—the Jewel.

He steeled himself for the inevitable hell of the junket, determined to make it through without being a dick and without thinking about himself. He could do this for her.

Byron took her hand when they stepped out of the car at the community center. It was small and warm but strong, too. Just being near her made him feel as if he was a better man than he actually was.

That was part of why he'd wanted to get away from her, but he knew that wasn't going to happen anytime soon.

He was going to marry her.

This woman, this force, was going to be his wife.

As unworthy as he was.

"This town, it's just like something out of the movies," Damara said to him when they were ushered inside.

The town had put together a potluck.

For a press junket.

He rolled his eyes. Leave it to Glory to treat an international affair like a night of church bingo. Although, he found he kind of liked it. It would make it easier to protect Damara. Once the town had claimed her for its own, she'd be one of them forever. They'd circle the wagons around her just like a group of pioneers under attack on the unsettled prairie.

They were seated at a long table on the stage. Bouquets of microphones had been strategically placed, and there were hundreds of cameras already in the room.

He spotted some of Renner's people already in place. He knew this building like the back of his hand, even if he'd been gone for years. He'd picked the lock to get into the indoor pool with a couple of girls on multiple occasions. He also knew where a couple of secret escape routes were.

As people filed in, the noise in the room became a buzzing roar.

He focused on Damara. She sat with her back ramrod straight, her legs crossed at the ankles and her hands folded primly in her lap. She was as serene as always.

Byron thought he was going to vomit.

For the briefest second, he thought he saw Austin Foxworth smiling at him from the crowd—with half his face missing.

His stomach gurgled.

Sonja stepped up on the stage. "Thank you for coming. I know you're all very excited to ask our couple some questions, but please listen to each other. Keep your questions respectful and polite. If you do not, Mr. Hawkins's fellow rangers will be assisting you with your exit."

His eyes darted back to the men he recognized as belonging to Renner. They nodded almost imperceptivity to acknowledge their kinship.

He swallowed his bile. He didn't deserve their protection.

But Damara did. He could choke it down for a while longer.

He nodded in return.

"We're going to let the couple introduce themselves. Then they'll be open for questions." Sonja nodded to Damara.

"My name is Damara Petrakis, and I'm so happy to be here in your country. Thank you for the warm welcome that's made me feel very much at home. I came to be here because my father had a dream of freedom for Castallegna. No more royals, no more right to rule. He wanted a country where the people were free to make their own choices. A democratic country." She took a deep breath. "But my father died before his dream could become reality. When I found out that my brother was on international watch lists and the men who'd been coming to our small island home were all criminals, I knew I had to do something. Especially when he sold me to one. The man your government sent to help me is the best of men. Good in every way that my betrothed was bad. Castallegna will always be in my heart, but so will America, and my fiancé, Byron Hawkins."

She was good. He'd give her that. She knew exactly what to say to both gentle them and to spike their curiosity about her escape.

"I'm Byron Hawkins. And the princess already said it all. She's good at these kinds of things. I'm more the strong, silent type." He flashed a cocky grin that he didn't feel. The crowd tittered. It was a part, just another role like Brian Hale, he told himself.

"The press release says that you were in Tunisia at the time of the Carthage Museum robbery. Was that you?" The first question. Not too hard.

"No, the only jewel I took was this one." Byron smiled over at Damara.

She demurred prettily. Cameras flashed.

"Grisha Kulokav says you tried to kill him."

Also not hard. "I did. And I would have if not for the princess's safety being my primary concern."

One of the reporters sighed, as if she thought it was the most romantic thing she'd ever heard.

"Kulokav and his brother both maintain that they're simply businessmen."

"His gulag tattoos say otherwise," Byron answered.

"His deal with my brother was to trade arms through Castallegna," Damara added.

"Were you afraid?"

"Not for a second." She looked over at Byron again. "We'd been in communication for months," she lied easily. "I knew Byron wouldn't let anything happen to me."

"When did you know you were in love?"

Damara fielded this one, as well. "We were floating in a small fisherman's boat in the middle of the Mediterranean, talking about the stars."

Another collective sigh filled the room, and Byron struggled to keep from laughing. That was what had happened, but the way she said it made it sound like something out of a movie.

"Do you think your father would approve of Byron?"

"Yes," she answered almost instantly. "I know he would."

He knew that was what she was supposed to say, but it twisted something in him because he knew her well enough already that he could tell she believed it.

"What do your parents think of the princess?" This question was directed at Byron.

Shit. He hadn't even thought of his parents. So he answered honestly. The fewer lies he told, the less he had to remember. "They haven't met her yet. This has all happened so quickly. But I know they'll love her just as much as I do."

Fat chance of that, but they'd go along with it or

he'd get Renner to throw them somewhere horrible for the duration of the ruse. They didn't hesitate to send him to Maur Hill so he'd have no hesitation, either.

"Just a few more questions," Sonja interjected. "Our new favorite couple has been through quite the ordeal in the last few months, the last several days especially. They need to get their rest."

"When's the wedding?" Another questioner asked.

"August fifteenth. It's my birthday," Byron answered easily. It was a fake wedding, so who cared when it happened?

"Why can't anyone see this for what it is?" Another voice sounded. "The princess is a radical, and she's using the United States to—" His microphone was taken away and two of the rangers grabbed the man and dragged him toward the door.

She stood. The princess held her hand up to stop them, and they paused. "I will answer this. I like to think of myself as a traditional radical." She smiled. "This was my father's dream. And these changes aren't unwelcome. The people voted more than seventy percent that they'd be in favor of this 'radical' thing called democracy. It's my brother who is a radical and a tyrant."

"Then how could you leave your people to run away and have this…romance?" he spat.

She smiled again, still calm and serene as ever. "Who are we to judge when love happens? I was leaving to find help and I found Byron Hawkins. I was already leaving. He just helped me. Protected me. And I love him. Knowing that an assassin could put a bullet in me at any moment, do you really think I should deny myself? Should any of us?"

The room was quiet, and the man had no answers.

"Thank you, gentlemen." She nodded to the men who held the naysayer and they led him out the door.

He was amazed at the way she handled the crowd, how easily she spoke of feelings and how very quickly she'd dug into the secret needs and desires of each person present.

She sat back down. "Any more questions?"

"When do we get to see the ring?" The tension had broken and everyone was once again focused on the love story.

She laughed. "As soon as he buys it for me. As romantic as it was in the middle of the ocean, there's no Tiffany's."

"What kind of ring do you want?"

"How do you buy an engagement ring for a princess on your salary?"

Damara was still unruffled. "Whatever he chooses will have emotional value over financial. I left behind hundreds of diamond rings in Castallegna. Stones mean nothing to me."

Oh, Christ, the pressure of choosing a ring. He was suddenly thankful for Sonja. She and Damara could pick whatever was best, and he'd smile and nod and go along with whatever they wanted.

"This talk of a ring has you looking terrified, Hawkins," a voice said from the back.

"What man isn't terrified of choosing the right ring for his bride?" He shrugged, playing up the hopeless male stereotype.

"Why did you bring her back to Glory?"

Byron answered this one. He knew why Renner had chosen Glory. "Because of the people. It's small-town Americana that I knew Damara would love as much as Glory is going to love her."

"That's enough questions for today, people. You all have my card. We'll work out something for future interviews. Thank you." Sonja indicated the junket was over.

A flood of questions erupted from the gallery, but Damara and Byron were ushered from the room and out a back door. There was still a crowd of people, but all they seemed to want was a view of the princess.

He couldn't believe how in her element she was. Most people would be exhausted to the point of tearful rage by now, but not Damara. She kept going; she kept smiling. Her face must ache by now, he was sure.

She even stopped to speak to a little girl in a wheelchair. Of course she would. That's what fairy-tale princesses do. He had a feeling that's what Damara would do even if she wasn't a princess.

"You're so pretty," the girl said.

"And so are you," Damara returned the compliment easily and sincerely. "What's your name?"

"Megan."

"What do you want to be when you grow up, Megan?" Damara eased down so she was eye level with the girl.

"A princess."

Damara seemed to know what her answer would be, and she probably did. She'd done this a million times. Yet her responses seemed no less real, no less genuine. If Byron didn't know better, he'd swear this was the first.

She took off the tiara that had been pinned carefully into her hair.

"Wherever I go, there are always other princesses in the crowd. I think it's my job to make sure they don't forget. So I give them a tiara. And whenever they start to forget or someone tells them they're not a princess, they'll have it to remind them." She positioned the tiara on the girl's head. "There you go, Megan. So you don't ever forget. Maybe someday, you can remind someone else not to forget, too."

Their security detail moved them along because the rest of the crowd had started to swarm toward the back in hopes of more pictures or getting some nugget for their publications that no one else had managed to obtain.

They were stuffed back into the car, and Damara immediately kicked off her heels. "Oh, my gosh, I hate those shoes. I'm going to burn them. Do you by chance have a blowtorch on you?"

Byron laughed. "I couldn't tell. You were amazing."

She waved her hand. "It's just a mask. A face that I put on and take off like makeup."

"It wasn't to Megan."

"No, it wasn't. But that part was real to me, too. It's important to me that women never let themselves be marginalized like me. I have a platform, so if I can use it, I will."

"Marginalized? I don't think you know your own power."

"I do what I can with what I have."

Her honest humility made him feel like even more of a bastard somehow.

"Freeing Castallegna is as much for me as it is my father," she confessed. "I think it would be amazing to have the freedom to do what I want simply because I wanted to. Some people think being a princess is all money and privilege, and some of it is."

"But you told Megan that she was a princess."

"A lot of little girls dream about being the story-book ideal of a princess. It doesn't matter what the reality is like. What matters is what they believe. I hope they keep their fairy tales forever. Like Disney princesses. They're all kind and good-hearted, and with enough hope and hard work, they get a happily ever after."

Byron didn't know what to say to that, so he changed the subject. "Are you hungry?"

"I'm starved. I'm always hungry."

"You haven't had your McDonald's yet. Do you want to?"

"Yes!" she cried.

The smallest, strangest things made this woman happy. He knocked on the window that divided the space between the passenger and the driver. "McDonald's. Drive-through."

"Whatever you say, boss."

The window went back up.

"Can we go see some sights or something? But with the heat on? I'm freezing."

He knew the proper response was to put his arm around her, but after everything it just didn't seem right.

Except her teeth were chattering.

"Do you have snow in Castallegna?"

"No. Greece gets snow in the mountains, but Castallegna is all spring and summer. We don't have fall or a real winter."

"Then you might be in for a treat, depending on how Kansas is feeling. The weather here is a little…bipolar."

"Polar?"

"No, like…emotionally unbalanced," he corrected.

"Oh." She laughed. "I see."

He felt like a pompous ass going through the drive-through in a government car with a driver, but whatever. He ordered, and she seemed fascinated with the whole process.

She ate her fries and she ate *his* fries, leaving him with both burgers.

"Um, those were my fries."

"Nope. They were mine. Obviously." She grinned. Damara had some salt on her lips, and the first thing he thought about was licking it off. "What? Do I have some in my teeth?"

"You've got salt on your lips." He tried to keep his voice steady and even, but it dropped an octave anyway.

She licked her lips and every swipe of her tongue sent a jolt of awareness through him.

"Did I get it?"

He could say all sorts of things—the worst and cheesiest would be, "Let me help you with that"—and then he'd kiss her, taste her, take her in the backseat of this car as though their relationship weren't a ruse. That it was real.

And she belonged to him.

She seemed to feel it, too, because she was suddenly so still. He didn't know if she was frozen, like some small mammal hoping he'd move on to other prey, or if she wanted him, too.

He didn't know why she would, not after the way he'd acted. He couldn't stand himself, so he didn't know how she could.

"It's easy to pretend, isn't it?" she asked without looking up into his eyes.

"It is. But there are parts of this that are more than pretend." When she didn't answer, he wondered if he'd broken whatever had started to bloom between them. "Aren't there?"

"There doesn't have to be. We're adults. We're capable of controlling ourselves."

"I'm glad you are."

"You seem to be doing just fine to me." She turned her head to look out the window.

"If you knew the thoughts running through my head," he confessed, looking at her, waiting for her to feel his regard and acknowledge him.

She didn't.

Part of him wanted to grab her and kiss her hard, melt that icy reserve, but then there was that part of him that knew this was how it had to be. How he said he'd wanted it to be.

But his lips moved without his permission. "Damara."

"What?" she whispered, still not turning toward him. "What do you want from me?"

"You could start by looking at me."

"No."

"Why not?"

She sighed. "Because I can't hide it, okay? I'll look at you, and you'll see right through me. You'll see everything."

He didn't realize he affected her so. "Isn't that only fair? You've already seen my wounds laid bare."

"No, I haven't. I know you've got wounds, but I don't know what caused them. You give me that part of you but hold back the rest. So no, I'm not just going to hand you that power over me."

He was both intrigued and tormented by the knowledge that he had some kind of power over her. Byron closed the distance between him, pressed his face against her neck and inhaled the scent of her. "You smell so good, Damara."

She didn't push him off, but she didn't invite more contact, either.

"How is it that you still smell like jasmine?"

"I guess that's just me. It's always been my preferred scent." This question she answered easily, though her body stiffened when he grabbed her shoulders. "I don't want her."

"What?" He leaned back.

She turned to look at him then. Her eyes bright and somehow still dark. "I. Don't. Want. Her. It's what you said on the phone."

"You don't understand." Byron didn't know how to explain it to her. He was trying to protect her, to keep her safe from everything, including himself.

"I understand perfectly. I don't know if you're just lonely, or you're trying to make the best of a bad deal, but I'm not going to sleep with you just because we're pretending a relationship."

He didn't understand—it was fine for her before. What had changed? Part of him was sure it was because she'd seen what was beneath the hero's veneer she'd painted over him. "You wanted me in Barcelona."

"And you wanted me in Barcelona, too." She shoved him away from her. "You wanted to be with me because…I don't know why. But you did. This? Now?" She shook her head. "This is something else. Maybe you're just lonely. But I'm not something that you can drag out and play with and then throw away when you don't want me anymore. Sonja wants you. If you're that hard up, you should give her a call."

The idea of anything to do with Sonja did nothing at all for his libido. She wasn't homely or unattractive, but she wasn't Damara. "There was a time when I could have any woman in this town. It's not desperation." But maybe it was. He was desperate to feel the way that only she made him feel. Desperate to be lost in her skin, her scent, her pleasure. Just her. He'd had one taste of her, and now he needed more.

"Then I suggest you call one of them." Damara crossed her arms over chest.

"If that's how you want it." This was probably best. He'd tried to be the good guy, tried to warn her off in Barcelona, but she hadn't listened and neither had he. He kept pushing, kept wanting, kept reaching for her because she was just so damn desirable. She was light when it was dark, sweet when the rest of the world was sour and soft when the world was hard.

"That's how you said *you* wanted it. I'm just trying to keep things in perspective."

"Do you really think you can go years without touch? That's how long this is going to last. This isn't a temporary thing." He was hurting her. Why couldn't he just close his mouth?

Because he still wanted her so damn bad; he'd do anything to have her.

She lifted her chin. "I went my whole life without it before you. So, yes, I can."

He couldn't imagine her sweetness, her bloom, all gone fallow because of him. She was made to be touched, made to be revered and worshipped with hands and lips.

Only she wasn't made for him. That's what he kept forgetting.

Damara turned away from him again, and there was a chill inside him he didn't know how to melt.

CHAPTER NINE

DO YOU REALLY THINK you can go years without touch?

Damara had thought so. She hadn't known what she was missing. But now that she did, now that she'd spent the night in his arms, she wanted his touch more than even another order of those French fries. More than anything.

Anything except her duty to Castallegna.

He was so close and smelled so good, so *safe*. The heat from his touch burned through her clothes, and she wanted to surrender to him. In that moment, when he'd talked about his difficulty controlling himself, part of her had hoped he'd just grab her and kiss her until she couldn't think—until all she could do was feel.

Years without touch, bound to him, yet so far apart it was worse than being alone.

How would she ever manage to keep from falling in love with him? She could tell herself it wasn't real, but living with someone, depending on them, it was what formed the bonds of marriage. Not that first spark of attraction, or even bliss in the bedroom. It was surviving each day together.

She couldn't look at him, because if she did, she'd break. She'd shatter, and fall into his arms like none of this mattered.

That would mean accepting he was going to break her heart.

Damara wasn't afraid of pain, but it was stupid to go flinging her heart at someone who didn't want it. So she was determined to keep her distance.

Even when she remembered what it felt like when he made her scream his name and dig her nails into his back.

When the car dropped them off at the house, she didn't want to go inside. He seemed to suck all the air out of the space. His presence filled each room and dominated the whole house. She couldn't breathe, and it was damn cold. Damara wasn't used to the weather.

"Do you think you could start a fire, please?" She nodded to the fireplace.

"Let me change."

"That's a good idea for me, too." She waited for him to go upstairs and come back down before she took her turn.

Damara wondered if he was going to sleep in the room with her again, or if he was going to try to sleep in the bed.

The man was putting his life on the line for her, the least she could do was be gracious about their sleeping arrangements. Although, she supposed the same could be said for what he wanted of her body. It was possible he'd die for her. Didn't she owe him?

No, her brain answered. She didn't. She was trying to rationalize her own body's wants with an excuse. If she decided to sleep with Byron Hawkins again, she'd go into it with her eyes open and a broom and dustpan at the ready for the shattered pieces of her heart.

She changed into a pair of fleece pants and a rangers T-shirt that had been so thoughtfully laid out on the bed. Probably by Sonja. Damara wondered if there'd be paparazzi trying to sneak into her bedroom and catch them in the act or something.

The shirt was much too large on her, but she liked it.

Damara brushed out her hair and went back downstairs.

Byron was working on getting the fire going. He was wearing sweatpants and a T-shirt. She'd never thought that sweatpants were something a man should ever wear in public. They were much too intimate and spoke of a certain lack of care for one's appearance.

Yet Byron in sweatpants was a whole other story.

All she could think about was getting him out of them.

He twisted to grab another log for the fire and his shirt rode up over his hip, giving her an unobstructed view of one of the loveliest parts on a man. She knew men weren't supposed to be beautiful, and she'd had the thought before, but he was. He was a work of art.

That line of muscle, or tendon, or whatever it was that led down from his hip like a beacon to his manhood—her tutor had called it an Adonis line.

The sight of it took her breath away and made her ache in places she didn't want to think about.

Damara told herself again if she wanted him, she should just take him.

I don't want her.

That cooled her ardor quickly enough, and she looked away from him.

"If you want to see something, all you have to do

is ask," he said when he finished, a cocky grin on his face.

"No, I saw everything I wanted to see, thanks." And she had, clearly. Including her own motivations.

"Are you ever going to forgive me for what I said?" he asked.

"Of course. You're already forgiven, Hawkins. I can't be angry with you for honesty."

"Will you ever let me explain?" His tone of voice slid over her in a way that made her think of silk and velvet, sheets and…

"No." She shook her head to emphasize the point. "We don't have to beat it to death. You said it. I heard it. I believed it. It's over."

"But it's not over, Damara. You won't even—" He seemed to be at a loss for what else to say.

"Sleep with you?" she added in a faux helpful tone.

"It's not even that. There's a distance between us now."

"That *you* wanted." She wrapped the blanket around her more tightly. He looked so defeated, and she wasn't trying to hurt him. She was only trying to protect herself. "Fine. You want closeness? You want intimacy?"

"I didn't go that far."

She made a sour face. "Yes, you did. Maybe you're uncomfortable with the word, but that's what it is. Intimacy. Say it with me."

He arched a brow in a way that suggested she might as well have asked him to write his name with a very large crayon and she couldn't restrain the laugh that bubbled up inside of her. His irritation amused her to no end.

She managed to control herself. If she let him make her laugh, they'd never get to the core of the problem between them. Or why things couldn't be as he wanted them. "Okay, don't say it with me. Tell me what happened in Uganda."

"No."

"See? This is why we can't have what you want."

His mouth thinned. "You know I bleed. You know I have wounds. Isn't it enough? Why do you have to pick at them?"

She exhaled heavily. "Because *you* won't stop picking at them." Damara wouldn't bring up what had happened in the bathroom that morning. He'd been so vulnerable then. They both knew it had happened, and she'd show him that she didn't have to tear at his wounds, his pain, if only he'd trust her with their source.

"I can't, Damara."

"I understand." She did, more than he knew. But even so, she wasn't going to sign up for a ticket straight to heartbreak station. At least, that's what her brain kept saying. Her heart just wanted to make it better for him. It wanted her to open her arms and welcome him to her embrace yet again.

And her body, well, she couldn't listen to anything it had to say. It had a vested interest in the decision that didn't benefit the rest of her.

"I'll be your friend, Byron. I owe you that, at least." She licked her lips. Her mouth had gone dry. "But I can't be your lover. It was no strings in Barcelona because I thought we'd never see each other again. I'm not as worldly as you are. I don't know how to do this and not fall in love."

"Am I so unlovable?" he asked quietly, almost so quietly that the fire flickering behind him was louder.

No, I am, she wanted to say. But he'd have another argument. "What would make you say that?"

He clammed up again, unwilling to talk.

"See? This is what I mean. You won't tell me anything about yourself."

He sank down on the couch next to her. "I'll tell you anything you want to know—just don't ask me about Uganda."

She hadn't expected that. Trepidation flickered over her like bee stings.

"So tell me why you think you're unlovable."

"You really go for the throat, don't you? I thought being trained as a diplomat, you'd be a little gentler." He gave a hollow laugh.

"You're an elite soldier. You're going to tell me you're afraid of your feelings?"

"Everyone is. Aren't you?"

He was right. She was afraid. "I suppose you've caught me there."

For a moment, she thought he was going to avoid answering the question. He was so quiet and still. "I don't know where to start."

"At the beginning?"

"I guess that would be when I was born. My parents were both part of the country-club set. She got pregnant. They had to get married. My grandfather paid her to marry my father. She never wanted to be a mother, and my father was more concerned about his duty to provide the two point five kids and the respectable facade of family to his law firm so he could eventually make partner."

She waited for him to continue.

"I got into a lot of trouble as a kid. I got into fights with other kids, and I slowly began to notice that they didn't care what I did. I was never punished for anything. Instead of running with a bad crowd, I ended up *being* the bad crowd. Girls wanted me, but only because I was *that* guy, you know?"

She didn't know. "I didn't have the same educational experience you did. I'm afraid you're going to have to explain it to me."

"I was like Bender in *The Breakfast Club,* only my dad didn't abuse me."

"Oh." She nodded. Damara had seen it, but only because her tutor thought it would be a good insight into American culture. If her brother had known she'd watched it, he would have had a stroke.

"He didn't pay much attention to me at all until I broke into the offices of his law firm. Then they dumped me in Maur Hill, where I stayed until I graduated and joined the army. I was recruited for ranger school right out of Maur Hill because of my delinquencies. All of my tests showed I had an aptitude for the job."

He said it like it was a bad thing.

"You know, men who do what you do, there's a reason that you're needed. You do make the world a better place. You did for me."

"Well, that's how I understand what you feel about no one wanting you for you. I felt the same way. Women wanted me for my reputation or my fast car. No one ever wanted to get to know *me.*" He leaned back. "The same is still true. When I was a ranger, it was because I was Special Forces. Then my cover for the DOD, it was because they thought I had money."

A heavy knock rattled the door and split the quiet camaraderie that had built between them. Neither of them moved.

"It might be important," he said.

"You should get it."

"I should." But still he sat there.

"I see you're in there. Open the damn door," a woman's muffled voice followed another round of banging.

"India." He laughed and roused himself.

She turned around on the couch and watched as a female police officer stepped inside. She was carrying a purple box, which she snatched away from Byron when he tried to take it. "Not for you."

The woman walked over to Damara without invitation. She was statuesque, golden and disgustingly gorgeous. She made Damara feel small and plain by comparison. Part of that might have been all the heat she was packing around her waist.

"Oh, is that a .40?" Damara asked.

The woman flashed her a large smile. "It sure is." She pulled the weapon out and handed it to Damara, barrel down.

Damara picked it up and curled her fingers around the grip. It was heavy, but she liked it. She hopped off the couch and held it up, lining up the sights and aiming out the window.

"Nice, huh?"

"I love it."

"Good. It's yours. But don't tell anyone I gave it to you since you don't have a license." India winked at her. "But being a foreign national, you can get away with stuff like that. Just say you didn't know."

"Really? For me?" Damara was pleased and found that she adored this other woman.

"These, too, if Sticky Fingers can keep his hands out of them." She handed her the purple box. "Sweet Thing" was printed on the side in scrolling white letters. "I'm India George, by the way. You met my partner, Caleb Lewis, yesterday. We're patrolling again tonight."

"Caleb said you were coming with doughnuts last night," Byron said.

"I was. But I ate them all." She eyed Byron. "Don't judge. I brought her a .40 to make up for it."

She flopped on the couch without invitation and took a doughnut out and shoved it into her mouth. "Really, you better try these or I'm going to eat them all again. They're called Better Than Sex doughnuts."

Damara's eyes widened. "If they're that good…" She took one out of the box and bit off a tiny piece. It melted on her tongue, sweet, then salty, and it occurred to Damara they were a lot like her experience with Byron.

She blushed.

"See what I mean?" India nodded and chomped again.

"Aren't you supposed to be, I don't know, *patrolling?*" Byron said.

"I'm serving and protecting right here. I gave her a .40. That's protection. I brought her Better Than Sex doughnuts from Betsy. That's definitely serving. What's the problem?" India looked very pleased with herself.

Yes, Damara decided that she liked India George very much. Especially when Byron reached for a doughnut and she smacked his hand.

"Nope, you wait until the princess has had her fill."

"I know three hundred and forty-two ways to kill you with a spork, George. Don't get between me and that doughnut again," Byron warned.

India laughed and held up her hand in mock surrender. "Fine." She grabbed another one. "Maybe you guys can wrestle for the last one." India winked at her and stood to leave.

"It was lovely to meet you. Do come back," Damara invited.

"Thanks. But, um, fair warning. I don't do the girlie friendship thing. Pedicures and shopping or whatever." India waved her hand around as if she was swatting a fly.

"Honestly, that's a relief. Those things are part of the job for me. They're part of my image and polish. Maybe we can go shooting and get more of these doughnuts."

"Betsy is Caleb's sister. She owns Sweet Thing and she'll make *all* the doughnuts you want. You should go see her about your wedding cake. When it's time." India winked at her again and left.

Byron locked the door behind her and sat back down next to her.

"You like her," he stated.

"She's wonderful."

"Mostly." He shrugged.

"Did you…"

"Sleep with her? No. She would've as soon as handed me my ass on a platter than paid me any kind of attention. She grew up hard, but she's a good woman."

"She's beautiful," Damara admitted.

"She is," he agreed. "But I've never had a thing for blondes."

"You're only saying that so I'll let you have that doughnut." She didn't want to talk about what that made her feel.

"Well, I didn't get one."

"They really are good," Damara teased. Part of her could see where this was going; they were going to end up in bed again and her heart would end up broken. She was on a collision course.

"Are they better than sex?" He eyed the doughnut and then his gaze slide over her with a languid heat. "I mean, really?"

"I guess you should eat one and see." She grinned. "Unless I eat it first." She grabbed at the box, but he was faster.

Damara knew he would be. This was an excuse for touch, for play. It removed the heavy weight of their earlier conversation. For now, she just wanted something to feel good.

And Byron, he felt good. *So good.* Better than the doughnut tasted, truth be told.

His body was so hard and hot—she loved how it felt to be pressed against him, even if they were scrambling to see who got the last doughnut.

She found herself straddling him, reaching for the box he held high above her head. Damara struggled for it, squirming against him.

His body reacted to her nearness. His arousal was nestled intimately against her. But he didn't grab at her or try to kiss her. Instead, he kept playing their game, kept moving the box just out of reach and that somehow made it okay for her to keep looking for more friction.

"That's got to be one damn good doughnut."

"You won it. You should eat it and see," she said breathlessly.

"Nah, I like this better." He gave her a lazy smile.

She did, too, but after all her talk about intimacy and opening up, she couldn't admit it. "We could split the doughnut."

He seemed to consider it for a moment. "Nope. Still like this better. You're hard-core all or nothing? Well, that's the way it'll be. With the doughnut, too."

She laughed. "This is dumb."

"You're the one on top of me, Princess."

Her breath came in short staccato bursts and that little voice that kept telling her this was a bad idea was getting further and further away—or maybe it was just being drowned out by the thud of her heart-beat and the need that throbbed through her.

Damara reached higher, pressing ever closer to him, her breasts brushing against his shoulders.

He dropped the box a fraction. "I tell you what. I'll give you the doughnut if you promise to eat it right here."

"In your lap?"

"Exactly as we are."

"You want to hold your arm above your head like that?" she teased in an effort to avoid answering him. Damara knew where this was going.

"I'll put my hands wherever you want me to." The

corner of his mouth turned up in the beginning of a grin.

"Okay. My doughnut. Your hands on the couch. Palms flat. No touching."

"You're a cruel mistress."

"Yes, I suppose I am," she agreed.

"As you wish." He handed her the box, and he splayed his hands out on the couch.

She pulled out the doughnut and examined it this way and that. His eyes followed her every action; the weight of his study was intense. She found herself very aware of every action, every breath.

Her tongue darted out to lick at the glaze, and his erection jerked against her. She blushed, but she'd come too far to stop now.

"Oh, really?" she asked him, her face warm.

"Oh, yeah."

She did it again and got the same reaction, but he held the rest of his body perfectly still and waited for her to do as she wished.

Damara found she liked having him under her command. There was something heady about having control over a man so strong. He could crush her, but he waited for her direction.

Damara licked all the frosting off the top of the doughnut. "It's so good."

"But is it better than sex?"

"You know, I think this is the part where I'm supposed to make you prove that it isn't, but I can't lie. It's good, but it's nowhere near as good as what happened between us in Barcelona."

"I wouldn't mind if you asked me to prove it."

"I'm sure you wouldn't. But we already had this discussion." She bit her lip and put the doughnut down.

"We did. And I've kept my hands to myself."

"Which is why you've earned a taste," her traitorous mouth said before she could stop herself. Damara lowered her mouth to his slowly, taking her time, enjoying the tension as it grew thick between them and their mingling of breath.

For a moment, it was a symbiosis. They breathed for one another, inhaling and exhaling together.

She brushed her lips against his ever so carefully, almost chastely.

"You said I could have a taste," he whispered against her mouth, and his tongue swept along her bottom lip. "Mmm. Sweet."

Now was the time for her to pull back, to take herself upstairs to bed and not think of this again.

She supposed what did that little voice in was the part where it said she wouldn't think of this again. She'd think of it all the time and she'd regret not taking what he offered.

What she'd said at the press junket wasn't a total lie. She didn't know what tomorrow would bring. It was a very real possibility that someone would kill her before she could finish what she'd set out to do in Castallegna.

She'd said earlier during the junket that an assassin's bullet could take her out at any time. If she only had this day left, what would she do with it?

Make love with Byron Hawkins.

It was almost as if he sensed her surrender, because he kissed her more thoroughly, even though his hands were still flat on the couch.

She pushed her palms up under his shirt, over his ripped abs, and down to that line she'd enjoyed looking at so much.

But Damara hadn't surrendered; she couldn't. She said she'd make love with him, and she couldn't do that by herself. He had to be making love to her, too. It had to be about their connection, not only physical fulfillment. She refused to pour herself heart and soul into a man who wouldn't do the same for her.

That was a kind of prison, and she wouldn't do that to herself.

"I can't do this." She scrambled away from him.

"You were doing just fine a second ago."

She debated whether or not she should tell him, but her mouth decided for her. "I was thinking about what I said at the junket."

"Which thing?"

"About being assassinated, not knowing when my next moments may be my last."

His lips thinned, and he clenched his jaw. "If you don't think I can protect you—"

"No." She shook her head. "It's not that at all. This has actually been a gift. It's helped me to see things more clearly. I know you'll protect me. I know you'd die for me. But you'll never live for me. You'll never give me all of yourself, and half just isn't good enough."

He scowled. "I told you I wasn't good enough in Barcelona. But you didn't listen."

"No, I didn't listen and neither did you. I didn't say you weren't good enough. I said half of you isn't good enough. When you're ready to give me everything, then I'll make love to you. Until then…" She shrugged. "I can't do that to myself."

"I told you it wasn't called making love. It's fucking." He might as well have been a beast for the snarl he lobbed at her.

"That's where you're wrong. For me, it's making love. And anyone I choose to give my body to, it will be because we are connected. Not just because it feels good and I'm sad or lonely or even afraid." She straightened. "I deserve better than that, and so do you."

"That's all I've got to give you, Princess."

"That's all you *want* to give me."

He shook his head slowly. "You're so naive."

"I guess I am." She'd rather be naive than so used up by the world that she had nothing left to give, not even to herself.

"Maybe you'll believe me now."

And maybe not. "I'm going to bed."

It was some time later, but she was still staring up at the ceiling in the darkness when he came into the room and made his pallet on the floor. He was close enough to touch but still so incredibly far away.

She replayed the memory of the ship in her head. *You can touch me.* It had been a tacit permission, a key to a forbidden door, because it unlocked her fantasies, her needs. There was no shoving them back into some dark unknown corner now that she'd tasted him. Now that she knew what it was like to be in his arms.

It wasn't just the place between her thighs that ached for him, but every piece of her. Her lips yearned for his, her tongue for the taste of his skin, her shoulders for his arms around them, her hips for his, pressing her down into the mattress… She craved the sight of him, the taste of him, the scent of him. It was everything about him.

Going without his touch was a little bit like dying. That descriptor sounded overdramatic even to her, but he'd brought a part of her alive, made her bloom. He was the light that nourished it, the sustenance that fed it, and without that, it withered and died. Although the time it had been given breath had been an experience unlike any other. Beautiful and harsh, soft and sharp, all at once.

He was close enough that she could whisper that she wanted him in her bed, and she knew he'd come. He'd touch her; he'd give her everything her body desired.

Except her pesky heart. That thing was making demands Byron had no way of meeting. She knew better than to expect a person to change into something they weren't. He'd been honest with her from the start.

Barcelona was different. He'd be a memory, something pretty to take out and remember, something to hold on to in the dark when she was alone.

But she wasn't alone now, even though she felt like it.

The part of her that was dying wanted to cry, but the rest of her that had lived without him for so long already was glad because this was safer. Without these feelings, she had confidence in what she was doing, a passion and surety that she could change the world.

Byron made her doubt herself because if she couldn't get one man to forgive the hurts of the past, how could she expect to do that for a country?

CHAPTER TEN

SLEEPING ON THE FLOOR was easier than taking the side of the bed she'd initially offered him, not that Byron anticipated he'd actually get to sleep—or if he did, it would be so riddled with nightmares he'd wake up screaming. It was easier to be awake, safer. For him and for her.

He pretended to sleep so he could be in the room with the princess and have a better chance at protecting her.

She was right to deny him her body. He'd been telling her all along that he wasn't good enough for her, that he'd hurt her. So now why was he hurt that she'd listened to him? It was better this way.

Part of him wished he'd denied her in Barcelona. She'd be happier now, and so would he. He wouldn't remember what it was like to touch her hair, the silk of her skin. The cadence of her gentle, even breathing as she curled up next to him in perfect trust. The trust was the most bittersweet of all. No one, except his team, had ever trusted him so implicitly.

From the moment they'd met, she'd had no doubts that he was the one, that he would save her. Even when he told her he hadn't planned on helping her, even when he told her that he didn't want to. It wasn't any sort of royal entitlement; it was just a knowledge that she had that he was the one.

He'd tried to tell her that he couldn't be trusted—this protection gig, it wasn't him. He was a breaker, not a fixer. She'd just smiled in that way of hers, and his pride wouldn't let him do anything but answer the call.

He knew he should try to sleep. He'd do a better job keeping her safe if he was rested. They had a whole team outside watching the house, and they were his brothers in arms. While he didn't deserve their protection, Damara did.

He half expected them to deny the detail. Everyone knew he'd lost his team. As ironic as it was, there were no secrets in the world of covert ops. Not about things like this. He wanted their judgment. More than that, he wanted their punishment. He deserved it.

But he wouldn't get it. They'd serve. They'd do the job they were ordered to do and complete the mission. Because they were rangers. He wanted to tear his skin off whenever they looked at him, as if that would somehow stop the burning. Byron knew it wouldn't, though, because it was a different kind of fire. It was hell.

He pulled himself out of the beginning of the spiral, away from the sounds of the screaming that had risen to a roar in his ears. Byron focused on that sound—her breathing. It lulled him and comforted him like nothing else.

Except now he was dreaming. Byron Hawkins knew he was dreaming because he was no longer in the house with Damara.

He was in the sweltering heat of the jungle, the

bites of insects like a thousand needles in his neck, sweat beading on his forehead and the buzzing in his ears.

It was always the same. He was in pursuit of the guerrillas in Uganda, and time stopped right before that moment when he murdered his team.

Because that's what it was—murder. Those men were dead because of him.

Yes, back to that time, that second, that breath before he spoke the words that ended them all.

He couldn't change it. Every time he dreamed, he tried to keep his mouth closed, tried to stop from speaking.

It never worked.

And the screams started again. Screams ripped from the bodies of men who'd walk into hell if it was their duty. Screams from men who didn't know how to scream.

This time, Foxworth didn't go with the rest of them. He held his weapon up against his chest like a baby.

"Recognizing that I volunteered as a Ranger, fully knowing the hazards of my chosen profession, I will always endeavor to uphold the prestige, honor and high esprit de corps of the Rangers." Austin Foxworth began reciting the Ranger Creed.

The one Byron didn't feel worthy enough to speak. The words were poison on his tongue.

"Say it with me, brother. Speak the words," Foxworth encouraged. "Acknowledging the fact that a Ranger is a more elite soldier, who arrives at the cutting edge of battle by land, sea or air—"

Byron found his voice and spoke with him. "I accept the fact that as a Ranger, my country expects me to move further, faster, and fight harder than any other soldier."

"Never shall I—" Foxworth stopped reciting when Byron stopped. "Speak the words, soldier."

"I'm *sorry.*" His apology spewed from him like a rancid geyser, but it did nothing to change the landscape around him. His sorry didn't bring them back, didn't soothe any hurts, and certainly didn't absolve him of any sin.

EXPLOSIONS RATTLED THE GROUND, sulfur filled the air and all the fires of hell burned around them.

"There's more to life than this, hoss." Foxworth nodded and his face had melted away, leaving nothing but the grinning rictus.

"I'm so sorry—I'm so fucking sorry." This time, the screams were Byron's. He was on fire, but he couldn't stop saying he was sorry, over and over, like some kind of benediction, even though he knew it wasn't.

"Say it. *Never shall I fail my comrades,*" Foxworth demanded.

"Never shall I…never shall I…" He roared in frustration. "But I did. I did fail you."

"Readily will I display the intestinal fortitude required to fight on to the Ranger objective and complete the mission, though I be *the lone survivor.*" The sharp finger bones of the skeleton dug into his wrist. "Never shall I fail my comrades."

And Byron spoke. Even though they sliced his tongue like razorblades, he spoke the words he did not feel, gave voice to his failure and let it live and breathe outside of him. "Never shall I fail my comrades."

He awoke sweat-soaked, the scent of jasmine in his nose and soft, cool hands on his face.

Damara.

"It's okay, Byron. You're here. With me. Just breathe."

The princess with all her strength, her courage and her sweetness cradled him against the dark.

She'd slipped down to his pallet and held him gently. She didn't ask him what he'd dreamed about. She just stroked her fingers through his hair and held his cheek to her breast. The steady thud of her heartbeat soothed him, anchored him into the world so he didn't drift away again back to that land of pain and fire.

He wasn't afraid of his nightmares; they weren't even the beginning of a just punishment for what he'd done. Through them all, no matter how many times he had to relive them, he knew they weren't real, and whatever he endured was nothing like what they'd suffered.

If he could trade places with them, he would've.

At least until Damara.

Byron was still convinced he was going to hurt her, that he was going to screw up and she was going to die. But he'd vowed to protect her with his life, and he would. It would be a good death if he died protecting her. So much better than he deserved.

Would it be so bad? Foxworth's voice asked in his head. *Would it be so bad to marry her, to take care of her, to love her?*

Even the voices in his head wanted her.

Yes, it would be horrible, he answered them. It would be the worst thing that could happen because even if he exorcised his own demons, they could never be together. She had a country to save, and when it was safe for her to go back to Castallegna, she had to go. Byron's life still belonged to the Department of Defense. He'd signed a contract. But he found himself wondering who'd be in Castallegna to continue protecting her. Who'd oversee the construction of the base, the operations…

He couldn't think about it anymore. Instead, he dressed early and went for a run, checking in with the security detail to make sure she was safe before he left.

He ran past the downtown area, not wanting to look at any of the small-town charm. He'd had enough of it as a kid. The air was cold on his face, chilly as it swirled in his lungs. He ran toward the edges of town. The part of the river that wasn't by the old grande dame Victorians, but the industry. The secret places of his youth. He saw they weren't so secret, or at least the kids there were like him. They were the miscreants, the misfits, the castaways.

They stood in a small group, smoking and laughing, huddled over a bonfire.

The ranger who lived in his head said to tell them to go home, to break it up. The kid that he used to be wanted to go join them. But the sad man he was in between just kept running.

He ran farther still to where the old train station sat abandoned, still waiting for city hall and the historical society to raise enough funds to restore it. Calliope music blared loudly and harshly through the space from the carousel museum.

Dawn had crested over the horizon, and he kept running, working his body as hard as he dared. There was a headspace he found in that kind of exhaustion that was the closest to peace he could get outside of Damara's arms.

Nothing could follow him there. Not guilt, not shame, not sorrow. It was this blessed empty white.

BYRON RAN UNTIL HE VOMITED, and then he ran some more, but the peace he sought was elusive. Further proof that true peace of any kind was denied him.

He turned his steps back toward the house, back toward his responsibilities and his failures. He hated being so at odds with himself.

He had to shut his brain off. Otherwise, Damara really was going to get hurt and it would be his fault because he couldn't keep his head in the game.

Sonja had given him a schedule, and there were more interviews and appearances on the docket for the day. He wondered when this was going to end. When they were going to get a chance to breathe.

When he got back to the house some hours later, the kitchen was full of smoke, it smelled like something had died and Damara was wearing nothing but the ranger T-shirt and crying.

It was enough to make him want to turn right back around and run. Keep running. He could handle Damara doing almost anything but crying.

That made him want to throttle something, but the only one there was Damara. He didn't know how to help her.

Stupid toast.

Stupid toaster.

Stupid princess. Without her crown, she was useless. Without her crown, without a cause, what skills did she have? Damara had never had time to learn how to cook. There'd always been staff to do so. But when she'd woken up hungry, she had tried to make toast. And failed miserably when the toast got stuck in the toaster and burned.

After everything Damara had been through, a stupid piece of toast to her absolute and utter horror had made her cry.

To make matters worse, Byron walked in on the mess she'd made of the kitchen and herself.

"What's wrong? What happened?" His sharp eyes immediately scanned the room for threats. "Are you okay?"

"I..." She sniveled. It was a loud, wet sound. Princesses didn't snivel. She allowed him to pull her against his body. She'd already come to associate his nearness with safety. It occurred to her that no matter how hard she fought this, she'd end up in bed with him again with her heart broken. Right now, she wanted to tell him she'd changed her mind. Maybe her brother was right. Maybe the only thing she could do was breed heirs.

"Whatever it was, it failed miserably," he teased.

She sobbed harder.

"Whoa, what's this? I was just teasing you a bit, Princess." His arms tightened around her.

Her comportment teacher was probably sitting up in bed from a dead sleep with the sure knowledge that

Damara had snotted on his shirt with her messy, ugly, unprincess-like sobs.

"I can't do anything," she managed between hitches of breath.

"What is this anything you're talking about?" He handed her a napkin.

"Anything!" He should know exactly what she meant from the wretched carcass of the damn toaster in the sink.

"You mean because you set your toast on fire?" His voice was calm and reassuring.

She nodded into his chest. Even after working out, he still smelled good, like he had on the ship. And she just wanted him to fix everything for her.

Over a stupid piece of toast.

Damara had to get herself together. She really wouldn't be able to do anything or help anyone if she lost her mind over a first attempt at a task she'd never been taught to do.

"Look at me."

Oh, God, no. She couldn't. Her eyes were puffy, her face was tearstained and her nose, oh, God, her nose.

"I couldn't give a shit less if you know how to cook or ice-skate."

She sniffed. "What does ice-skating have to do with it?"

"Exactly. Nothing. Who cares? So you burned the toast. And the toaster." He shrugged. "So you take a cooking class if you want to. I can't cook. We can eat takeout forever."

She sniffed again. "But you can do other things."

"So can you."

"I can be a princess. No one cares if I know how

to plan a seating chart so you can invite a man's wife and his mistress to a fund-raising ball. I never wanted to be a damsel in distress."

He stroked her back with long, smooth motions. "Damara, I don't know if someone forgot to tell you, but you have *never* been a damsel in distress. There have been times when you've needed a team effort, but that doesn't make you a damsel in distress. Remember how you told me that asking for help doesn't make you weak?"

She had said that, hadn't she? Damara nodded. "It's stupid. I shouldn't have gotten this upset."

"With the amount of stress you've been under, it's really not a surprise."

"You've been under the same amount of stress as I have and I don't see you sniveling into my shirt."

"Damara, if you'd let me snivel into your shirt, I'd find a reason to be there."

She chuckled. "Stop making me laugh."

"Truthfully, I only have one person I have to keep safe. You have a country. That's a little bit more pressing than toast."

"I'm still hungry." She hated how helpless she sounded, as though she expected him to fix it for her. But she supposed that she did. She kept waiting for him to ride to the rescue, but she was going to have to rescue herself. He wasn't always going to be there. He didn't want to be responsible for her safety even now. The sooner she could take care of herself, the better.

"Why don't we pick up some doughnuts from Sweet Thing and go to The Bullet Hole?"

"What's The Bullet Hole?" It sounded nefarious.

Of course if it came with anything from Sweet Thing, she was in.

"It's a shooting range. You can practice with that .40 George brought you. I happen to know you're a lot better with weapons than kitchen appliances."

It made her wonder about the future. Was this it for her? If she couldn't help her people, was she going to stay here and be his wife? What would she do with herself? How would she contribute to their household, or would he have to take care of her?

As a little girl, she used to dream about what it would be like to be just a girl—not a princess. Now that she was faced with that possibility, it was terrifying.

So was the thought of being married to a man who didn't love her, and she'd had a much longer time to get used to that idea.

She couldn't let herself think this way—about the what-ifs. The doubts. If she couldn't find one way, she'd find another. It didn't matter how many times it took, she would do this.

She studied him. Damara hadn't expected this kind of interaction with him after last night. She hadn't expected him to be cruel, but he seemed so warm and open. It was probably because she'd been crying. Most men, her brother being the exception, would do anything to get a woman to stop crying.

Damara sniffed. She hated crying and endeavored not to do it. Her tutors had told her that princesses didn't cry where anyone could see them. Her father had told her that was utter rot. It was okay to be moved by something, hurt by it, overwhelmed. It was okay to show pain and compassion. Being royal wasn't supposed to make you inhuman. If anything, her father had taught her it had to make her more human.

"So what do you say, Damara? Do you want to go?"

Shooting. He wanted to take her shooting. That was something she could do, something she was good at. Damara nodded. "Yes, I'd like to go shoot things."

Damara didn't want to kill or hurt anyone, but she wasn't going to let anyone do those things to her, either. She needed to keep honing her skills. "Maybe you'll spar with me later?"

He raised a brow. "Are you sure you want to do that?"

"Because you think you'll beat me?" She sniffed again indelicately and put a hand on her hip.

"No." His hand was dangerously low on her spine. "Because I think we'll both like it way more than we should."

She fought her physical reaction to him.

Self-respect seemed a cold comfort when his arms were so strong and the heat of his palms scalded her through to a place beneath her skin.

"Maybe we will. It'll be a good teaching tool to learn to focus through distraction." Her hands found purchase on his shoulders.

"You're a dangerous woman, Princess." His voice was low and throaty.

All her instincts wanted her to lean in, to tilt her face up to his and part her lips. She wanted to invite him to kiss her, taste her, take her upstairs and— She tried to turn it off. But she knew she was right. If she could learn to fight through that kind of distraction, she could learn to fight through anything.

She smiled at him, trying not to think about the

shape of his mouth and what it felt like on hers. "So what does a princess wear to shoot things?"

"What did you wear on Castallegna?"

"A dress."

He arched a brow. "What are you going to wear to spar in?"

"This?" She looked down at the shirt.

"That's cheating." His eyes raked over her.

She liked this easy back-and-forth between them. Damara wished she knew what to do to make it stay this way. If she gave in to her body's desires, they'd still be in the same place they'd been before. There'd be immediate gratification but nothing solved for her more tender feelings or her future.

How she wished things were different, that her people were free and Byron, too. Free from the pain and sorrow that chained him down. He was as much a prisoner as any of them. The thought of him dying before he had a chance to fly turned her stomach. Grisha and Vladimir wouldn't stop in their pursuit of her. They'd use anything they could to get at her, and they wouldn't hesitate to kill Byron Hawkins.

"You look like a storm cloud. What happened?" he asked her.

She looked up at him and knew if she confided her fears that he'd think she saw weakness in him and that wasn't it at all. "Just thinking too much. You know, the wishing in one hand, but the other one seems to be filling up really fast."

He laughed. "It does that. Get moving if you want to go blow things up."

She took the stairs quickly. It would be nice to do something that was practical but fun. Damara couldn't remember the last time she'd done something simply because she wanted to—Barcelona aside.

Damara rather imagined this to be like stealing a moment where she didn't have to be a princess, he didn't have to be a ranger, and they didn't have to worry how their actions impacted a country or who could see them. This didn't have to be about anything but the enjoyment of the action itself.

Too bad she couldn't approach going to bed with him the same way.

But, oh, what if she could? What if she could see it just as pleasure for the sake of pleasure? If she could just surrender to sensation.

She bit her lip and sat down on the bed, wondering what would happen if she were to call out to him and tell him what she wanted.

No, she didn't wonder. She knew. She'd find herself flat on her back with her ankles around his waist and the best orgasm she'd ever had. That's what would happen.

The after was really what she wanted to know about. How was it so easy for him to switch his emotions on and off? How could he be so intimate with her, so connected as they spiraled together, and then when it was over, it was like it had never happened?

Or worse, that it had and it didn't matter.

CHAPTER ELEVEN

BYRON FELT ONLY a tiny flash of guilt enjoying the view from behind as she ran up the stairs in his T-shirt. It was obliterated by lust at the sight of all that delicious skin he'd touched but was now denied.

And it was his own fault, he knew. All he had to do was give her something he didn't have, and she'd surrender to him.

He was more determined now than ever not to break her, not to be the reason the light went out in her eyes. He shook his head. The woman wasn't afraid to stare down a Russian thug, but burning toast made her cry. She was a bundle of contradictions.

He trudged up the stairs after her, giving her ample time to get ready so he could change. A quick shower wouldn't be remiss. He couldn't believe he'd hugged her and she hadn't fallen over dead.

She popped out of the door, wearing another of his T-shirts and a pair of jeans that should have been illegal.

"I, uh, I'm grabbing a shower," he managed, trying not to stare at her curves. He finished his shower and dried off, his cock still painfully aware of their every interaction.

He supposed what happened next was his fault for not making sure she'd gone downstairs. Or maybe there was part of him that wanted to show her what she was missing. He knew she liked looking at his body—and it made him feel strong, worthy, when she stared at him like that.

When he got out of the shower and opened the bathroom door, she was sitting on the bed. He could have called out to see if she was still in the room, but he hadn't.

Her eyes widened and her mouth made a soft little O shape that made him imagine it doing all sorts of things on his flesh.

The proper thing he knew was to cover himself, but she didn't want him to—not the way her eyes raked over him like hot coals. He knew he should say sorry, something, but there was a spell over them both.

"You're so…hard."

It sounded like something out of a bad porno, but not when it came from her lips. It made him proud of his body and the work he put into it. Like it was good for something more than killing.

"Because I was thinking of you," he answered in a measured tone. He forced himself to walk over to the closet and pull out clean clothes.

She reached out her hand to touch him, and as much as he wanted her to, she'd already told him strings were definitely attached. Yet she made contact before he could bring himself to stop her.

Damara's palm was flat on his abs and she dragged it down oh, so slowly.

And as she'd observed earlier, he was definitely hard. Everywhere.

"This is going to happen, isn't it?" she asked in a

small voice, referring to the irrefutable draw between them, the desire.

"Not if you don't want it to." He never wanted her to think that she owed him something, or that she had to sleep with him. He wasn't that kind of a bastard.

"Is it wrong that I do, but I don't?" Her hand was still on his oblique, tracing ever closer to the center of his need.

By God, how he wanted her to touch him, the sweet silk of her palm wrapped around him, that wide-eyed look on her face, her dewy lips—he closed his eyes and gritted his teeth.

This was his chance to be the good guy. He'd been offered it in Barcelona, but he'd taken what he wanted for himself instead. He could have her now; she'd let him push her back on the bed and make her come so hard she screamed the house down.

But that wasn't what she needed right now, and, deep down, it wasn't what she wanted. He'd sworn to himself that he would protect her from all threats foreign and domestic, including himself. He opened his eyes and forced himself to make eye contact.

"No, it's not wrong at all. It's how I feel, too."

It was the first time he'd said that in a long time, acknowledged any sort of emotion aside from rage or guilt. It was a piece of himself—a small one—but he hoped it could be a kind of balm for them both.

"Really?" She finally dragged her gaze up to meet his.

He closed his fingers around her wrist, and, even though he wanted to push her hand lower, he brushed his lips across her knuckles and placed her hand back in her lap. "Really," he admitted.

"I'm sorry," she said when he'd turned away from her to dress.

"I knew you would be." He didn't want to acknowledge that being right was a kick to the balls.

"Not about Barcelona. About you being stuck with me." Her voice was so small and quiet. He knew what she was feeling because he'd be feeling the same way if the situation were reversed. He'd made her feel useless and unwanted. But he didn't know any other way to keep them from surrendering to the fire.

"We already determined there is no one else I'd trust with this job."

"I don't want to be your responsibility," she said softly.

"And I don't want to be something you regret. So we're even."

"I don't regret you, Byron. I just wish you weren't so pretty."

"Pretty?" He arched a brow. His chest might have puffed a fraction of an inch. No one had ever said he was pretty before. He'd been told he was hot, dangerous, all manner of things, but never pretty. Pretty was for kind things. No one had thought that about him.

"I just want to look at you all the time. I can't help myself. Whether it's the scars on your hands, or... or..."

"Or when I'm naked?" he offered, trying not to think about how easy it would be to cross the line. They both wanted to.

She blushed. "I used to have something called decorum. I'm not sure where it went. I can't believe I said that to you."

"When you're running for your life, decorum

seems useless." He was happy to be back to safer subject matter, but he couldn't stop thinking about what she'd said about the scars on his hands. He'd never thought about them one way or another, but she seemed to actually like them. That led to him thinking about what it was like to put his hands on her body—the contrast between them. Her perfection and his…not.

Byron kept thinking that this tension between them would dissipate. She said she didn't want to want him, and he knew better, so why couldn't they stop?

She seemed to know what he was thinking. "I guess we should find a way to deal with this if we're going to be married."

"Being married doesn't have anything to do with it, Damara. It's just a piece of paper, a legal shield against your brother and anyone who wants to take you away from my protection. Do you understand? Signing our names to that paper doesn't change anything between us."

"Isn't it forever? Do you want to live this way forever?"

"It doesn't have to be. We get you safe, your people safe. Then if you want to divorce me, that's what we'll do."

"What about what you want?"

He didn't dare think about what he wanted, deep down in that place where things secret and forbidden were kept hidden. What he wanted wasn't possible, so thinking about it, talking about it, breathing the idea into the corporeal world wasn't an option.

"That was shot to shit a long time before now." He couldn't bring himself to say anything else until he saw something fragile in her eyes. "Don't mistake me. It's my honor to protect you, Damara. You're physical proof of the good in the world, and, after all the death, it's good to know it was for something." Byron had to pull back. He couldn't risk sharing anything else. He'd probably already spilled too much. "Get your shoes if you still want to go."

He fled downstairs to pull on his boots and put some space between them.

If he'd never left Glory, it would be such a normal thing to do, to take his woman to Sweet Thing or The Corner Pharmacy for breakfast on a lazy morning. Except he'd never done things like that with any woman. The only time he'd ever gone to breakfast with one had been a stripper who worked the little joint hidden on a country road between Glory and Lawrence.

She'd paid.

He'd left a failure in the back of a police car and he'd returned the same. Maybe not in the back of a police cruiser, but it was a government car and the rules were the same. Do what you're told, or you're going to prison.

He had no doubt if he screwed this up with Damara, Renner would follow through, but that wasn't the worst of it. The worst was that if he screwed up, if he failed again in any way, Damara would get hurt. He could stomach any outcome of this little scenario but that one.

He kept waiting for that earworm to push to the forefront again. He kept expecting to hear Austin Foxworth condemning him, but he didn't. He heard nothing but his own doubts and fears.

She was deceptively fast, darting back down the

stairs wearing those illegal jeans and a soft sweater over his T-shirt. They clung to her luscious little curves in a way that made her outfit sexier than if she'd been wearing lingerie.

He especially liked her boots with the fur on top.

"It's not *that* cold." He grinned. She looked as if she was preparing for the Iditarod.

"*And* I'm wearing a coat. It doesn't ever get this cold on Castallegna. I can't seem to get warm." She snuggled down into the sweater.

It would have been an easy thing for him to pull her against his body and offer her his warmth. It's what every instinct inside him screamed to do. As if he was failing again somehow because she was cold. Instead of touching her, he stuffed his hands in his pockets. "When summer gets here, you'll be wishing for the cold. We don't have the ocean to keep the temperature mild. It gets hotter than the devil's ball bag."

"Is that a meteorological term?" she quipped.

"It is." He nodded seriously.

"So, we can just go out—we can do that? I've never been able to just go somewhere because I wanted to."

She was so damn beautiful, but she'd been a pretty bird in a gilded cage. He tried to remember that. And like a bird who'd never gotten used to her wings, she was likely to fly too far, too high, and not know how to get down without crashing. It was his job to make sure she didn't.

"Yeah, we can do whatever you want." They had some time. It wouldn't hurt to indulge her.

"We don't have to take a car or…" She shrugged.

"If you want to walk to Sweet Thing, it's not that far."

"Will there be coffee?" She perked.

"I'm sure there will." Byron took a moment to check in with the security detail again to tell them where they were going.

They walked down the old-fashioned sidewalks and crossed into downtown, the area he'd deliberately avoided on his morning run. It hadn't changed much since he'd been gone. It was almost a caricature of small-town goodness with the cobbled sidewalks and wholesome storefronts.

"Your hometown is lovely, Byron."

Byron guessed it was okay for antiquing and quilter types. He'd always wanted more adventure. He shrugged. "It's quaint."

"I bet you were miserable here as a child. Not enough excitement." She laughed, still taking in all the small-town charm.

"Maybe I was." He nodded. It had been more than that—he'd just never felt as if he belonged anywhere.

After the press junket and all the to-do that had been made about his return, people waved at the princess (they still stared at him as if he were a leper), but they weren't mobbed. It was as though she'd already been welcomed into the fold.

He knew what was next.

Casseroles.

Bundt cakes.

Three-layer macaroni salads.

Maybe they should just turn around and— Nope. Any hope he'd had of dragging Damara elsewhere died a cold death when they smelled the bakeshop.

Damara inhaled deeply. "That smell is divine."

"You can tell Betsy you think so. I'm sure an endorsement from a princess wouldn't hurt her business."

"Is she your friend?"

"Everyone knows Betsy. She's Caleb's sister."

She didn't say anything else until it was time for her to choose her pastry. All the patrons in the shop were staring at them. Their stares reminded him of his every sin. He wanted to rail at them, to growl and rage. He wanted to demand they stop studying him as if he were some infectious virus.

"What do you recommend?" Damara asked when it was their turn.

"Princess Damara! I'm so honored." Betsy Lewis squealed. She came around from behind the counter, wiping her hands on her apron, and embraced Damara as though they'd been friends since they were kids.

"You must be Betsy." Damara allowed the hug.

Byron looked around the shop. Many people averted their eyes, until he saw Jack McConnell sitting in a corner. He knew the other man had returned home a hero. Jack was everything he wished he could've been. Prosthetic limb and all. His team had come home. He found it hard to meet the other man's eyes, but when he did, he saw the same horrible knowledge reflected back at him.

The same self-doubt, the same fears.

Byron nodded in acknowledgment, and Jack returned it.

He wondered how the other man could have that much pain and sorrow when he was a hero? It made him think that maybe everything wasn't as it seemed, perhaps for both of them.

Betsy promptly loaded Damara down with three

of those purple boxes, at which Jack stood and made his way over.

"Hold on now—you can't give away all the maple bacon doughnuts. Those are mine, Sweet Thing," Jack interrupted.

There was something in the way he said those words that Byron knew he and Betsy were together. Betsy had followed him around in school like a love-sick puppy. But they both seemed better for it.

"India brought over some Better Than Sex dough-nuts last night. I can see why she ate them all the first time."

Betsy arched a brow. "Oh, really? She told me Caleb ate the first box."

They laughed. "Byron told me if I keep eating all these doughnuts and French fries I'm going to get fat."

Betsy glared at him. "You did not."

He nodded. "I did." Then he grinned. "But she doesn't care." Byron was still aware of stares boring into his back. He'd learned to live with whatever they thought of him.

"And neither should you," Betsy admonished.

He held up his hands in mock surrender. "I don't care if she's fat as a piglet." He cast her a sly glance. "As long as she doesn't care when I let the six-pack go."

Damara made a face. "Does that mean that Adonis line will go away, too?"

"Most definitely." She was so good at playing the game, for a moment, even he believed their banter was real.

She put the boxes down and the expression on her

face was one of abject disappointment. Almost like a child who'd been told no lolly before bed.

"Damara," he said quietly into the shell of her ear. "I'm only kidding. Eat yourself into a sugar coma. I like the sounds you make when you're eating these doughnuts."

He also liked watching the blush stain her cheeks and pretending that this banter meant something more, that it wasn't just a show for the world.

"They're bad about making us blush, aren't they?" Betsy asked, shaking her head.

"How much do we owe you?" Byron asked. He wanted to get away from the genuine love he saw between Jack and Betsy, their bond, because Byron was still playing pretend, still dressing up like something better than what he was.

"Nothing at all." Betsy beamed.

"India suggested you might like to make the wedding cake," Damara offered.

"Won't you be accepting bids?"

"No. I want you," Damara said. "If you'd do it."

"Of course. I'd love to." Betsy grinned even wider. "Really? I mean, this is a big deal."

"Yes, really."

"If she has her way, it'll just be doughnuts and French fries," Byron said, trying to keep the tone light in his own head.

"I'm seriously considering it," Damara teased.

"We better get moving if we want The Bullet Hole to ourselves for a while."

"You like to shoot?" Betsy asked.

Byron realized all eyes were on them, and he

nudged Damara. “I like mixed martial arts, too. I’m afraid I’m not always a very proper princess.”

And he felt the judgment of all those eyes sear deep into his bones. Damara could do no wrong, but the people here would never forget that he was just bad to the bone.

CHAPTER TWELVE

BYRON HAWKINS WAS BUILT like a god with the mouth of some dark knight turned poet, Damara thought as they reached The Bullet Hole. The things he said, the things he made her feel, it was as if he turned every emotion to ash and then filled her back up again. Her heart ached for him as much as the rest of her did.

She didn't think he realized how deeply he experienced things. The more he tried to shut them out, the more they cut into him. He was tragically beautiful, but not like a piece of art. He was real, he was flesh and he bled inside.

Damara was tempted to think if he'd just open up to her that she could help him shoulder his burdens. Yet, she wasn't as altruistic as he believed or as she wanted to be. Some of her reasons were purely selfish—something a princess wasn't supposed to be.

She couldn't help but wonder why it wasn't okay for her to want something or someone just for herself.

Except she knew why, and she knew why it couldn't be Byron Hawkins. He wasn't ready to be with anyone.

And that realization hurt, especially as she listened to the playful banter around her.

She shoved a doughnut in her mouth, hoping the

sugary goodness could actually patch the wounds that had ripped themselves open.

"Are you going to taste it?" He eyed her.

No. They were the Better Than Sex doughnuts and those made her think about the night before, and right now she really had to focus on what she had to do for Castallegna.

Except at the moment, they were one and the same. She had to marry him for Castallegna. She had to put him and herself through this ruse for Castallegna.

She was glad they were going to a shooting range. She'd get to blow off some steam.

Her stomach did a little flip when she realized they were completely alone on the range.

He flashed her a grin. "Your safety is a matter of national security. I asked Renner to close it for the day and bring out some big boys for you to play with."

If she'd ever thought she'd be allowed to go on a first date, this was what she'd want to do. She closed her eyes, trying not to be affected by the gesture.

"I just thought you'd need to know how to use some of the heavier weaponry. If the *Bratva* is running arms through Castallegna, this is probably what's going to be available for you to use." He gestured at the array of weapons before them. "You don't look pleased."

"It's just, this is so kind. This is exactly the kind of gift I'd want, if you'd asked me." She tried not to make too big a deal of it, but it was. It meant a lot to her.

"Good. Let's blow shit up."

He led her closer to the weapons. "This is an AK-12 Kalashnikov. It's a carbine rifle. They've just recently been phased out of use, so those weapons had to go somewhere. Most likely to men like Grisha and Vladimir. Because of your size, this is going to be harder for you to manage. So hold your hands, here and here."

Byron posed her so that she had a better grip of the weapon, moving her around like a doll. She couldn't help but think about that morning when she'd seen all the hard body she was now pressed against so intimately. He smelled so good, and all she could think about was touching him when she should've been focused on the weapon in front of her. He was right. They could be running this very weapon through her country right now. If she was faced with one, what would she do? What could she do?

"Want to try it out?" he asked, curling his finger over hers and around the trigger. "You can fire six hundred rounds a minute at fully automatic. Or you can set it to a three-round burst, or semiautomatic. Right here." He showed her with his other hand.

When Byron released her, she felt his absence acutely with a chill that was more than skin-deep.

"Ready?"

Her phone buzzed in her pocket, as did Byron's. He scowled and leaned away from her to answer his own. "It must be important."

She answered. "Hello?" Damara could hear that Byron's call had been linked to hers.

It was Renner. "Approximately three hours ago, another ship like *Circe's Storm* in the Mediterranean sent out a distress call. Satellite recon shows it was 'escorted' to Castallegna by armed ships that have been linked to other incidents of piracy. Vladimir Kulokav announced to investors today that they'll be opening a shipping station in Castallegna as part of his new venture with his brother-in-law. The Council ratified your marriage to Grisha."

Damara knew her brother would be angry, she knew on a logical level that he'd do anything to get what he wanted, but it was still a knife in her heart.

"Princess? Are you there?"

She nodded until she realized he couldn't see her. She would have to speak. She didn't want all the things she felt to choke her voice; she didn't want them to know just how much this hurt her. Even after everything, he was still her brother. "I'm here," she managed in a small voice.

Byron met her gaze, and she shied away from the knowing there. She suddenly understood why he didn't want her to see when he was hurting—how weak and vulnerable she felt.

"I never signed anything. I never agreed. The law says—" she began. Damara hated how she sounded.

"Your brother changed the law. Two Council members who dared to oppose him were found dead this morning. Suicide, but we have proof that it wasn't," Renner offered.

She narrowed her eyes. If he had proof of this, why hadn't he done something about it? "Do you have people on Castallegna?"

"Yes."

"Then why don't they manage my brother?" She regretted it as soon as she said it because Byron had offered to "manage" her brother several times and she'd declined.

"The same as he doesn't want to cause an international incident, neither do we. But Interpol and the State Department have linked him to Kulokav's seedier ventures, like human trafficking, and they're both now wanted men. Your brother is wanted in Monte Carlo for murder."

Damara felt as if she'd been punched. The hits just kept coming. Her brother, these things couldn't all be him. They just couldn't. Except she kept seeing the boy he'd been rather than the man who'd taken his place.

"So what do you want me to do?" she asked, dreading whatever was to come.

"We need to move up the wedding. You need to be a citizen of the United States. And you need to call your brother. We'll record the conversation and use sound bites in the media campaign," Renner instructed.

She looked at Byron, and he nodded his approval to the plan. Of course, what else would he do? No, this had been the plan all along. It was a mission, a strategy.

She'd let herself forget that.

"Okay," Damara agreed because there was nothing else to do.

Byron tried to put his arm around her, but she declined the support. He'd told her that she had to depend on herself, to trust only herself, and that's what she would do. She pushed away from him. She couldn't let herself rely too much on the strength she derived from his touch because it wasn't always going to be there.

"I assume you've got someone waiting to patch me through?" she said.

The line went dead for a moment before several clicks and ringing. The phone was like a brick in her hand, and her stomach rolled and twisted. She thought she was going to vomit, but instead she closed her eyes and breathed.

"I'm surprised you called," Abele said after the first ring.

His voice made her stomach churn again. It made her homesick and heartsick. His voice was both familiar and warm but terrible, too.

"Your actions asked me to call." She didn't know what else to say.

"I asked you to marry Grisha Kulokav, and you didn't do that." His voice was low and silky, with an undertone that promised violence.

Damara was sure she didn't know the man speaking to her through the phone.

"Marrying a man and picking up the phone are two different things, my brother." She hoped to remind him that she was his sister and that at one time, he'd loved her.

"Not so much. Both were for the good of my heart."

Liar, she wanted to scream. "I'm sorry if I've worried you, but I'm safe."

"Your husband will be looking for you."

"My *husband* is in the next room. Or didn't you hear about the secret wedding?" She couldn't resist needling him, driving home the fact that he didn't get to choose who she married and that she wouldn't let him do this to her or her country.

"Grisha is willing to overlook your mistake. The stupid bastard actually likes that you tried to kill him. He's even willing to take you now, even though you've spent your worth on that dirty American."

The blooming confidence shriveled and burned

like a flower too long in the sun. "Obviously, he must think I have some worth if he still wants to marry me."

That's all she was to him. A path to different alliances, wealth and power. He no longer saw her as human, if he ever had.

She couldn't help but remember those times spent together as children and how he'd been her best friend growing up, her constant companion. He'd protected her, coddled her and loved her. Now he was someone else entirely.

"No, sister. You lost that chance. He doesn't want to marry you, but he'll keep you as his whore. His mistress. I've given you to him. By Castallegnian law, you are married. But it will be like Khan in the days of old. He will take you and do with you as he pleases."

"There's something I've been wanting to ask you since this started," she dared.

"Oh, and what is that?" He seemed amused.

"If you think women are worthless, that I am worthless aside from my womb, why did you bother to teach me to read, to think? Why did you give me books filled with Aristotle and Plato?"

He was silent.

"Maybe you disapprove of who I am, what I've done, but you had a hand in molding me, Abele." She hoped to remind him of their shared memories, their shared joys. She hoped somehow it would wake him up to what he was doing. It would remind him that he loved her and she loved him.

"And I will unmake you."

His words stabbed her. "Why do you hate me so much?" She was afraid of the answer, but she needed it all the same.

"I don't hate you, but you will learn your place. Just as I have learned mine. Our mother was a whore who spread for any man who'd take her. I won't let you do that to our line. You are no longer the crown princess of Castallegna."

He was insane. "I don't know what you're talking about."

"I am not our father's son!" he spat. "But nevertheless, I am king. And you, sister, have made yourself a criminal by defying me. I'm demanding your immediate return to stand trial."

Terror knifed through her. She knew he was evil, she knew he'd done horrible things, but part of her had always thought she'd be able to make him see reason. If he got her back to Castallegna, it wouldn't be a trial. It would be a thematic production where the tragic princess dies in the end.

"Come home and face your punishment. If I have to come retrieve you, I can promise you it will be much more terrible than you can imagine. Your ranger might be tough, but there's only one of him and I have all of the *Bratva* at my disposal. I hope your keepers listening on the line heard that. Because they're on my list, too."

The line clicked, and Abele was gone.

Damara stood frozen and sick with grief.

"I'll have your marriage license messengered to the house. All you have to do is sign it, and I'll rush the paperwork through for your citizenship. We can't rightfully keep you from him unless you're a citizen. We'll spin it that you abdicated your crown to be with Byron."

Her fingers were curled so tightly around the

phone, she'd lost feeling in the tips. "No, we won't. I'll sign the papers. I'll marry him. I'll even abdicate my crown, but I'm not doing it for anyone but the people of Castallegna. I'm doing it for democracy, and that's not a spin. It's important that my people know I haven't abandoned them. Making up a pretty romance was a great idea as long as it worked, but push came to shove. So I'm shoving back."

"Princess, I really think—"

"Didn't you hear? I'm not a princess anymore. I've agreed to everything you've wanted, and I understand that in some cases, you know more than I do about such things. I'm content to be guided by your experience. But not in this."

"You're risking support," Renner pleaded.

"Then I'm risking it."

"Then all of this will be for nothing," Renner said in an attempt to manipulate her.

"If her people are stuck with that bastard, then it will be for nothing. She's made up her mind," Byron said in her defense.

"Fine. Get back to the house. Sonja will meet you there."

She clicked the phone off and stuffed it back in her pocket, still numb.

"Let me serve you now, Princess."

"Like I told Renner, didn't you hear? I'm not a princess anymore."

"Yes, you are. Being royal is just like family. It's not always blood that makes it so. Or what any piece of paper says. Your brother is a festering boil on the ass of humanity. Nothing he says should affect you."

"After everything, he's still my brother." Damara

wished she could turn it off. She wished she could forget that fact, but she couldn't. She wanted to hate him, but she couldn't do that, either.

"That's the only reason he's breathing now—trust me on that," Byron said softly and pulled her close.

Damara did believe him. She knew the man who held her was a deadly weapon, but beneath all of that, she knew he was a person with dreams and fears just like anyone else. She wanted to dissolve in his arms. She wanted him to be a white knight and save her, but she knew what he'd do to save her. Byron Hawkins was a good man, but he was no white knight. Real men weren't.

"Promise me you won't kill him."

"I can't make that promise, Damara. I won't lie to you."

A chill skittered down her back. "Even knowing I couldn't forgive you?"

"If Renner tells me to kill him, I don't have a choice."

"Yes, you do. We always have a choice." She knew she should break away from the embrace, but he was still her lifeline. She couldn't let go. She'd lost everything else.

He closed his eyes and leaned his forehead against hers. "All right, Damara. I'll defy everyone for you—my country, my boss, myself. On one condition. If he hurts you, you release me from my promise."

"You could say what he's doing right now is hurting me."

"I could, but I'm not dancing around anything here. If he makes an attempt on your life, kidnaps you or otherwise lays hands on you, I will put an end to him, promise or no. Release or no. Period."

"I guess I'll have to be content with that." She cupped his cheek. "Thank you for even that concession."

"Always the diplomat, aren't you?" There was no malice in his words, so she wasn't sure what he meant.

"I don't—" She shook her head.

"You didn't get exactly what you wanted, but you thanked me anyway. You soothed over whatever doubts I had and cleared away the debris that might have turned into an argument."

She cocked her head to the side. "Why would we argue? You've stated your position. I've stated mine. And we came to a compromise that neither of us is happy with, but we can both live with. What's there to fight over? This is the way of the world."

He laughed with honest mirth. "You always surprise me, Damara. For how innocent you are, at times you're very worldly wise." He shook his head. "I didn't expect you."

"Well, that was obvious when you told me that you thought the Jewel was a stone."

"No, I didn't expect that, either. But sometimes what we don't expect—it's better."

She didn't dare let herself feel any of the things that flowered sweet and warm inside of her. They were all better left in the dark. If they never saw the sun, if she never acknowledged them, it wouldn't hurt so much when she had to shove them back down and hide them away from both Byron and herself.

"Sorry to cut this short, but we should get back to the house."

She nodded.

The walk back wasn't nearly as lovely. It was filled with a heavy silence. Marrying him hadn't been real. She'd thought that somehow everything would come together and it would all work out.

Part of her had wanted to believe in the spin they had crafted for the rest of the world, that he'd fallen hard for her while saving her. But that was just her being a naive girl who didn't know any better. She'd wrapped him up in the pretty colors of her fantasies and damn if he hadn't tried his best to live up to them.

Her hands shook, and she shivered.

Sonja pulled up to the house as they approached, her thin face pinched and grim.

Once inside, Byron said, "That was fast."

Sonja spread the papers out before them, and Damara froze.

She picked up the pen and looked at the document that would bind her and Byron together. Her hands were still shaking.

For all her talk, she didn't know if she could do this to him, knowing it wasn't what he wanted. Her eyes were drawn to his face. She was both curious and afraid as to what she'd see there. Damara knew if she saw dread or misery, she wouldn't be able to sign.

She'd have to find another way.

He grabbed the pen out of her hand and scrawled his signature in black ink; then he handed it back to her.

She signed, intensely aware that with every swoop and curl of her signature she was changing her life irrevocably. No matter what happened now, she would be Byron Hawkins's wife. Even if it only lasted a day, a month, a year or five years. She would have joined her life to his.

And he to hers.

If Abele was removed from power, he'd be a crown prince of Castallegna. He could be king.

She paused and looked at him again.

He wouldn't be a bad king. He was a good man. But was he good enough to relinquish that kind of power?

He was. She knew it in the marrow of her bones.

She finished signing.

"I now pronounce you princess and ranger. Many happy returns," Sonja said, her voice as grim as her expression. "I hate to drop a bomb and run, but we still have to make your marriage an event for the world to see, and I need to reschedule that satellite interview." Sonja took pictures of the papers with her cell phone before stuffing them back in her briefcase. "I'll be working from the carriage house office." She nodded her head toward the back of the grounds where the security detail was lodged.

It was official. She was married.

To the man of her dreams who didn't want her.

"I'm sorry," she said when Sonja and the rest of the crew had left. "I know what you're sacrificing."

"And I know what you're sacrificing. We agreed to this. Actually, you bullied me into this," he teased.

"It's not funny." She felt her lips thin.

Byron tilted her chin up to make her look at him. "I'm not giving anything up to do this, Damara."

"But you said—" She remembered how he'd said he didn't want her. She wished she could forget. Even after everything, that still played on a constant loop in her head.

"I say a lot of stupid shit. You'll learn that soon enough." He laughed, but it was awkward and uncomfortable. "First of all, this is my job. It's what I do. Your safety, your people, they're my mission. Serving you—" he smirked, and she blushed "—is how I can best serve my country." Then he was serious again. "It's an honor to do so."

She wanted to cry. She was so stupid. Of course she was a mission. She couldn't ever let herself forget that. But there were moments that she did. Like now, when he offered her succor and protection against the world.

But he did not belong to her and she wasn't that to him—never could be that to him. He wouldn't let her.

"That's not supposed to make you unhappy, Damara."

"Supposed to?" She shook her head. "This isn't anything that we haven't been over."

"I'm sorry I can't give you what you need."

"No, you're exactly what I need." She only wished he could believe it— No, even if he believed it, he didn't want to be what she needed. He was still too busy punishing himself for his crimes. "All that matters is Castallegna."

CHAPTER THIRTEEN

Byron hadn't planned for Damara, not in any way, shape or form. She was chaos and light.

Most people thought of chaos as something bad, especially for someone like him who had regimentally planned his life around structure and protocol. He operated within these confines to make sure the only people he could hurt had it coming.

He didn't grieve that—it was just how things had to be. But Damara had changed that. She gave him purpose, she gave him—

She gave him hope.

Hope for a future, hope that he could be more than what he thought he was.

It had damn near killed him to promise not to kill her brother outright. It offended Byron to the blackest part of the soul he wasn't sure he had that the bastard drew breath in the same world as Damara. Or that his words could still wound her so deeply. After everything she'd done, how resolutely she fought, he was the chink in her armor.

And Byron wouldn't let anyone hurt her.

Protecting her was the best thing he'd ever done; the only thing he felt was honorable. Now she was his wife.

He knew he was at cross-purposes with himself.

If he killed her brother, there'd be no reason for her to stay married to him. She'd be safe.

Byron knew eventually he'd lose her either way. He'd rather know she was safe and living some wonderful life than keep her clinging to him out of fear.

His mind had been made up.

Abele Petrakis had to die.

But he wouldn't break his word because he wouldn't have to. He fully expected that Abele would do something to hurt Damara, and then Byron would be free to do what he should have done on day one and kill him.

Of course, if he'd done it then, he never would've had this time with Damara. He couldn't regret it.

Having come to that decision, a sense of peace filled him. This was what he was trained to do, and he would do it well. Damara would be safe.

He shuffled his feet and stuffed his hands in his pockets. He'd decided to kill her brother and had married her. Now he had no idea what to say to her.

From the look on her face, she felt the same way—uncomfortable and awkward.

"Strange, isn't it? We had no lack of conversation in the middle of the ocean running for our lives, but here in our house, after getting married, neither of us has anything to say."

"I'm not sure what there is to say. You're my husband now. It feels so strange to say."

"Especially since I'm not a prince." There was no rancor in his voice. They both knew she'd been groomed to marry another royal. Her whole life had been changed in the past few weeks.

Her expression was grave. "You will be, if Abele is removed from power. Actually, you'll be a king."

"Nah, I'll just be Byron Hawkins. Former ranger and current bodyguard."

She nodded slowly. "I think you're the only man on the planet who would give it back."

"It's not mine." He shrugged, uncomfortable with the light he saw in her eyes.

It made it uncomfortable because he wanted it to stay there. No one had ever looked at him like that before. It was as if he'd hung the moon and stars and there was nothing he couldn't do.

It was such a pretty lie. If he wasn't careful, she'd have him believing it and confessing his sins to her. And then she'd see. She'd know…

All he could do for her now was make her safe.

"Don't look at me like that," he commanded. It felt too good, even knowing it was a lie, the way she seemed to raise him on some pedestal of virtue.

"Like what?"

"Like I'm a good man."

"You are!" She went to him, placed her hand on his cheek. "You're a better man than you know."

"No." He shook his head. "I'm not."

"Why do you say that?"

He couldn't tell her. He still couldn't admit his failures. It would mean watching that light in her eyes dim. So, instead, he spoke of the things that didn't scare him. "Because I remember what you said to me, that you didn't want me to touch you without knowing all of my sins. But when you look at me that way, it makes me want to kiss you. And I know if I did, you'd wrap your arms around my neck and let me take you upstairs."

Her eyes widened; her lips parted. "And maybe

I was stupid to try to deny this pull between us. I'm going to get my heart broken anyway."

That wasn't what he expected her to say. He thought she'd be angry or indignant. Not this acceptance. This wasn't what she wanted. He knew that.

Byron was trying to put distance between them without extinguishing that light—he couldn't bear to give it up.

Yet, if he killed Abele, he knew he'd have to. She'd never forgive him. There were so many things he'd done that weren't worthy of forgiveness, and many where there was no one left who could forgive him.

She walked toward him, that terrifying expression still on her face.

The doorbell rang, clanging through the house like a death knell.

But neither of them moved.

"Hawkins," one of the security team yelled through the door. "You and the princess have company to welcome you to the neighborhood. And Bundt cakes."

"So it begins," he said ominously.

He opened the door, and it was just as he feared. Soon every surface was covered with casserole dishes, desserts and three-layer salads made out of things that should never be called salad. Or put in people's mouths at the same time, for that matter.

The Ladies Auxiliary, with their large purple hats and myriad of baking dishes, had detonated an explosion of all sorts of homemade dishes in his kitchen.

Damara watched with bright eyes as Mrs. Cresswell, his former math teacher, dished up plates of everything and handed it to them.

Half the time, her class had been the only one he'd bothered to attend.

Damara was getting a heaping serving of his past whether he wanted to share it with her or not.

"Come give us a hug, kiddo," Mrs. Cresswell said.

He embraced her, and she patted his back reassuringly. She still smelled like roses. He remembered that her room always smelled like that rose perfume. It reminded him of the time she'd caught him pulling the fire alarm. He'd been meticulously removing the plastic covering that was supposed to repel such activity when he'd smelled her rose perfume. He'd thought for sure he was busted.

All she'd done was sigh and motion for him to hurry up. She'd said it was a nice day outside and they could all use a break, but if he did it again, she'd rat him out.

She probably should've turned him in to begin with.

"You've done well for yourself. I always knew you would, once you found an outlet for your…talents." She smiled.

"Have you had anyone as bad as I was since?" He raised a brow and Helena Sutterfield sniffed indignantly.

"Johnny Hart gave you a run for your money—that's for sure." She shook her head. "Brilliant with numbers but no ambition."

He considered. "You know, I think your class actually saved my life a couple times."

She lit up. "Maybe you'll come speak at the school and you can tell them that. I hear from kids all the time that they'll never use advanced math in their everyday lives and it's a waste of time."

"You never know when you'll have to calculate the gross national product of a country in relation to a mobster's investments and how much you'll need to pretend to make to get him to take a meeting with you. And then to discuss market trends without sounding like an idiot."

She held up her hands. "See, ladies? What did I say? He was really a good kid underneath all that trouble."

Her praise made him uncomfortable.

"A good kid? He's the best of men," Damara said.

Now it was more than uncomfortable. He itched. Damara's praise had given him a rash.

"I bet the princess here has no idea just what a little hoodlum her ranger used to be," Helena announced.

"Oh, I think I might. You don't get the skills you need to rescue princesses without getting your armor dinged up just a bit." Damara smiled at him.

No, no, no. He could not let her make this okay. It wasn't. Because then she'd have him thinking those thoughts again. That he wasn't born bad. But he was. He knew he was.

"Frankly, we were all surprised," Helena said.

"I wasn't," Mrs. Cresswell said.

"Then you were the only one." Helena sniffed again.

Damara bristled beside him. "In my country, it's rude to enter a person's home and say disparaging things about them. I can't imagine it's much different here. Is it, Mrs. Cresswell?"

The woman laughed. "No, dear. It's exceedingly rude." She eyed Helena.

But Helena Sutterfield wasn't about to be intimidated or put off. "Rude would be the time he—"

"Helena, really," Mrs. Cresswell interrupted her.

She was right, though.

He realized this was why he liked covert work so much—he could be someone else. "No, by all means." He held out his hand in invitation. Let them say what they would about him, let them warn Damara off him as if he were a rabid dog that needed to be put down. Maybe that would make it easier to stay away from her.

Helena looked back and forth between them, but she shoved a bite of gelatin surprise in her mouth instead of speaking.

Which Byron had to think was a first.

"Ladies, I'm going to share a secret with you, but you must promise not to tell anyone else." Damara quickly changed the subject.

They all looked at her and nodded, appearing to be eager for whatever gossip the princess would share with them.

"Byron and I didn't want to wait anymore. So we got married this morning."

There was a collective gasp.

"We're still going to have a ceremony, but—"

"You're newlyweds and you'd like to enjoy your privacy," Mrs. Cresswell said with a knowing grin. "Well, ladies. Let's leave our young prince with his princess."

Byron rather thought getting them together to do something as a group had to be like herding cats, but

Mrs. Cresswell managed it. Probably the same way she managed him. With a flurry of hugs and well wishes, the ladies were gone.

"How do you do that?" he asked her.

"What?" She turned to look at him.

"Make everyone want to do things for you."

Damara shook her head. "I didn't realize I did."

"Thanks for getting rid of them. I know they mean well." He was secretly grateful she'd gotten rid of them before they could sour her on him, before they could tell her all the horrible things he'd done and why he'd never be anything better than what he was.

"So you ran with a bad crowd, huh?" She smiled.

"I *was* the bad crowd, Damara."

"I meant what I said. I don't care that you were some bad-boy kid." She shook her head. "You're a good man."

"Stop saying that." He was almost pleading.

"Why?"

He turned to look into her eyes, hope and fear warring inside him. "Because I might start to believe you."

DAMARA WAS DONE fighting herself.

Even if she never gave her body to him again, her heart never had a chance. The connection she shared with him wouldn't ever let her be free. She wasn't naive enough to think she was in love with him already, but she'd already tripped over the ledge and she was falling hard and fast.

And she knew he wouldn't be there to catch her. She would hit bottom and she'd hit it alone.

It was really quite something to make the choice

knowing he'd never be hers. Never feel the same way about her that she did about him.

He'd already touched her once. Didn't they deserve to have some pleasure, something that felt good? If that's all he had to share with her, she'd take it. By handing down edicts she'd been trying to change him, and she knew you couldn't do that with people. You had to accept them as they were.

Byron didn't want to cut himself open and show her his pain, and who was she to demand that he do it? Why was that her place? It wasn't. The same as he couldn't make her choices for her, she couldn't make his for him. His pain was his. Why did she need to dig around in his wounds?

They were married now; they might as well reap some of the benefits.

"That look on your face is even more terrible than the one before." He took a step back, hands in front of him as if that could protect him from whatever she was thinking.

"Is it?" she asked, not really looking for a response.

"You've come to some kind of decision, and from the set to your jaw, I don't think I'm going to like it." He shook his head.

"You'll like it. You'll like it a lot." She hoped. "You said you wanted to kiss me before the Purple Hats showed up. So kiss me."

"I thought we decided that was a bad idea."

"Changed my mind." She wet her lips.

"Because someone said something to me you thought was mean? The world is full of cruel people." He stepped back from her.

"It is, but it's full of good people, too." *Like you,* she wanted to add.

"Are you going to kiss everyone Helena Sutterfield was mean to? Even if they deserved it?"

He was still trying to do the right thing, trying to take care of her and protect her from herself. But he needed to understand that you could never protect a person from their own wants, desires, angels and demons. They were always present. "Do you remember when you said I could see anything I wanted?"

His eyes closed. "You're offering me what I want most knowing I can't give you the same." She could see his pulse beating in his neck, and she wanted to touch her lips to that place.

"I don't care anymore, Byron. You said if I wanted to see anything to just ask. I want to see *everything.*"

"Then let's go upstairs to the bedroom where there's no camera."

She'd forgotten about the cameras. She was so used to being on display, to being watched, that she'd put them right out of her mind. Damara took his hand, rough and calloused as it was, in her own soft one.

Then she closed the door behind them.

Desire warred with nervousness. "Show me," she commanded, leaning against the door for support. She wasn't going to back down now.

"You like being in charge so much, maybe we should play princess and the bodyguard." He arched a brow.

"Isn't that what we're doing?"

"Not like this." He pulled his shirt off. "See, you give me commands and I'll do anything you want. I'm at your service."

Service. Made her think of all the ways she could require his talents.

"Is this a thing? People do this?" She blushed thinking about it.

"People do lots of things to get off. We could switch it up. You could be *my* bodyguard."

He was totally naked under his jeans, but she knew he would be.

She didn't know it was possible for her mouth to water and go dry at the same time. Every inch of him was gloriously perfect. Even the scars from knives, bullets and other violence. That was what she'd liked best about his hands—that they were scarred.

He was a weapon, and he was offering to let her wield him as she wished.

"As if anyone would ever believe that." She snorted.

"I would." He stood proud, unabashed in nakedness. Allowing her to drink in all of him.

"Only for pretend."

"No, I saw you handle that guy in Carthage. You know how to fight. You're small, but you're strong and fast. With the right training, you're capable of doing anything I can do."

This was why he was dangerous. He believed in her. Not just what her name could do or her position, but the woman underneath.

Oh, she was in so much trouble. Her eyes were drawn down to his arousal.

She wanted to touch him, taste him, own him and *be* owned by him.

"What's it going to be, Your Majesty? How shall I serve you?"

"Maybe all I want to do is look." Her voice was

hoarse, guttural and completely unlike her. *That didn't sound very commanding at all.*

"Maybe. And maybe you want me on my knees between your thighs."

Jolts of white-hot lust scalded through her. "Yes, I do."

"Then what is your command?"

She couldn't find the words. She was still afraid of what it would mean for her—for them. She didn't want to tell him to fuck her, but she couldn't ask him to make love to her either. And "take me" was too trite.

But he didn't move forward, didn't take control. Byron waited for her.

He wasn't letting her off easy. She'd have to articulate exactly what she wanted from him to get it.

She understood now what it was like to be on display. Damara thought she knew, but she didn't.

"Worship me. Make me believe I'm the only woman you'll ever touch again. Make me feel like being your woman is better than being a princess."

"As you wish."

"You keep saying that to me."

"What should I say?"

"It's just… It sounds like it means something different than the way you speak it."

"Do you want to talk about my vocabulary or would you like me to demonstrate my cunning linguistics?"

"Demonstrate." That was the easiest answer of the night.

He moved toward her, and she was entranced with every part of him that was on display. Byron held out his hand in invitation to the bed. She sat on the corner gingerly, feeling more inexperienced than she had that night in Barcelona. He hooked his fingers around the waist of her pants. He held her gaze as he pulled them down her body.

She decided she liked him stripping her much better than stripping herself.

"You can still change your mind," he said, his lips hot on the inside of her knee. "You should change your mind. You should tell me to stop, because you deserve better than this."

She shivered with need. "No, I think we're both getting exactly what we deserve."

Next came her panties and still he didn't look away. No, he met her stare—all dark intensity—even as he dragged her forward to the edge of the bed and drew her feet up onto his shoulders.

Even as he dipped his head.

Damara remembered how much pleasure he'd wrought with his tongue in Barcelona. She knew what he could do to her, and the anticipation was an erotic treat all on its own.

She was torn between wanting to watch his every motion and hold that connection with him and surrendering to the sensation. He pulled her farther forward so that he supported her weight and she couldn't see him but for his dark hair.

He was like a bird of prey, flying higher and higher until he dived in for the kill. Even as she flew with him, they were twisted in some death spiral toward culmination. Making love with him was like watching a master paint on canvas. His hands and mouth the brushes, her body the canvas and her ecstasy the paint.

It would be a masterpiece for them both. She writhed and arched, moaned for more.

Again, as before, she felt as if she were a bowstring that had been strung so tight she'd snap, but he pushed her further until her whole world narrowed to a tiny pinpoint of light collapsing in on itself until it exploded outward in a bomb blast. She experienced every sensation, every bliss, all at once.

He eased her legs down and rose up to kiss her on the mouth. She tasted herself—sweet.

"I want to do the same for you that you did for me," she offered shyly between kisses.

"You don't have to." He almost sounded afraid.

"I want to, Byron. I really want to." She took him firmly in hand, as she had in Barcelona, but this time, she was going to do all those things with her mouth.

Damara reversed their positions on the bed.

She realized that for Byron Hakwins, a growl could mean so many things. Usually, it meant he was angry, but that low rumble in his throat when she took him, the jerk of his hips and the way his fingers curled gently but firmly around her shoulders told her everything she needed to know.

Damara still hadn't finished exploring him, so she decided to indulge. She traced his length, learning what was sensitive, what he liked and what he didn't as she went.

"Damara—" Even though he growled again, it was as though her name were a curse or a blessing—she wasn't sure which. But she hoped for both. She wanted to make him feel so much pleasure, he thought he would shatter, and maybe she did want him to shatter. Just a little bit.

And she'd pick up the pieces again, the same as he'd done to her in Barcelona.

Being as new to the love game as she was, she might have been unsure of herself, but Byron wasn't. Byron believed she could do anything.

So maybe she could.

"What you do to me—" His whole body was taut even as his hips surged forward. He tried to pull away, but she wouldn't let him. She was determined to have all of him. Even his culmination.

He spasmsed and cried out her name as he spent his seed.

Damara was very satisfied with herself, indeed.

She'd given him these moments, this bliss. This was something that the future couldn't steal from them. It would always be theirs. Damara slid down into the crook of his arm. That had become second nature to her. She tried not to think about how she'd miss sleeping next to him when it was all over.

She'd miss a lot of things. The way he touched her, the way he made her feel…not just in the bedroom, but as a woman. As a princess, too.

He made her feel as if she could do anything.

CHAPTER FOURTEEN

THIS MOMENT, RIGHT HERE, was the best thing Byron had ever experienced. It was better than sex, better than his first kill, even better than when he'd finally realized what his purpose was—killing. Destruction.

Simply lying in bed with Damara Petrakis— No, his wife. Damara Hawkins.

Guilt bloomed.

She'd told him no, but he'd pushed and coerced and seduced until he'd gotten exactly what he wanted and made her think it was her idea.

Yet he continued to bask in the warmth of her arms, the softness of her body pressed against him and the comfort she offered.

For him, this was happiness. Or as close as he'd ever been. The worst part was knowing it couldn't last. Part of him wished he'd never had it at all. Then he wouldn't be able to miss it when it was gone.

He tried to remind himself that she was just a mission and this heat between them was a bonus, but he knew it was more than that. So he had to cut it out like a cancer before it had a chance to spread.

Even though he didn't want to break free from the cocoon they'd wrapped themselves in, he forced himself to get up.

"Where are you going?" she said sleepily.

"Shower."

She stretched lazily. "I'll join you."

"I don't think that's a good idea." He swallowed hard, hating his own words.

Damara sat up and pulled the blanket around her. "Why not?"

"You know why not." He didn't want to do this—he didn't know if he could.

"Look, you don't get to make these choices for me."

"No, I don't. I get to make them for *me*."

He tried to turn away from her, but the soft defeat in her voice cut him too deeply when she spoke. "So, you got me. You got through my defenses and got me to surrender. Now you don't want me anymore?"

It would be easier if he could say that he didn't, but he couldn't hurt her that way. Not with the sorrow that already tinged her voice. "I want you too much."

"Then why can't we have this?" Her eyes were wide, her mouth drawn as she waited for him to explain it to her.

"It'll make it harder for us both when it's over."

"Why does it have to be over?" she cried.

"When your brother is deposed, who is going to lead your people?" His voice was gentle, but the meaning behind his words was like an anvil.

"They will."

"Damara, they trust you and they need you. The whole point of all of this was to keep you safe until you could return home. Don't you want to go home?"

"More than anything."

That was the only answer he needed, and the one he expected. He nodded. "The world loves you and your people love you. Don't demand I love you, too. Because I can never have you, not really."

He didn't wait for her answer. Instead, he turned on the water in the shower and tried to ignore the ache in his chest.

But he wasn't alone. She didn't listen. She crept into the shower with him anyway.

"One day, Byron. Just give me the rest of this day. Maybe if we do everything, feel everything, it'll be enough. Maybe we'll stop wanting each other like this."

"It will never be enough."

Now she was the one pushing, demanding, manipulating his weaknesses as he'd done to her. He supposed it was only fair that it was her turn to take what she wanted from him. She wanted this day, and he'd give it to her.

"Make love to me, then fuck me and then make love to me again. Fill me up with memories so I don't forget." Her words were a transgression, something he'd never thought he'd hear her say. It was illicit but intimate, almost at cross-purposes.

The water cascaded over them, and he pushed her hair out of her face gently. She twined her arms around his neck, her skin slick and warm.

Every touch was more intense, every breath was somehow sweeter.

He couldn't let this, or her, mean any more to him. Byron had to think of this as a mission. The best course of action would be to deny her, but he couldn't—wouldn't.

He had to step up his timetable so he could finish this mission.

Byron turned off the water. "This shower sex works in fantasies, but in real life, it's not so much fun." He guided her to the bed.

DAMARA MEMORIZED THE taste of him—it was different now than in Barcelona. The first time he'd kissed her, it had been wonderful, but now there was familiarity to the act that added another layer to the sensation.

He kissed down her neck slowly, nibbling and nipping at the tender skin of her throat. She clung to him and pulled him even closer. She wanted her body to remember what it was like when he held her—the way it felt to press her breasts against the wide expanse of his chest, his flesh inside hers and the thunder of his heartbeat under her cheek. She wanted all of those things to be absorbed on some primal level that she wasn't even sure was possible.

He moved down to her collarbone and then the swell of her breast. Byron gave every inch of skin his undivided attention. There was no centimeter more important than any other. He filled his hands with her pert breasts, but he didn't linger. It was as if he sensed what she needed, or maybe his body had accepted what her mind already knew.

That this was indeed the last time.

Or maybe he was just that skilled at giving her what she wanted from him.

He moved down her chest to her belly and veered over to her hip, the outside of her thigh. Every place his lips touched was brought to stark and vibrant life, each touch receptor vibrating with bliss.

Byron moved his way down her leg, all the way down to her ankle and then back up to the inside of her knee. She giggled, but he didn't stop. He pressed his lips to her mound, then continued his journey to her other leg, her other hip, all the way up her ribs to her shoulder. Down the inside of her arm.

He was making love to her with his lips. Not getting her off, not to drive her higher; this is what he would do with her if he knew he could never do it again.

He was committing her body to his memory the way she'd done with him.

She didn't think her heart could break more than once, but it did. Over and over again.

Byron reached over to the nightstand for a condom, but she stayed his hand. "I don't want any barriers between us tonight."

"Are you sure?" His tone was gruff, his lips swollen from their explorations.

"More than anything."

He went back to his pursuit, kissing and tasting, exploring her body.

The arousal was secondary for her. Yes, he made her want and he made her wet, and she knew her release would be dazzling—fireworks and symphonies. But this part, where the emotion dwelled, that was what she needed, what she drank like a wanderer did water in the desert.

She didn't want to wait anymore. She wanted the next level of this sensation. "Please, now."

Their gazes had joined when he sheathed himself inside her, and it was like a kind of trespass to experience these feelings while looking each other in the eye. It added yet another layer to the insanity, the connection.

And it felt like nothing else. She felt so full of him, but still she wanted more. She'd never get enough of him, or the sense of fulfillment she got only when she was in his arms like this.

She locked her legs around his waist as if that could somehow draw him even nearer to her, pull him deeper or give her more of him than she already had.

He gripped her hips and rolled them so that she was on top of him, and she got exactly what she was looking for. She'd taken him as deep as he could go.

Damara braced her palms on the mattress and pushed down with her hips. His hips thrust up to meet her, but still he didn't look away or close his eyes.

Her hair fell like a curtain around them and it was almost as though it was hiding them from the rest of the world. If only.

If only what?

If only she wasn't a princess and he wasn't a ranger? Then they wouldn't be who they were. Then this might not be so perfectly imperfect.

She didn't hold anything back from him now. She didn't try to hide from him; she let him see whatever he wanted as he looked into her eyes. Damara loved the play of expressions on his face as he neared completion. The way he sought it out but fought it at the same time. The tight cords of muscle in his neck as he strained against the pleasure and against her.

Even the slightly tender spots on her hips from where his fingers had gripped her just a little too tightly.

Every time she touched the tender flesh she was reminded of what had transpired to make it tender.

He grabbed her hard around the waist.

"Roll over."

She complied without question, lifted herself off of him and lay on her stomach.

"Up on your hands and knees," he commanded.

Damara did as he instructed, and his arm wrapped around her waist, his chest hot against her back. She shivered, waiting to see what he would do to her.

"You said you wanted me to make love to you, then fuck you, then make love to you again, right?"

"Yes."

"This is the fucking."

She gasped when he entered her again with a powerful thrust. At this angle, it hit a new place inside her that made her cry out.

He didn't stop; he didn't ask her if she was okay. He knew she was. He knew she wanted more. Already he could read her body like a map.

He drilled into her without mercy, but she wanted none. She met his thrusts, pushing herself back against his hips and thighs. Every time he went deep, sensation spiraled through her belly, her cleft and even down to her toes.

Damara curled her fists in the blanket and gasped.

He tangled his fist in her hair and tugged, just enough to get her to lift her head but not enough to hurt.

She loved it.

"More!" she demanded.

He increased the speed and tempo of his thrusts, slamming into her and giving no quarter. Her sheath spasmed around him as new bursts of sensation ricocheted through her.

Byron swore, and he pulled her back against him hard as he spent.

He dropped down on the bed next to her, a fine sheen of sweat on his forehead and his eyes closed.

She twisted so she could face him, and Damara kissed his cheek. The corner of his mouth.

He moaned. "Woman, are you trying to kill me?"

"It would be a good death."

"Yeah, but I need a minute."

"Just one? Or did we break it?" She grinned against his mouth.

"It's unbreakable."

"Good. You still owe me another round." She tried not to cry. It would be stupid to cry, but with her body still shaking with the aftermath of what they'd just done, she was wired with emotion. The first time had been a warm-up. The second time had been about lust. And this time, it was about everything.

Byron pulled her against him, his hand a brand on her back.

She nestled into him, fitting perfectly, as if they'd been made for each other. She thought he was just being sweet, but after a few moments he pulled her leg over his hip and angled her so that he could push inside her again.

He pressed his forehead against hers and slowly began to move.

Damara hadn't known he was capable of such tenderness.

Byron slipped his hand between them and brought her to a devastating bliss before they dissolved in each other's arms.

For one day, her marriage had been one of heat and passion. It had been real.

And just like that, it was over.

CHAPTER FIFTEEN

WHEN DAMARA CAME downstairs the next morning, she wasn't sure what she expected to find. She was thankful that some of those purple boxes from Sweet Thing were part of the package.

Two of the purple boxes had been demolished—their smashed and battered tops, not to mention *empty* remains, were on the counter by the waste can.

The last box was being guarded by Byron, uniform fatigues, weapon and all. It would have been funny if it wasn't so tragic. She saw the living room was full of people. She was glad she'd bothered to dress before coming downstairs. She plastered on her princess face.

"Good morning, ladies and gentlemen. From your faces, it appears we have a situation. Let me get my coffee and we'll get started."

Sonja handed her a paper cup, and Damara sipped the dark brew. It was slightly bitter, even with the sugar and heavy cream. But it was exactly how she liked it. The coffee fortified her. She helped herself to something from the purple box. She didn't want to face impending doom on an empty stomach.

Byron released the box into her care, and she let herself enjoy the moment. Then she said, "What's happened?"

A man in a suit who she didn't know, but who had been part of Renner's team when she'd met him on the tarmac, typed some buttons on a laptop. The big-screen TV came alive.

With her brother's face.

He was still as handsome as ever. Strong jaw made to look even sharper by the high collar of the imperial jacket he wore. His eyes were large and dark, and they'd always been his secret weapon. No matter what he said, how blatant the lie, he always seemed so earnest because of those eyes. She knew her brother would employ whatever means necessary to get what he wanted.

Although she was surprised that he'd sent a public plea. And surprised that it brought Renner and company all the way to Glory from D.C. for a group viewing.

Perhaps Renner had been right and Abele didn't want to risk angering the international community. That would be a first for him. He had to have some other motivation. He'd probably already installed the Kulokavs in some official position on Castallegna.

Damara watched the screen in front of her and the image of her brother talking to her, imploring that she see reason and return home like a dutiful, loyal citizen of Castallegna.

The part at the end was the best, where he begged that if she wouldn't return home, she at least call him and let him know she was safe.

He looked so sincere.

Damara wasn't stupid. He was planning something.

Most likely her death.

And it broke her heart.

Abele had been a different person when she was a child. He'd been caring, attentive and everything a big brother should be.

It had been Abele who'd taught her how to read, helped her escape her comportment tutor. He'd been her rock when their mother had died. Their father was a good man, but losing his wife had torn something vital out of him.

Abele had picked up the pieces.

Damara didn't know what had happened to them. A descent down a slippery slope that had started with a little stumble. He'd gone away to university in Greece and he'd come home a different man. Then their father had died and the Abele she knew and loved was gone.

When one of her tutors had told her about the torture, the disappearances, she hadn't wanted to believe them.

Until she'd seen it for herself.

She narrowed her eyes. "He's wearing my father's sash."

"What does that mean?" Sonja asked.

"It means he's declared himself king," she answered. "And since I've already called him, he's setting the stage for something else."

"Known associates of Kulokav's tried to enter the U.S. this morning, but they were stopped and detained by customs," Renner said.

"He really wants me dead. He's not going to stop until he kills me." Saying it out loud made it more real somehow, drove it home into that place in her heart that still loved her brother. She bled on the inside, a bile of pain and loss.

"You already know my solution for that," Byron said grimly.

"He's a king. You can't just kill him," Renner said, as if he were explaining to a child why he couldn't have another cookie.

"Yes, I can. You'd just prefer I don't."

"I think the princess would prefer you don't, as well," Renner said meaningfully.

Damara chose not to answer that. Instead, she said, "So what's our next move?"

"We do the satellite interview today. Then we move up the wedding," Sonja said.

"Didn't we already do that?" Byron asked.

"The production. There has to be a ceremony so all the little girls can wish they were Damara. The people need to see the beginning of your happily ever after," Sonja supplied.

Damara nodded. "Okay, let's make this happen."

She couldn't look at Byron, but she didn't need to look at him to feel the weight of his stare.

He was right—it hadn't been fair to either of them last night. She shouldn't have asked that of him, and now it was all she could think about. Especially now that she had irrefutable proof that Abele wanted her dead.

She'd seen Vladimir's associates in the palace, and they were the same ones who'd been seen talking to villagers who'd gone missing. She didn't need them to spell it out for her.

Damara wondered if she'd ever see Castallegna again.

It made her wish she were a different sort of person. Someone who could say that, yes, she wanted a man dead. Yes, she wanted her brother dead.

But she didn't. She wanted him to be safe, to be well. She wanted him to be like he was when she was a little girl. Damara knew it was time to mourn that boy because Abele would never be him again.

Sonja led her back to the stylist, who had clothes laid out for her and was waiting to do her hair. The cosmetics had been splayed out just as she'd asked previously, a ritual for her to calm her nerves.

"You know, it's okay that you don't hate him," Sonja said quietly.

"Is it? There are so many lives in danger because of me."

"No, it's not because of you. It's because of him. Your people will have hope because of you. You can do this. Look at how far you've come already."

Damara didn't feel as though she'd come very far at all. She felt as if she'd screwed everything up beyond fixing. If she'd just been quiet, done as she'd been told— No, she couldn't doubt herself. If her father had taught her anything, it was that while she had to be aware that she wasn't infallible, she also couldn't second-guess herself.

Her phone rang, and a sense of foreboding slipped over her like a shadow. She knew without looking that it was Abele.

"I didn't think you had it in you, sister."

Abele's voice chilled her blood to ice. "Had what?"

"Are you afraid?" His voice was silky with the implied threat.

"We all have our resources, Abele." She assumed he meant his goons being detained at customs.

He laughed. “Is that so? We’ll see about that in person very soon.”

“I’m sure we will. I’m not afraid of you.” But if she were being honest with herself, she was. She was terrified of the stranger that lived in his skin.

“You don’t have to be afraid to die. And if you cost me this partnership with Kulokav, you will.”

“You should worry about yourself, brother,” she said with more confidence than she felt. “You could be in a sniper’s sights as we speak.”

He laughed again. “I suppose I could be. But I’m not. If you wanted me dead, you would’ve sent your ranger after me. If you thought he could do it.”

Her brother didn’t know her at all. That was both comforting and heartbreaking at once. “I grieve for you, Abele. I do. I grieve the loss of my brother, because you’re not him.”

“This is your last chance, Damara.”

She ended the call, numb.

“Was that him?” Sonja asked.

Damara nodded. “He didn’t say anything new.”

“I’ll tell Renner. I doubt we’ll get any more information off the line, but we can try.”

Damara pulled on her princess costume—the expression, the hair, the makeup—and she went back to face the camera feeling as helpless as she ever had.

BYRON READIED HIMSELF for the satellite interview that would air on all the major news networks. He still didn’t want to put on the ranger uniform, but it was all about the image.

He still didn’t think he deserved it.

But he kept thinking back to his nightmare, and it was strange that he found a sort of ease in it.

Someday, he'd find the courage to write those letters to each of the families of the men he'd lost. He'd always wanted to, not just to say that he was sorry because he knew that was never enough.

He wanted to tell Foxworth's wife that he couldn't wait to come home to her and their children. He wanted to tell Barnes's daughter that her father was a hero. That he knew what lay in store for him, but he faced it without fear because he wouldn't abandon his fellow rangers. He wanted to tell them all that they deserved so much better than what they got, and maybe one day, if he could ever forgive himself, he might ask them for the same. To forgive him for what he'd taken from them.

To forgive him for living when those they loved didn't.

Byron didn't know if he'd ever be able to say those things out loud, but he'd finally been able to acknowledge them. They'd always been there, waiting in the shadows and the dark to tear at him with claws and teeth.

But he ripped at himself deeper than they ever could.

The constant loop of screams in his head was still there, but they weren't as loud and insistent.

He checked himself in the mirror, and he saw a ranger staring back at him. He wanted to recite the creed, for Barnes, for Foxworth, for himself. For them all. Only, he still wasn't ready. He still hadn't earned it.

Sonja checked them over and decided that Damara

needed a bit more lip gloss before she was camera ready. Then they took their positions in the sunroom—the new couple relaxing at home.

A large monitor had been set up for them to be able to visually engage their interviewer. Byron didn't like that they were accepting calls for questions, but he wasn't the PR person. He had no idea how this would help their cause, but he knew someone was going to say something awful. That was just the nature of people, especially if they could be anonymous. "Ready to go?" Sonja asked.

Damara nodded, and the screen buzzed to life. The reporter on the other side of the screen gave her intro.

"I'm Melanie Moon, and tonight, we have a live satellite interview with the princess and the ranger. Thank you so much for being with us, Princess Damara and Lt. Hawkins. So let's get right to it. Everyone wants to know more about you both and your amazing story. Mobsters, royalty and intrigue. It sounds like some kind of novel. How did it all happen?"

Damara recounted the same story she'd told at the press junket, how they'd been interacting for months before she made her escape. She sounded completely believable. Who knew she'd be such a good liar? He'd been taught the body language and the microexpressions to look for when people were being dishonest, and Damara had none of them. For that moment, she must've found a way to make herself believe everything she was saying.

"You've definitely got some critics. What do you have to say to them?" Melanie asked.

Damara flashed what he'd come to call her princess smile. It wasn't fake, but it wasn't exactly real, either. "I don't have anything to say to them. There's always someone who wants to judge you. I've done what I thought was best with the resources I had. And that's all any of us can do."

"So true, Princess. So true." Melanie nodded. "Lt. Hawkins, do you have a response?"

Byron fell back into the same character he'd adopted at the press junket. "She's the diplomat with the pretty words. I'm just a soldier, and my words probably aren't appropriate for live television." He flashed his best bad-boy grin. It was all he had in his arsenal and probably the most believable anyway.

Melanie laughed. "Okay, I have another one for you. How do you feel about the threats that the king of Castallegna has made against your life?"

Byron hadn't known that they'd released the call to the news outlets, but it made sense.

"Let me play it for the audience."

He tightened his fingers around hers to offer his support. Hearing this once today had been enough to last her a lifetime. Now she had to hear it again on live TV with everyone watching her pain. Her brother's betrayal. It was an open wound, and they were inviting everyone to tear it wider.

After it finished, Byron said, "I put my life on the line for my country every day. It's the least I can do for my wife."

Melanie's expression told him that was exactly the right answer. "Wow, it looks like you've lit up the phone lines, Lt. Hawkins. Why don't we take a call? Hello, caller. You're on with Melanie Moon and the princess and the ranger. What's your question?"

"You're married?"

Byron grinned at the camera. "As of yesterday morning. In fact, I have a little something I forgot to give her." He pulled out the ring and slid it on her finger.

The tears in her eyes might have been real as she held up her hand for the audience to see.

"Was that your question, caller?" Melanie asked.

"I was going to ask if he had any single friends that were like him."

He didn't have any friends, single or not. But he knew to play up to the audience. "I'll see what I can do for you."

Melanie seemed irritated at the question. It was obvious she was hoping for something a bit more hard-hitting and worthy of journalism, rather than the dating habits of the American girl. "Next caller."

"This is a pretty fairy tale you've got for yourself, Lt. Hawkins."

He recognized the voice. It was heavily accented. Russian. He signaled to Sonja, and she started tapping madly on the screen of her phone.

"Yes, it is. I'm very grateful," he answered neutrally.

"What about your team, Lt. Hawkins?"

Oh, Christ. His first instinct was to declare the interview over, but he couldn't. Not if he wanted to keep Damara safe. They could run a trace on the call from the news studio and figure out where Kulokav was.

Byron didn't say anything else. He pursed his lips. He had to remember that the world could see him. Everyone could see him. They'd be able to see his pain and his guilt.

He'd just been thinking about how he wished he could tell their families…

"Your team in Uganda, Hawkins."

Fuck, how had they found out about that? It was classified. Top secret. No one had access to that information. His brain churned around the logic, the mission, but his guts ached and revolted, demanded that he give the emotion, the attention, it deserved.

"What about them?" he asked, his face stony and hard as he fought the tidal wave washing over him.

"I just thought you'd have something to say about it since you're here and they're not. How'd that happen?"

Damara bristled. "Sometimes those in a position of leadership and power have to make hard decisions. Choices that lead to other people's pain, but they're for the greater good. Or they're the only thing you can do—"

"I live with that guilt every day. There isn't a day that goes by that I don't wish I could change what happened."

"Princess, so you admit that sometimes a leader has to make hurtful choices?"

Byron knew where this was going, and he also knew that even if he wanted Melanie to cut the call, she wouldn't. This was too juicy. He knew he had to turn it back around on himself.

He knew he had to face his demons there where everyone could see.

"You asked me a question. Do me the courtesy of allowing me to answer."

"By all means, Lt. Hawkins," Melanie said.

He took a deep breath. The memory barged to the forefront of his mind, stark and awful. The screams, the fire—and the absolute knowledge that it was his fault. "We were in pursuit of a guerilla faction. It was a trap. My men died. The official inquiry exonerated me, but I feel their loss and I regret what happened every day." He was as succinct as he could be.

"What were you doing in Uganda?" Melanie asked.

"That's classified." *Damn them. Damn them all.*

"And you've lit up the switchboard again, Lt. Hawkins."

Damara's fingers threaded more tightly with his and she tugged lightly to get him to look at her.

When he did, she spoke a wealth of things with her expression. It was written as plainly as words in a book that if he wanted to stop, if he wanted to end this, he could.

No, he could do this.

Or so he thought. Then Melanie spoke again.

"We have Belinda Foxworth on the line."

He couldn't hide his reaction to hearing her name. He imagined his face must have looked much like an animated clay figure as it was formed and destroyed and reformed by all the emotions that riddled him like so many bullets.

Byron was frozen to the spot. He wanted to run. He wanted to fall on his knees and beg her forgiveness. He wanted to do something besides sit there and silently bear the weight of what he'd done. But there was nothing else for him to do. He was caught in a trap of his own making.

"Lt.—Byron? Can you hear me?" Her voice was gentle and sounded just like Foxworth had described it to him. Like the chiming of small bells.

"Yes, ma'am," he answered. God, this was the culmination of everything he'd hoped for and everything he couldn't face. But he owed it to her to bear whatever she wanted to fling at him. If she wanted to rage at him on national television—he owed her that and so much more.

"I don't blame you. His children don't blame you. It wasn't your fault."

That was the last thing he'd expected from her. That kindness, those words, they drained the life out of him, sapped the strength from his bones. If Damara hadn't been there holding his hand and rooting him in the real, he would've crumpled like paper.

He found he had no words. Not just that he didn't know what to say, but that he couldn't speak them even if he did. His throat was so tight, his tongue thick and useless.

"I want to invite you and the princess to come visit me at the ranch. It would mean the world if you'd come. Austin spoke of you often and well."

"Thank you, Belinda." He managed not to choke on his answer.

Melanie was quiet for a moment, and then she began speaking. "An emotional time now for Lt. Byron Hawkins as—"

"I'm sorry. Excuse me." He left the interview. He had to get away from the cameras, away from that raw pain and the horrible feeling that was forgiveness.

He'd thought he wanted it, but he didn't. Byron couldn't punish himself enough for what he'd done, so he needed her to do it for him.

He should have known that Belinda wouldn't blame him, not after the way had Foxworth talked about her.

She was a light; she was a jewel. She was…everything he'd thought about Damara.

Her hands were suddenly on his shoulders, and he turned around to face her.

"Let's go to Texas. Let's go right now."

"Have you lost your mind?" He couldn't go to Texas. Not now, not ever.

"Probably. I had Sonja get Belinda's information. I've got her address, and I told her we're coming."

"I can't."

"You *can*." Damara nodded. "You owe her and yourself that much."

"In case you forgot, there's a threat against your life."

"No, I didn't forget. But I'd like to. If we take one day to go to Texas and see her, it's not going to hurt anything."

"I just can't face her," he confessed.

"She's not angry with you—she doesn't blame you."

"Not, but I do, and she should." *Oh, she should.* If she'd been there, if she knew what he'd done…

"That's the great thing about emotions. You don't get to choose how other people feel," Damara reminded him gently.

"Wouldn't it be easier if we could?"

"No, I don't think so. There's a reason we feel the things we do. Lessons we can't learn otherwise. Even the things that hurt."

"Damara, I can protect you. I can kill for you. I can die for you. But don't ask me to do this."

"I'm not asking for me. It's for you." She reached up and cupped his cheek.

“Then let me do it in my own time. Right now is about protecting you.”

“And I wish it wasn’t.”

“But it is and wishing it wasn’t isn’t going to change anything. For either of us.”

CHAPTER SIXTEEN

IT WAS SUDDENLY all too much for Damara.

The situation was so far beyond her control that it made her wonder if she'd ever had a shot at making a difference, both with Castallegna and Byron.

Damara was furious.

Furious at the news outlet, furious at Sonja. And most of all, she was furious at her brother for making Byron a target. She hadn't realized what he'd been through and the weight he carried around with him. She didn't want to be the one who dug into his soft places with sharp things. She didn't want anyone to hurt him.

From what it seemed like since they'd come back to Glory, Byron had no one. Renner used him for what he could. He had no friends. All the time working for the DOD, he'd never made any real human connection with anyone.

To Damara's way of thinking, she was all he had.

Did she think she was going to swoop in and save him by dragging him to Texas to face the pain he carried with him? She couldn't do that for him. And even if she could, it wasn't her place.

"I've got to get out of here for a while."

"Damara—"

"Look, I just can't be here… and this… It's fine. I need some space. Some quiet."

"I'll go with you."

"I need it away from you, too."

"Tough luck, Princess. We don't have to talk, but if you think you're leaving here by yourself, you've got another think coming."

"I just want to feel normal."

"Let's go feed the ducks."

"We need to talk about arrangements," Sonja interrupted them.

"I just can't right now. I really don't care what you do. It doesn't matter. Whatever works best for the spin, right?" Damara replied.

"You don't want to at least pick out your dress?" Sonja took her hand.

Damara shook her head. "No. Choose whatever you think is best."

She couldn't think about planning a wedding to a man she wasn't going to stay married to. The deal had been sealed when she'd signed the license. This was just pouring perfume on a goat, as her father liked to say.

"Why don't you give us a little while? We'll be back in a few hours, and Damara can approve everything then."

Sonja looked back and forth between them and nodded slowly. "You can take my rental." She handed her keys to Byron.

As soon as she stepped outside, she tried to use her breathing exercises to calm and center herself, but everything was still too close, too tight.

Too much.

He was the one who'd just been through an emotional ordeal, and she was the one who couldn't keep it together. Damara was embarrassed and ashamed, but that did little to help her.

"Hey, it's okay. I get it," he said once they were driving past the outskirts of the main downtown area toward a small park entrance. "I'm surprised you haven't been more upset before now. This is a lot for anyone to handle."

"Not you."

"It's my job to handle it," he reassured her.

"Mine, too."

He scrubbed his hand over his face. "You expect too much from yourself. You say that you're just an ordinary woman, but you're not. You are every inch a princess."

"And I'm still in my tower."

"I'd say you're a long way from your tower." He eyed her. "But you don't have to do anything right now but come feed these fat little bastards." He pointed at the ducks.

There was a vending machine with little pellets just to feed the chubby white birds.

"The palace swans bite. Do these bite?" Damara asked, cupping the food in one hand.

"If they do, they'll get drop-kicked like a football."

"Byron!"

"When I was a little kid, my babysitter used to bring me here so I'd have something to do while she made out with her boyfriend. She'd give me crackers to crumple up and throw on the water. The ducks decided they didn't need me to get the bag." A duck nipped at his fingers lightly, begging for more, and there was no drop-kicking. He indulged the animal and gave it some more. "I guess it was kind of funny to watch, all those ducks quacking at me, flapping their wings and nipping at me to get the bag, all the while I was screeching like I was dying." He shook his head. "I had nightmares about ducks for years."

"And this is where you wanted to bring me?" She laughed and looked up at the sky and then down at the patient ducks at her feet. "I guess mine are better mannered."

"I should hope so. They heard what I said about drop-kicking."

The knot in her chest started to unravel, and she sat in the grass, food in hand.

"I don't know if I'd sit down with them. It wouldn't do for me to return the princess to the palace covered in duck droppings."

She laughed. "No, they wouldn't dare. They don't want to be drop-kicked." One bold duck allowed her to stroke her hand over his feathered head. "My father used to take me to feed the swans when matters of state got to be too much for him."

"You said they were mean?"

"Cruel to a point, but they were so beautiful."

"He didn't take Abele?" Byron asked carefully.

"No. He didn't like the swans." She remembered Abele never wanted to go with them. "I miss my father so much."

"He'd be proud of you, I'm sure."

"I don't know. I'm not proud of me."

His hand flew forward, and she blocked it with her forearm without thinking. He did it again, and she repeated the block, the ducks scattering as they squawked and fought over the flung pellets.

She hopped to her feet, understanding what he was doing. He was trying to show her that she had skills.

And she did.

Damara darted behind him and feinted to the left. He blocked her easily.

“Again,” he said.

She could tell he was restraining himself. “Don’t hold back.”

Byron startled her with a kick, but she caught his leg and sent him sprawling.

He laughed as he rolled to his feet. “See what I mean? There aren’t many people who can do what you can do.”

She wanted to say that he was the one who’d just been through something and he shouldn’t be worried about making her feel her own self-worth—he should be focused on his own. But maybe this was what he could do with what he was feeling. He’d already said he didn’t want to talk about it, but Damara couldn’t leave it alone.

“There aren’t many people who can do what you can do, either.”

“I used to believe that.”

“Until Uganda?”

“There’s more to life than this, hoss.”

“What?”

“It’s what Austin Foxworth used to say whenever things got dicey. It was his way of saying it would get better, that we could make it better. But we—I—didn’t.”

This was as close as he'd come to sharing anything with her.

"You made it better for me. I never would've made it out of Tunisia without you."

"You'd have found a way."

She was surprised by all the faith he had in her when he had so little in himself. The knot in her chest started to tighten again, and she flung herself back in the grass, looking up at the sky.

"I'm still looking for a way. I don't see how I've done anything but make it worse."

"You've shed light on the situation. That goes a long way."

"I'm sorry you're stuck with this—me."

"I've had worse assignments."

That wasn't what she wanted to hear. *Don't demand I love you, too,* was what he'd said. That was exactly what she wanted to demand, even though them being able to stay together was a hopeless fantasy.

"I'm sorry about everything else, too." Everything he didn't want to talk about.

Suddenly, he was on top of her. "What are you doing?"

"Stay very still," he whispered into her ear. "I'm going to kiss you and you're going to reach for one of our phones and you're going to squeeze the power and sound buttons at the same time. Do you understand?"

She didn't, but she'd do as he asked. Damara fought the urge to look around for the threat.

"I never should have brought you here alone." His lips brushed her cheek, and it was no chore to push her hands down his sides and reach into his pocket for his phone. "The phone will transmit an emergency signal. No matter what we do, he's going to shoot. Do you understand what that means?" His voice was so calm, so quiet, as if he were soothing her to sleep rather than asking her to accept he was going to be shot. That he could die protecting her.

Terror knifed through her.

"Don't be afraid, Damara. I won't let him hurt you. Remember how you pounced to your feet earlier? You're going to do that again and you're going to stay behind me. We're going to run for the car. It's only about twenty-five feet." His breath was warm against her ear.

"No, we're not." She choked on the words. Damara wouldn't let him die for her. She'd known when she'd asked him to help her that it was a possibility, but it seemed fey and misty, something unlikely to actually happen. Yet, here it was unfolding before her in some red-tinged nightmare.

"Yes, Damara. That's the only way. You're going to get in the car and you're going to follow the nav to Fort Glory. You're going to tell the exit/entry staff who you are and they'll get you to a secure location. We have to assume the house has been compromised." He said this as calmly as if they were still talking about wedding arrangements.

"I won't leave you," she said stubbornly.

"Yes, you will. The emergency signal will bring the cavalry running."

"You're asking me to let him shoot you. For me."

"Did you forget that's what I'm for?"

Faced with losing him, she couldn't. Damara knew in that second it didn't matter how many safeguards she'd put around her heart. She loved him. She loved him more than herself, more than Castallegna. She wouldn't trade his life for a thousand. But she'd trade her own.

"Maybe this is what my people need. Maybe they need a martyr to rally behind and they'll overthrow Abele."

"And maybe you've lost your damn mind. We both have a better chance of surviving the farther away he is. If we stay like this much longer, he'll risk getting closer. If we run, he'll shoot on my terms."

"No."

"I won't let you become another voice screaming in my head, Damara."

She was afraid, terrified. She'd hear him saying that forever.… When he jerked her to her feet, she didn't scream. She ran behind him as instructed and even though she heard a series of pops, she thought they were fine. She thought they'd made it safely and he'd missed.

But the shooter hadn't missed.

Byron stumbled against the car, a smear of his blood thick on the door, but he jammed the keys in the ignition.

"Drive."

Bile rose in the back of her throat, and she froze. She'd never seen so much blood.

"Fucking drive, Damara."

Even though the shooting had stopped, she kept her head down and shoved him in the backseat, his blood staining the pristine interior. "Don't die, Byron. Please don't die."

"You better hope I do, because I'm going to throttle…" He choked and blood gurgled at the corner of his mouth.

"I love you," she blurted.

"Don't do that, either."

That was when it occurred to Damara that she wasn't the target at all—it had been Byron all along. The three shots to his chest were all center mass. The shooter hadn't been aiming anywhere but at Byron. This was Abele's warning to her. Even if he didn't kill her, he'd hurt anyone who dared to help her. Or anyone she loved.

Damara did as he instructed. She put the car in the Drive and typed "Fort Glory" into the GPS.

She hated the voice on that thing, the silly bitch so calm while Byron bled his life out in the backseat of a rental car.

"Don't die. You can't throttle me if you die." He didn't make any sound. "Talk to me. Stay with me."

"Bossy," he mumbled.

"Yeah, that's me. Tell me all about it." She had to keep him talking.

He mumbled something she couldn't understand.

"I read a story about a navy SEAL who got shot, and he plugged the wounds with his fingers. Don't tell me he's got the drop on you."

She was met with utter silence.

"You promised me in Barcelona that everything was going to be okay. This is not okay, Byron. Do you hear me?" She tried to tether her emotions, to push them down. If she was hysterical, she couldn't help him, and she definitely wouldn't be able to drive on the wrong side of the road. She'd probably broken so many laws…but it didn't matter. The only thing that mattered was getting Byron help.

The GPS said they were only three minutes away from the entry gate. She turned into the lane. As soon as they were out of traffic, she opened the door.

"I'm Damara Hawkins and have Lt. Byron Hawkins. He's been shot."

CHAPTER SEVENTEEN

Byron dreamed of Austin Foxworth again. For the first time, he wasn't on fire. They weren't in the middle of the jungle, and there was no cacophony of screaming playing like some sick movie score in the background.

"You're not supposed to be here," Foxworth said.

"Me? You're the one who's dead. I'm here to save the princess."

"You already saved the princess. Now save yourself."

Byron shook his head. Every nerve ending in his body hurt, even places he was sure didn't have nerve endings. Like his eyelashes. He opened his eyes slowly.

There wasn't a single part of his body that didn't hurt.

His chest felt as though there were a hundred-pound brick on it, and there was a bunch of crap in the room making an ungodly racket. Apparently, he was hooked up to all of it. The more the dark sleep world faded, the louder it got.

A memory of what had happened flooded back. He probably would've died if she hadn't forced him into the backseat.

It would have been a good death, one he would've

been content to have. Only there wouldn't have been anyone to keep her safe. He struggled to turn his head and take in his surroundings. He was in the army hospital; at least she'd followed his instructions and fled to the base.

It was his fault they'd been in that situation anyway. If he'd been thinking, he wouldn't have taken her there. He wondered how the shooter knew where to find them. He'd been careful watching for a tail.

Damara was curled up in a chair in the corner, her feet tucked under her. Her face was drawn and pale, dark circles under her eyes.

I love you.

Christ, having that in his head was almost worse. He knew he didn't deserve it. He didn't know what to do with it anyway. It was like a bubble she'd handed him and expected him not to break.

Her eyes fluttered open, and he saw all his failures reflected back at him in her pain.

She flung herself on the bed and buried her face in his shoulder. "You're alive."

"Unless you kill me," he mumbled. He wasn't ready to face what her words meant.

"I could kill you. If you'd died, I couldn't live with myself."

He managed to raise his arm and stroke her back. "That's a bit of a contradiction there, don't you think, Princess?"

"You promised me in Barcelona it would all be okay. I told you in the car and I'm going to tell you again, this is not okay. This is the farthest from okay that it could ever be."

"I told you I'm not so good at keeping my promises."

"I swear, I'm going to punch you in your bullet holes."

He laughed, and it hurt like a bastard.

"I couldn't stand it if you died for me. Because of me."

This was leading down that road he didn't want to follow. "If I'm okay with it, you should be. You're not the one who has to do the dying."

She shuddered against him, and he realized that she was crying. "Hey, don't cry." God, his mouth was dry. His lips felt stiff, as if they were ready to crack. "I didn't die. I'm—" he took stock of himself "—mostly fine."

The wounds in his chest smarted, it hurt to laugh, it hurt to breathe and it hurt to have Damara half on top of him. Even with holes in his body, she still made him harder than steel.

"I'm going home, Byron."

"What? I don't think I heard you correctly." She couldn't go home, not yet. Not until he'd killed Abele.

"I'm going home."

"Because of me?" *Dear God, don't let her say it's because of me.*

"Because of me." She splayed her small palm on his cheek. "Because I can't do this. I can't let anyone else get hurt because of me."

"What about all the people who will be hurt when you go home and there's no one to show the world what your brother is doing? What then?" The monitors started beeping furiously, an audible censure against raising his blood pressure.

"I'll have to find another way. Look at the grouping of the shots. He wasn't even trying to shoot me, Byron. It was you."

"Yeah, well, he's a piss-poor shot. I'm not dead."

"I— No." She shook her head. "No."

"What did you think would happen, Damara?" he said quietly. "This is what men like us do."

"You're nothing like Grisha, Vladimir and certainly not my brother."

"I'm just the other side of the coin, Princess."

"You don't know your own worth."

He inhaled and exhaled slowly. "That's you. Do you really think that Renner is going to let you leave just because you want to? Because things got a little dicey and you can't hack it?"

"Yes. He doesn't own me."

"Now you're being naive. All the resources and man-hours he invested in you and this operation? No, Princess. It doesn't work that way. You set a chain of events in motion and for good or ill, you have to see them through."

"You're telling me I can't go home?" Her voice was almost childlike.

"I'm saying you can't go home without me." A calmness had settled over him. She'd said she loved him. It had taken root inside of her, and he had to prune it to the quick.

She sat up and leaned away from him. "And you won't take me unless you're going to kill my brother."

"However you measure it, Princess, someone's thread is getting cut. That's just how this has to end. I made you a promise on the condition that he didn't try to hurt you. So, I'll take you home, but I'm going to kill him. Then you'll be safe."

"I'll never forgive you," she whispered.

"I know." He did know it. Byron was under no illusion that he'd take her back to Castallegna and, once her people were free, she'd forgive him because she realized it had to be done. Damara wasn't an end-justifies-the-means kind of person. Lucky for her, Byron was.

"And you don't care, do you?" Her voice dripped with the acid of the sudden knowledge that she wasn't going to change his mind.

He cared, but he couldn't tell her that. Not now, not like this. "No, I don't. Your safety is paramount here. After he's dead, you will be safe."

"What about the *Bratva?*" She was trying to appeal to his logic, to get him to find another course of action.

"They'll see their destiny lies elsewhere. They don't want the world's attention on their operations. Frankly, I'm surprised Vladimir hasn't met with an unfortunate accident. It was on his watch that all of this made international news. He can't keep his house in line. I don't have to kill him. His own people will do that."

"Please don't do this." Her eyes sparkled with tears.

"I think you should go."

She shook her head. "I didn't leave you at the park, and I'm not leaving you here."

"You're not going to change my mind." He thought that she understood that.

She nodded slowly. "Yes, I will. Because you're a good man, with a good heart. But I don't have to talk about it anymore right now."

I love you. In all truth, she might have saved her brother's life yet again if she hadn't told Byron that she loved him. It was a two-birds-with-one-stone scenario. It would be the worst thing he could do and the best. She'd be safe, and she wouldn't be in love with him anymore.

The thought of it tightened around his heart like a noose. He couldn't let himself think about what that meant. Byron knew he was doing the right thing because it felt awful and wonderful at the same time.

The door creaked open and Damara whipped out a 9 mm and pointed it at the door.

"It's just me." Renner held up his hands. "Don't shoot."

"I'm not taking any chances."

"Where'd you get that thing, anyway?" Renner closed the door behind him.

"I'm not telling. But it's mine." She practically dared Renner to take it away from her. Byron's money was on the princess for that round.

He laughed. "Fair enough."

"Don't laugh. It's not funny. He could have died," Damara growled, fierce.

"Yes, he could have. So could you. As soon as Byron can stand, we need to have the ceremony."

"I'm not doing this," Damara said.

"Pardon me, what?" Renner was like a king cobra who'd just turned all his attention on a baby rabbit.

But Damara wasn't intimidated. "I said I'm not doing this. I won't risk him."

Renner's eyes narrowed, and Byron could see the ruthlessness that he'd had to cultivate to be successful at his position.

"She'll do it," Byron interrupted. "We were in the middle of discussing how this is going to go down when you came in."

"I was in the middle of telling you it wasn't."

"And we were discussing how you wanted to go home. I'll take you home for our honeymoon," Byron said.

"Please don't make me do this."

"This is what you signed up for. I thought you assured me that you'd do whatever it took to save Castallegna?" Renner's voice was gentle, but the meaning of his words was sharp.

Byron struggled to sit up. "Dan. I've got this, okay?"

"No, your princess and I need to be very clear with each other."

Byron leaned over so that he was between Renner and Damara. "No, you and I need to be very clear with each other. I said it's handled. My job is to protect the princess, and I'll do it, even from you."

"What about yourself?" Renner asked him. "Did you tell her the details about Uganda yet?"

"That's just cruel," Damara answered for him. "He doesn't have to tell me. I don't care."

"You should. I think you two have forgotten what this is. It's not real. Get your heads in the game or this whole thing is going to fall apart." Renner slammed the door on his way out.

"Damara, did you not hear anything I had to say about this? This isn't Castallegna, and Renner might as well be a king with all the power he has at his disposal. He usually uses his powers for good, but he is not the kind of man you want to cross."

"Did you mean what you said? That you'd protect me from him?"

He closed his eyes for a minute. He was afraid of what she was going to ask him. "Of course I will," Byron said on a heavy exhale.

"Then don't ask me to risk you. If you're gone, then what will I have? Who will keep me safe?"

"You'll keep yourself safe because you're strong, confident and capable. You don't need me, Damara."

"Maybe I don't need you, but I want you."

"I haven't changed my mind about killing your brother."

"You will."

He knew he had to tell her about Uganda. She had to know. Renner had used it against him like a weapon. If he thought that would keep Byron from doing this one good thing, he was sadly mistaken.

"If you still want to hear it, I'll tell you about Uganda." His voice was harsher, lower than he meant. He tried to speak clearly, to own his crimes, but his vocal cords didn't want to obey him. Neither did his memory.

Byron shied away from remembrance like he would a hungry lion. He didn't want to think about it. He couldn't, but he had to. Just like he was asking Damara to face some ugly truths, he had to face his own.

She leaned over and carefully placed the gun in the drawer of the nightstand and turned her attention back to Byron. Gone was the fierce warrior angel and in her place was the soft, kind woman who'd held him to her breast when he'd been coming apart at the seams.

Damara nodded slowly. "Tell me."

"It was summer," he began, remembering the

smells, the heat, the constant sting of bugs on the back of his neck, his arms. “We, my team and I, we were on a mission to roust some guerillas that had been attacking villages. We found them. Or they found us, rather. They attacked the camp and fled, leading us deep into the jungle. I gave the order to pursue.”

He inhaled a shaky breath, feeling as if someone had dropped a piano on his chest. It was more than just the gunshot wounds. It was the weight of his crime, the wages of his sin. His throat constricted. “And it was a trap. An ambush I should have seen coming a mile away, but I didn’t because I was so keen on completing the mission. We’d been in the area for weeks, getting nowhere. I thought if we could just…”

“It’s not your fault. Your men chose to follow you.”

“They trusted me, and I broke that trust. You know how you don’t want anyone to get hurt because of you? My whole team died. Slaughtered. Tortured. By the time I saw what was happening and called a retreat, it was too late. I’m the only one who survived.”

“What were you supposed to do? Follow them to die?”

“If I had any honor, it’s what I would have done.”

“And then who would have told Belinda Foxworth that her husband wasn’t coming home?”

He cut a sharp glance at her. “Like that’s a good thing?” Byron tried to keep a snarl out of his voice.

“It is when that’s all there is. Now she knows to bury him. She’s not waiting, in vain, sitting by a window watching the road and feeling her heart leap up in her chest every time she sees a strange car or the telephone rings. Each time, it would choke her with hope and despair. Those things can’t coexist. Eventually one or the other wins, and either way there's no healing. No grief. So now she can honor the man he was, she can love him, she can miss him, but she can live, too. There's no shame in surviving."

"It was cowardly."

"Death isn't always an honor. Sometimes, most of the time, it's the easy way out."

Byron had held on to his pain, his guilt, it had been like a life raft buoying him up in a black, oily sea. Without it, he was drowning.

"I dream about them. I hear them screaming in my head on an endless loop."

"Their pain is over, Byron. Don't you think yours should be, too?"

"No. I deserve to suffer for what I've done. For reaching too high. I thought I could be more than what I was, but I learned that lesson."

"The boat, when you talked about getting your hand slapped." She pushed her hand through his hair. "I'm so sorry, Byron. For pushing you to this, for taking what I wanted when I didn't know what you'd been through."

"Oh, Princess. That's not on you. I just want you to understand why."

"Why what?"

"Why it's okay if I die protecting you. I don't think it'll square my accounts, but maybe there's a little bit of redemption for me with every person you save."

"When you dream of them, what do they say?" She wore a wistful look.

"Austin Foxworth says that there's more to life than this while his face burns away," he said in an even tone that belied the horror.

"You have that in your head and all this talk of weddings and public relations must turn your stomach."

It had at first, he'd admit. "That doesn't matter now, Damara. We're so far past all of that. We're already married, but we have to have the ceremony. It'll be televised, and then there will be no doubt in the world court of opinion that it happened. This is to protect you."

She looked down at her hands. "I feel so ashamed."

"For what?"

"For putting you through this. For balking when it got tough. I just—" She shrugged.

"You have a soft heart. But that's also why you have me. To do things that your heart can't."

She leaned down on his shoulder. "I'm afraid."

"I know." He didn't tell her it would all be fine. He wasn't going to lie to her again. Either he was going to die or her brother would when this was all over.

"You need time to heal," she said after a long period of silence.

"I don't have that luxury. I'm sure as soon as I can stand, they'll shovel me into a monkey suit and you into some lace and a veil."

"And then you'll take me home," she said with a certain finality.

"Yeah. Then I'll take you home." And one way or another, he'd never see her again. But that was probably for the best, for both of them.

He wondered what she'd been thinking when she'd said she loved him. If she'd imagined a future with him that could never be. Or if it was just to get them through because she couldn't bear the thought of him or anyone dying for her.

No, he knew in his bones without even asking what the answer was to that question. Damara felt everything deeply, completely.

He used to think that if he had one wish, one moment he could change, it would be Uganda. But if he did, then he wouldn't be the one here with Damara.

If he had one thing that he could do differently, one course of history he could change, it would be to make this right for her. To take away her pain, to make her safe.

He couldn't take her pain, but at least he could make her safe.

CHAPTER EIGHTEEN

"CHRISTMAS DAY," SONJA said to her across the cafeteria table at the base.

"Are you insane?"

Sonja looked at her. "Why would you ask that?"

What kind of question was that? "He was *shot,*" Damara answered, as if the PR rep wasn't aware of the fact.

"He's fine." Sonja waved it off. "He's a former ranger, honey. You can't keep them down unless you put them down, if you know what I mean."

"There's no way he's going to be ready to be on his feet." She shook her head.

"He's already been on his feet. Did you really think a man like Hawkins would be content to lie there and *convalesce?*" She said this last as if it were something dirty.

"It'll have only been a week on Christmas Day."

"And we can't show any weakness." Sonja eyed her. "You understand that, right?"

This whole thing had gone so far afield from what she'd wanted, how she'd planned. Damara supposed she really was that naive girl Byron had accused her of being. She was still a pawn, and she'd done nothing but exacerbate the situation.

"Yes, I understand." She nodded.

"So, we're going to have the ceremony here, at the Main Post Chapel. It's really a lovely building."

Damara didn't think there was anything in the world that was worth Byron Hawkins's life. Nothing. Not Castallegna, not capturing Kulokav. And not her.

Nothing.

At least when she thought they'd have to be apart, she'd know he was still in the world. Still flashing that cocky grin and still saving damsels in distress.

Morbidly, she wondered how many nights Belinda Foxworth had stayed up bargaining with heaven for the exact same thing. What had she offered in trade for Austin Foxworth?

And why hadn't it been enough?

"Hey, I'm losing you. Front and center." Sonja snapped her fingers. "We're down to the wire."

"I know. I'm sorry." Damara sighed. "I'm trying."

"You're distracted because you're worried about Hawkins."

"Aren't you?" She wondered how the other woman could be complacent in this insanity of a plan.

"No. That's not my job. My job is to get you married. I know it sounds a little coldhearted and mercenary, but it's what has to be done. Renner tells me that you're going back to Castallegna? Do you have a plan?"

"I thought that only PR was your job?" Damara asked.

"We can't very well release to the press that you're going to Castallegna on your honeymoon."

A fake honeymoon was apt for a fake marriage. "I don't even know how we're going to get back on

Castallegna. It's not like we can just fly in. This has all fallen apart." She shook her head.

Sonja's face softened. "Look, I know this has to be tough. But you're letting your brother and the Russians get in your head. That's what they wanted. The shooter could have easily used a much higher-caliber weapon. They didn't want him dead. They wanted to show you that they could hurt him, and they did. They wanted you to scramble, and you are. But let's scramble on our terms, okay?"

"PR campaigns are very much like waging a war, aren't they?" Damara asked her.

Sonja grinned. "Yes, they are. They're the ones who bloodied the waters, so let's give them a shark." She paused. "I've been in meetings with Renner. I promise you—Hawkins can take it. He'll be medically cleared before you go. He'll still have a wound, but he's not like other men. He's more like a junkyard dog. Mean as hell, and, if you tear him open, you'll just make him madder."

Damara wondered if Sonja knew just how right she was about that. No wonder he'd been pushing her away because Damara was the one who kept trying to tear him open.

There was a part of her that wanted to call Grisha and surrender. If she did that, Byron would be safe. But she was sure that was a little-girl fantasy, too. There was just no way for this to end but badly.

"So, what do you think of the dress?" Sonja prompted.

Damara looked down at the pictures spread out in front of her. The pretty white ballgown with holly trim around the neckline and the red sash at the waist that turned into part of the train. It was lovely.

But it made her think of her mother's simple Grecian dress. She'd worn no jewelry when she'd married Damara's father until he'd placed a ring on her finger and a crown on her head. There'd been jasmine petals under her feet.

Her heart constricted, and she missed Castallegna, her mother, her father and the way her brother used to be.

"It's fine." She nodded.

"We can get something else," Sonja rushed to assure her.

"No, really. It's fine." She plastered a smile on her face and forced her attention to the arrangements. This was something she had control over, something she could do. It wasn't much, but it was enough to make her mark and that had to be worth something, at least in her own head.

She wrote down a list of the things she wanted from the cake to the reception. "I want a closed reception for the town. No press. Only locals. The town has been good to me, and I'd like to do something special for them." For Byron, too. Maybe he'd stop thinking so little of himself if the town could show him the man he'd become, not the boy he once was.

"I think we're done for the day." Sonja gathered up all the papers and began organizing them with sticky notes, highlighters and folders.

"Thank you for all you've done." Damara took her hand and squeezed.

"My pleasure. Usually, I'm hired to clean up things we'd rather not know about. It's not a nice job, but it pays well. And this, this was something good. What's better than a fairy tale?"

"The truth?" Damara raised a brow.

"Honey, you're going to get the happily ever after. You're a princess who is all the things a princess should be. And you're already in love with the prince."

"The prince has to love himself first, and I don't know if that's going to happen. Even if it does, we're from two different worlds."

"I guess that will be for you two to work out." Sonja finished packing up. "I'll walk you back to the room. They've moved him to a labor-and-delivery suite so your stay is more comfortable."

This was the last thing she wanted to think about. The very last. It was too close to all the things she'd dreamed of and none of the things she'd have. But she followed behind Sonja anyway.

They paused at the empty nursery, and Damara was glad it was empty. Damara didn't want to take a chance that a child would be hurt while she and Byron were being sheltered there. She placed her hand on the window anyway, thinking about what it would be like to have her own child. Not now, not tomorrow, but someday.

"Aren't you worried Hawkins will catch you day-dreaming?" Sonja teased.

No, she wasn't worried about that at all. She'd been trying to picture children with some nameless, face-less someone, but all she could see was a little girl with his eyes and her hair. His strength and her heart.

As if that would ever happen. If Byron didn't even want a commitment, he'd never want children. She dragged her hand away from the glass and followed Sonja to the room.

"I'll leave you two alone. I have some paperwork to catch up on." Sonja left.

She was right; it was a much nicer space. The room was done in soft, dark colors. There were two cushioned couches, a bed large enough for them both and a fruit basket as well as other sundry items all set out for them. It was almost like a hotel.

Byron stood in a pair of clean black fatigues, bare from the waist up.

Her mouth watered, and she felt instantly guilty about all the thoughts in her head. He was an injured man, and yet, standing there with his muscles all hard and flexed in the soft light, Damara needed to touch him.

More, she needed the reassurance of his body, the heat of his skin, the steady beat of his heart.

He turned when she entered and the sight of the angry wounds on his chest drilled deep into her. She ached for him physically, as well as in her heart. She supposed they were one and the same.

"I'm glad to see you've been taken off all the machines. That means you're improving, right?"

"I'm fine." He nodded.

"So says you with the holes in your chest."

He shrugged, his massive shoulders rolling with the action. "They don't feel good, but the docs sealed them with that surgical glue."

"And what happens if someone hits you there?"

Byron raised a brow.

She walked toward him slowly, her brain screaming at her that this was a bad idea, but she just had to touch him. Damara wanted to feel his heartbeat beneath her fingers.

He was frozen, didn't move or even blink as she looked up into his eyes and pressed her palm over his heart.

The words bubbled up again and she didn't want to say them, but she'd decided love was much like soda. It was sweet and carbonated, dancing around and exploding outward when rattled by a thought or a sensation.

She bit her lip.

Yes, she loved Byron Hawkins.

It was true—it was the first time she'd ever felt this for anyone. She knew love and lust could be easily confused, but when she imagined her future, he was there. Not just as some soldier on a mission, but as a true husband. A partner. A lover. Her best friend.

He'd quickly become all of those things. She could tell him anything. Anything but this because she knew he didn't want it.

She'd always thought that love was something that should be shared, given freely with no expectation of anything in return. She'd thought it was stupid to keep those feelings to yourself because, after all, what could be bad about love?

But she saw now that it was a burden to know that someone loved you if you didn't reciprocate the feeling. It was awkward and uncomfortable for both people. Just like that soda she'd used as a comparison: If no one was going to drink it, why bother to open it? All of that wonderful, fizzy, bubbly carbonation just disappeared into nothing.

Wasted.

So she'd hold it inside, keep it tightly sealed in its bottle and it could fizz happily but quietly.

Maybe she wasn't a silly little girl, after all. She was strong enough to love him, to be in love with him, and not punish him for not feeling the same thing in return. He had enough to bear on his shoulders, and she knew that he cared for her in his own way.

He'd said he'd kill for her and he'd die for her. There was devotion there. So what if it wasn't love? She'd planned on living without it, so nothing had to change. She'd just enjoy these feelings for what they were, an experience that was a gift because she'd thought she'd never have these feelings.

"Damara." Her name sounded like a warning, and his fingers closed around her wrist.

But he didn't stop her when her hand moved down to his abs or back over his chest, up to his shoulders. He stood there, stock-still and waiting for whatever she'd ask of him.

"I'm just checking," she whispered, almost as if she was afraid someone would hear her.

"For what?" he whispered back.

"That everything is still present and accounted for. Everything still works."

"Oh, it works." He leaned down to her ear. "It works really *hard*."

Her face flamed. "Of course you'd say that. One of my bodyguards told me that men were like the monkeys in an experiment she'd read about at university. When given the choice between buttons that would provide pleasure or food, they'd hit the pleasure button until they starved to death."

He took control of her explorations and pulled both her hands down to his abs. "I've been eating. That's not starving, is it?"

She laughed. "No, but you're hurt."

"Yeah, I'm in all kinds of pain. Right here." He pushed her hands lightly toward the waist of his fatigues.

She didn't need any further guidance. "You think so? Is this your reward for saving the maiden fair?"

"No." He put his hand over her heart the same as she'd done to him. "This is my reward for saving the maiden fair."

She knew that he meant her breath, her heartbeat, her life, but he was so right. All of her belonged to him.

"The Jewel of Castallegna." He brushed his lips against her cheek.

She shivered, loving his touch but not his words. "No, I'm not the Jewel any longer."

"It's not just the shape of your face or the curve of your hips, Damara. It's you." He pushed her T-shirt up over her head and tossed it to the floor. "There's a reason you're the Jewel of Castallegna, and it has nothing to do with the pretty sheen of your hair or your lovely breasts."

She knew what it was. It was what was between her thighs, her womb, because she would ensure the succession of the throne. Or so it had been thought.

"Whatever you were thinking about that made you scowl like that, it's not true."

Damara decided she didn't like this game. These things were still too tender, too raw. She didn't want him to see them because she feared if he did, he wouldn't have the same opinion of her. He'd realize that she was just a woman with no special powers. She couldn't do the things he did, and she was just a damsel in distress with more ideas than ways to implement them.

"I saw that you were the Jewel because of the light that's inside you, and it shines so bright, glitters. Just like a precious stone caught in some brilliant light."

"You sound like a poet." She couldn't bring herself to comment on the content of his remark, so she focused instead on the words themselves.

"I've never been any better with words than I am with people, Damara. That's all you." He kissed her mouth with a tender reverence she didn't know he was capable of.

In that moment, Damara believed she was the most beautiful woman in the world. The most treasured.

The most loved. It was such a pretty fantasy; it was so easy to surrender. She let herself forget that she was a job, a mission, and that it was "his honor to serve her." She forgot that he'd said he didn't want her, because right now, he did.

And it made it that much harder to swallow the words on her tongue. So instead she surrendered to the sensation, lost herself in his hands, his mouth and his touch.

She let herself drown in the connection between them, that moment when nothing mattered but each other. It was as if her body was not her own; she writhed and arched, begged and moaned. Damara would do anything to keep feeling the bliss he gave her.

She learned that he liked it when she used her nails on his back just a little bit, that he liked it when she was loud, when she spoke of the things she wanted him to do to her. She learned that the more she turned him on, the longer he played with her, taunted her and dragged out her pleasure.

His body was becoming more familiar to her, and it no longer seemed taboo to touch him anywhere she chose.

Damara loved dragging her hands over his biceps, and his back—his shoulders. She especially loved his butt. It was perfect for grabbing and kneading while he thrust into her.

She loved everything about him. Especially his scars. They were what made him perfect. His flesh wasn't ruined, but it was obvious he didn't sit in an office for a living.

With his scarred hands on her breasts, teasing the puckered buds of her nipples, she'd have sworn he hung the stars in the sky.

He moved inside her, his body seeming to be too big, too hard for her to accommodate, and yet she did and took the utmost pleasure in it.

Especially when he buried his face in her neck and they clung together while passion racked them both.

BYRON'S CHEST BURNED like a bastard, but there was no way he'd turn her down. The clock was quickly ticking down on their time together, and he wanted to remember everything about Damara that he could.

For all her talk that he was some kind of poet, he wasn't. He was a simple man with no way to express the complex things she wrought in him. He tried to tell her with his body what he couldn't—shouldn't—with words. If he told her that he loved her, it would only make things harder for them when they had to go their separate ways.

Part of him wanted her to know. She'd changed him. He'd never think he deserved her, and he still bore the guilt of his past actions and failures, but thus far he'd been responsible for her. He'd protected her.

He'd kept her safe.

That wasn't something he'd thought he was capable of doing.

He looked at her face and decided that maybe even in her heart, she was his. That was a dangerous thought. If he allowed himself to think of her as his, he didn't know how he'd ever let her go.

Byron wasn't a good enough man to acknowledge his love for her and then release her. He was too selfish.

Although he supposed this trip to Castallegna would do it for him.

Her unwavering belief in his goodness would be crushed. At first, he thought it would melt away like spun sugar. There were lots of things about Damara that were delicate and sweet, but once spun sugar was gone, it just dissolved, leaving only a sticky residue that faded. But not her belief in him. It would be more like glass or iron nails. After it was broken, it would stab into her.

Byron was in love with his wife, and when she walked down the aisle, it would be a mockery of everything he wasn't supposed to want. But he knew it was as close as he'd get to ever having the real thing.

She opened her eyes and looked up at him. "What?"

"Just thinking."

"Stop it."

He laughed, but there was no mirth. "I wish I could sometimes."

She sighed. "Me, too."

"You're my wife, Damara," he said before he could think better of it. He should have kept his mouth shut. No reason to point out the obvious because it was like a bramble of thorns. There was no way to pick it up, to interact with the fact without it slicing into tender things.

"There are worse things to be."

It was just a piece of a paper, a contract that was as easy to dissolve as the spun sugar he'd been going on about in his own head. Spun sugar and poison. It didn't mean anything.

Only, it did mean something. It meant everything.

He wanted to blame the holes in his chest for all of these feelings. It was as though they'd burrowed through all his defenses, leaving wounds not only in his chest but in that place where he locked down all the things he didn't want to feel.

"What's wrong, Byron? Are you in pain? Did we tear something open?"

"No, Princess. I'm fine." He'd meant to use her title as a way to put some distance between them, but it had become an endearment.

"No, Ranger. You're not. Tell me." Her palm was on his heart again, as if she was checking to see if it was still working.

It was working overtime, working harder than it should. He couldn't shut the damn thing off. "I'm sure this wasn't what you'd imagined would happen when we met in Tunis."

She laughed, the sound sweet. "Oh, you'd never guess at some of the things that go through my head. I really am a silly little girl sometimes."

He remembered when she'd spoken of starlight and heroes, wishes and hope. He'd be those things for her, just not in the way she wanted. It was all he could do.

"Your heart is beating so fast. What are you thinking about?"

"Things better left for the moment they happen." Any other answer that had sprung to his lips was better left to dust.

"Oh." Her voice was a whisper. "When you decide to take a life, how do you do it?"

"What?" He peered down at her.

"How do you know it's the right thing? How do you know—I mean…it's forever." Coming from anyone else, he might have thought the question to be rhetorical, some introduction to a debate, but from Damara, she really wanted to know.

"Yes, it is forever," he acknowledged.

"Are you going to answer the question?"

"No."

"Why not?"

Why not? Because he couldn't answer her. He couldn't put those things in her head, the things he'd seen. Worse, the things he'd done. "Because it doesn't matter."

"I think it does. I mean, you don't just grab a list of names and throw a dart at the wall. Right?"

"I do what my commanding officer tells me to do."

"*You* were a commanding officer. If you'd caught those guerrillas, would you have killed them?" She searched his face for some deeper meaning to his answers.

He didn't know if she was looking for his redemption or a way to make it right, but he didn't have anything to offer her.

"If I had to. Ideally, they'd be tried for war crimes and human rights violations." Yes, ideally, justice would be served. But in his reality, he'd have rather just slit their throats and been done. If they'd crept up on them in the night, if they hadn't tried to take them back to stand to pay for their crimes…

"They killed a lot of people?" she asked softly.

Scenes of the villages those guerillas had raided flooded his mind. Those were images he'd never get out of his head. Even with all the horror he'd already shared with her, this was a step further than he'd take her—or anyone else. "Horrifically."

"Then why can't my brother be tried for his crimes?"

He tried not to bristle at her question. "Because as long as he draws breath, he is a threat to you and Castallegna."

"What if he were sent to prison in—"

"*Bratva* can get into any prison, Damara. They can find him and use him, or be used by him wherever he's sent."

"Maybe like the days of old when royalty was bad I could just lock him in a tower." She sighed. "Please don't hurt him, Byron."

The plea in her voice was almost enough to make a man forget his vows, his honor. He'd lost it once before. He wouldn't lose it again.

"We shouldn't talk about this now."

"When will we talk about it, Byron? When we're flying into Marseille? When we're docking at Castallegna? When I'm crying at a state funeral over my brother's body?"

They wouldn't talk about it; there was nothing left to say. He'd do what had to be done and that would have to stand for his goodbye.

His chest hurt, and it was more than just his healing wounds.

"I'm going to tell you this just once and then we don't have to speak of it again. I want you to take this with you when this is over. Remember it."

He reached out and touched her cheek.

"When you walk down that aisle on Friday, with Christmas candles burning and the smell of holly and evergreen in the air, that's the only time that's ever going to happen for me. I never wanted to get married, have a family. So, that's okay. And I know this is a farce, but for those few hours when we say our vows, when we have the reception, when we do all those things that people are supposed to do, *it will be real.*"

Her bottom lip trembled.

"It could be real forever," she whispered. "If you wanted it to be."

"By not doing my duty? By you not doing yours? There's no happy ending for us. The best we can hope for is to save Castallegna and you."

"You could stay." Her voice was so quiet he almost couldn't hear it.

"I couldn't. What would you do with me? What would I do with myself? There's a darkness in me, Princess. It's why I'm good at what I do." He didn't make mention of Abele again, but he knew that she wouldn't want him there after he did what had to be done.

“I could stay with you.”

“Damara.” He realized he sounded as shocked as the school principal who’d caught him selling his dad’s smokes for a dollar each in the boys’ bathroom.

“I know. I couldn’t, could I? No matter how much I want to.” Damara shook her head slowly as if the facts of the situation had just become something solid and tangible.

She buried her face in his neck. He’d give almost anything to keep her there.

CHAPTER NINETEEN

IT WILL BE REAL.

Those were the words that Byron Hawkins had said to her about their wedding. He loved her. This ceremony that was just supposed to be a show, a publicity stunt, a tool—it had sped way past pretend a long time ago.

"Are you ready, Damara?" Sonja stood outside the dressing room with her trusty clipboard.

She laughed nervously and checked herself in the mirror. "Not quite." Damara still had to apply her cosmetics.

"I told you that we have someone to do that for you." Sonja clucked over her like a mother hen.

"No, no. I need to do it myself. I'll be out in a few." Damara leaned forward in the cup of her hands, studying her face in the mirror again.

"I wish you were here, Mama." She sighed at the mirror. "You, too, Papa. And you could tell me what I'm supposed to do."

She'd dreamed of her wedding day when she was young, thinking about the handsome prince and his crown. He'd be strong and smart, kind and gentle. Her mama would dress her hair and help her with her dress, and her papa would walk her down the aisle, his steady hand guiding her toward her future.

Damara supposed she'd gotten part of it right.

Her prince was strong, smart and gentle with her. There was a kindness in him that had been beaten down, crushed out of him, but that made the beautiful things inside him all the more precious.

She picked up the tube of red lipstick, and it glided smoothly over her lips. Damara remembered her mother showing her how to do it just so, all those hours at her knee before state functions.

Damara took one last look at herself, looking for traces in her own face of people she'd loved and lost.

She saw her mother's eyes, her father's nose. More than that, she felt their presence in her heart. Her love for them was with her, so that would have to be enough.

Whatever happened from here on out, Damara knew that this was real for her, too. She'd pledged her heart to this man, and it was no farce, no act. And when it was all over, she'd carry him in the same place she carried the memories of her parents.

She finished applying the rest of her makeup. When she opened the door, she saw Sonja standing there with a tiara of twined holly and roses.

"You look beautiful, Princess." She affixed the tiara to Damara's hair. "I think we're ready."

Dread knotted her gut. Not because of what it would be like to walk down the aisle to face the man she loved, but what came after. She exhaled, trying to push all her doubts and fears away. She had faith in him and herself.

"I think I'm ready."

"Dan is here to walk you down the aisle." Sonja opened the outer door.

Damara supposed it was only fitting that the man who'd put them together in the beginning was the one to give her away. She slipped her hand into the crook of his arm.

"You look stunning, Highness." Renner stood tall and proud, his every step smooth and sure.

But everything faded from her awareness. Everything but the man in front of her.

She didn't hear the music, didn't see the roses and holly all over the chapel. It didn't matter. None of it did except for the man standing at the end of the long red path.

He was supposed to be wearing his dress uniform; instead, he was wearing a suit of dinged-up armor.

It was not at all shiny.

And it was perfect.

She brought her hand to cover her mouth to keep from crying. The symbolism there, what it must have cost him to be there with his heart, his darkness, all of him on display in front of everyone—the world—as he pledged himself to her.

With this armor, he was telling her all the things that she already knew, but he was telling everyone else, too. This was all he was; this was what he had to offer. Dinged-up armor. He wasn't Prince Charming, he wasn't a knight in shining armor, but what he did have was hers.

So many cameras flashed it was like a starburst above her head, but she moved forward looking only at her groom. Her feet carried her forward faster than they were supposed to. She practically ran down the aisle.

It was very unprincess-like, but Damara didn't

care and neither did the onlookers. They seemed to be taken with her obvious love for her groom. She flung herself into his arms, and he kissed her.

For a moment, this was everything wonderful and a dream come true. If she could carve it out of time and put it away in a box like a piece of tulle from her dress, she would. She'd keep it forever.

She melted against him, and the roar of the crowd clapping and cheering in the chapel was almost deafening. The minister coughed politely to draw attention to himself. When she would have acknowledged him, Byron refused to let her go.

He finally broke the embrace and they faced the minister.

"That part is supposed to be last," the minister stage-whispered. A titter sounded among the crowd in response.

But Damara's whole world had become Byron Hawkins—all her senses were focused on him. He was all she heard, all she saw, all that she breathed in as if he had become her very air. She wasn't even aware of herself nodding or speaking in the right places, until it came time for his vows.

He dropped to his knees in front of her and took her hand. "I can't pledge you anything that doesn't already belong to you. I can't promise to share my dreams when we already traded them under a starry Mediterranean sky. I can't promise to give you my heart because it already beats in your chest. What I can offer you is a man in dented armor who will defend you, your life and your honor to the death. I can offer my queen a champion."

She nodded, pulled him to his feet and kissed him again.

A queen's champion.

He'd admitted his love for her and declared war on her brother all in a single breath. Yet it didn't surprise her. That was just how he did things. She shouldn't have expected anything less.

Before the minister could instruct him to kiss her, she was in his arms again and his poet's mouth crushed against hers. Their life together could have been so beautiful, if only they'd been allowed to live it.

Byron swept her up into his arms, and, rather than let her walk out of the chapel on her own, he carried her out to the waiting car that would take them to the community center for a small, informal reception.

Damara didn't speak. All she could think about was how he'd said today would be real for him.

The town had come out in support and to celebrate. Even with the heavy security at the front door, the community center had a small-town, homey feel to it with banquet tables lined with potluck dishes. All sorts of casseroles and things Damara hadn't heard of. None of which Byron wanted to let her taste without first allowing him to taste it.

She found it easy to lean against him. His body was so large and warm. She could burrow into his side and hide there forever. She wouldn't have to face what was coming. No matter how she planned and plotted, she couldn't see any outcome where she didn't lose her brother *and* Byron.

She could almost hear her father's voice telling her that no matter how much she may have wished it, life was not always fair. She could do her best to level the playing field, but sometimes it didn't work that way.

Hiding with Byron was what she'd been doing. All along, when she started to believe the fantasy with him was something real.

But no, he'd said this was real to him. He meant every word.

Yet, in the grand design, it meant next to nothing because they couldn't be together.

Even so, when the music played for their first dance, Damara moved into his arms easily. They spun around on the dance floor as if it were a cloud rather than wood and wax.

"Thank you for this," she whispered in his ear.

"Don't ever forget what I said, Damara."

Her heart constricted. "Never. I'll keep this memory with me always."

She was only vaguely aware of the camera flashes, but she didn't find them intrusive. She wanted as many pictures as possible so there was proof that this day had happened. And she wanted them not just so the world would see but for long nights when this was just a memory, faded and yellowed like old vellum.

"Are you okay?" She referred to his wounds.

"It wasn't as dire as all that. I've had worse." He tightened his grip.

"Then why did you pass out in the car and bleed everywhere?"

"Not one of my finer moments. But if the shooter really wanted me dead, I would be. They didn't hit anything vital. It hurt—I'm recovering. They patched me up fine. Don't worry about me."

"Easy for you to say. What would you have done if *I'd* gotten shot?"

"I don't think that's a question you actually want the answer to."

He guided them across the floor so gracefully, so smoothly, it was hard to remember that they were dancing and not flying. It occurred to her that her husband danced the same way he drove a stolen Patingale—as though it was art.

"I don't need you to answer it because I know."

"Do you now?" he whispered in her ear.

"Stop trying to change the subject."

"How am I trying to change the subject?" His breath was warm on her neck, and she shivered in his arms with delight.

"You know exactly what you're doing. Let me remind you, Lt. Hawkins, that turnabout is fair play."

"That's what I'm hoping for."

"You're a bad man." She laughed but then stopped, realizing what she'd said. Damara had spent all her time trying to convince him that he was no such thing, and now a few careless words might have undone all that she'd wrought—if anything. "I didn't mean that."

"Today, it doesn't matter. Today, I'm going to make love to my wife, just once. Once before this is all over."

"Yes," she whispered and clung to him just a little more tightly.

Their embrace was broken when Renner tapped on Byron's shoulder. "May I have this dance?"

She wanted to say no; she wanted to sneak away with Byron and hide them both from all the things the rest of the world demanded from them.

But she put on her princess face and smiled. Byron stepped back and allowed them the dance.

She didn't know why she expected him to be awkward or bumbling. He wasn't. He moved with a certain skill and grace. Damara rather imagined that planning a covert operation was much like dancing. "You're an excellent dancer."

For the first time, she saw Renner give her a genuine smile. "My wife forced me to take ballroom lessons when we got married."

"Smart woman."

"Yes, she was." A brief cloud of sadness passed over his face, and then his hard facade was back in place. "At seventeen hundred hours, you and Hawkins are going to slip away toward the kitchen. You're going to giggle, you're going cuddle and you're going to look like any other young couple in love. If anyone notices, they'll believe you're eager to be alone together. But you're going to slip out the back door. There's a car waiting to take you to the airport."

He spun her around and then brought her back in close. "The Italians have lent us the use of their navy to secure your harbors. Interpol is willing to assist. And I have some men on the ground. A small operation. You're going back to Castallegna, Princess. Are you ready?"

"Yes," she answered in a voice with much more surety than she actually felt.

Of course she wanted to go home, but that meant so much more than just going home. It meant her time with Byron was over. It meant that she'd have to face her brother. It meant that she'd have to make hard decisions. People could get hurt. People could die.

Byron could die.

Or he was going to kill Abele.

It occurred to her again that there was no way that this could end happily. The best she could hope for was a democratic Castallegna.

"Are you really ready?" he asked. "I've seen the way you two look at each other."

"I said I'm ready. I know my duty, and Byron knows his." It was an effort to keep the sting out of her voice.

"Despite what happened in Uganda, Hawkins is a good man."

"Have you told him that?" She didn't bother to hold back the sharp edge to her tone.

Renner pulled back from her, looking almost startled. "Why would I do that?"

"Because no one else has."

"Haven't you, Princess?"

"He doesn't listen to me when I say it."

"I think maybe he does. Otherwise, he wouldn't have donned not-so-shining armor for you."

She didn't like the way Renner looked at her. As if he knew something that she didn't. "What better for a queen's champion?"

"Are you a queen?" He raised a brow.

"I suppose I will be for all of five minutes. I wasn't kidding when I said I didn't want a title. I will bring my father's dream to Castallegna." That was when she realized it wasn't only her father's dream. It was her dream, as well. She wanted this for herself, too.

"I know you will." He guided her back to Byron, his expression that of a doting, benevolent relation. "Enjoy your dance."

Byron swept her around the floor once more. "Did he tell you the plan?"

"Yes."

"Are you ready?"

"Not really, but when I think about it, I don't think I ever would be." It was an epiphany she wasn't happy to have had. Nothing could ever be easy.

He gave her a bittersweet smile. "No, you wouldn't."

"How do I do that?" She looked up at him and actually expected him to have an answer.

"The same way you hid on the plane to get to Tunisia. The same way you got on that bike with me. The same way you escaped *Circe's Storm.* You jump."

"And just hope for the best?"

"Hope for the best—plan for the worst. If you're lucky, they meet in the middle." He drew her close again. "But you have me. So you know I'll catch you when you jump."

"How long do I have you?"

He didn't answer her. "It's almost time to go, Damara."

"One more time around the floor?" She wanted to make this moment stretch as long as she could because when it was over, it was over.

"Once more."

She glided with him to the symphonic strains, loving and dreading each step. Damara let herself feel his muscles move beneath her fingers and committed every sensation to memory. She'd have tattooed it there with a hundred needles if she could've. Their bodies were in a perfect synchronicity, playing on each other like a violin and a bow, their friction producing a beautifully haunting song. And when he led her to the kitchen entryway, she shed her woman's heart and became the princess she had to be.

CHAPTER TWENTY

BYRON TRIED TO shut off his emotions and focus on the mission.

Slipping out to the car had been easy. A couple of older matrons noticed as they slipped through the kitchen, but they'd eyed the couple with the kind of knowing smiles that made Byron wonder just what kind of trouble they'd gotten into in their youth.

It was strange the way they treated him now. He'd left a pariah and returned a hero. It was what he'd wanted, for the people of Glory to finally see something more in him than just the delinquent.

Now that they did, he felt like a fraud. He was just the bad kid gone a little worse who managed to turn it into a living.

Yet, there was still a use for him. Maybe not in Glory, but in Castallegna.

He was going to kill a king. Then she'd be safe. He thought about her smile, her eyes, the way she fit against him. The way some kind of higher knowledge seemed to be balanced with her innocence. Then he thought about Grisha, and what men like him did in the world. What men like him did to women.

He would die, too. This time, he'd make sure. So would his brother.

So would anyone who compromised Damara's safety.

Petrakis and Kulokav didn't know it yet, but they'd just opened the gateway to hell and the devil was about to come calling.

The car drove straight out on to the tarmac and to the waiting plane. Damara changed out of her wedding dress once they were on board. He instructed Gregson to register a flight plan to Barcelona, but in reality, they'd be landing on a small Greek island not too far from Castallegna.

Then Byron would bring the fight to their door. His blood coursed hot at the thought; his adrenaline spiked as his body prepared for war.

Damara must've seen the darkness in him because she asked, "What's wrong?"

He looked at her, wearing the same style of fatigues she'd been wearing when they'd met. Their circumstances seemed to have come full circle. "I'm taking the Jewel back where she belongs. She won't be mine anymore." He didn't want to fight about her brother, not now when this was all the time they had left together.

"She'll always be yours," Damara confided, face alight with the passion of her convictions. It was like he'd thought when he'd first met her—it was the ones who burned with a cause that were dangerous. How very right he'd been.

How he wished that it were true, that the Jewel would always be his. Some part of her would belong to him. For a moment, he'd allowed that to be true. But now he had to set her free. This was the best thing he could do for her, because he knew that she'd spread her wings and be more glorious than anything that could be for the likes of him. "I want you to get married for real, Damara. I want you to have a family. I want you to be happy."

"Happy is with you." She said it so sure of herself. As if her answer was never in question. As if there was no other answer.

He couldn't imagine it, no matter how he wanted to. "Do you really want to be Belinda Foxworth?" He wouldn't do that to her, even if it was what she thought she wanted. Watching the road for a traveler who never came home, heart aching and unsure, lost and alone, wondering why he didn't come back. No, he'd never want that life for her.

"If that's the way it goes." Damara shrugged. "I'm not afraid of what I can't change, but I am afraid of what I can. That maybe I don't know the difference."

Everything about her sliced him deep and stitched him together at the same time. Her words were so honest and heartfelt, and he knew exactly what she meant. He wanted every moment with her. "Technically, this is our honeymoon. All twelve hours of it. Come with me to the lavatory."

She shook her head. "No way."

He made a show of bouncing on the couch. "Right here, then?"

"No." Her eyes widened. "Someone will see."

"Someone will not see. There's just you and me and the pilot, and he's busy flying the plane."

"Not a chance." But she looked around the cabin as if she expected to see someone else on board.

It occurred to him then that he'd never touch her

that way again, but she deserved a better goodbye than being shagged in an airplane lavatory.

Sometimes, he could swear she could see right through his skin and into his soul. It was as if she knew his train of thought and she couldn't bear it. Either his sadness or her own. She stood as prim and proper as if she were going to an officer's ball and headed back toward the lavatory.

"This may not work."

"You're right. I don't know how people do this. Maybe they're all much smaller men than me. But I couldn't take a p—use the facility in here if I tried."

"You don't have to start watching your profanity now, Lt. Hawkins. Wasn't it you who said this was called fucking?" she teased, lightening the mood.

"Indeed, I was." God, the feelings again. When would they stop? He was brimming with them, and he wanted to tell her he loved her. Because he did. When all the dark places in him had emptied out, all that was left was his love for her.

He didn't know how or why it had happened, but it had. His brain began running down logical reasons for the anomaly. That it was normal for people who experienced high-stress situations together to feel bonded. The adrenaline rush of fear was a lot like love. What that said about the world, he didn't know.

Or didn't want to think about.

The wedding was over. When they landed, so, too, would be their "honeymoon." It could go no further than right here. He had to turn off these feelings, root them out of himself before they turned malevolent and devoured him from the inside out.

She giggled and squirmed, pretending to try to get

away from him. But when he would've let her go, she locked her arm around his neck.

"This is getting to be a habit. So are we playing princess and the bodyguard?" He tried to think only about the physical, so he didn't have to feel all this sorrow.

"No, we're playing husband and his new wife." He kissed her before she could say anything else. Byron supposed that was cowardly, but he just couldn't talk anymore and he didn't want to feel anything but her.

He pushed her up against the galley and he broke the kiss to turn her. She placed her hands on the sides of the counter. Byron pushed her fatigues off and pulled her panties down to her ankles.

Byron ran his hands along her silky hips and thighs; he couldn't get inside of her fast enough. He slipped his hand between them to ready her, but she was already wet for him.

"You really like this." He thought of a hundred other scenarios he could play out with her if he'd had the time. If she were really his. Oh, the things he'd do to this body—he loved the sound of his name on her lips and she'd be screaming it to bring the rafters down. If only, if only…

"Oh, yes," she said, her voice breathy. "Now do it."

He'd joked about liking her to command him, but he didn't think there was anything sexier.

This wasn't just about sex. Or the heat that flared between them. It was about everything else, too. As much as he didn't want it to be. He couldn't fight it anymore. He knew it was going to hurt when she was gone, when he had to leave. Hell, it hurt now. There was no avoiding it. He was already in so deep he'd drowned in her.

After sheathing himself in the condom from his wallet, he drove deep inside her.

She cried out but pushed back against him, meeting his every thrust. She filled his senses, touch, scent, sound, sight and taste. The taste of her mouth was still on his tongue, the jasmine scent of her.

Her sweet warmth pulled him deeper, taking it all but giving him everything.

He lost himself in her every time he touched her. There was no beginning, no end, no nothing but the focused point of sensation where their bodies joined.

Byron was starting to need this with her, to feel this connection and this link. This was more than a need for his body—it was a need for his heart.

And when it was all over, he had to let it be just that.

Over.

THE PLANE LANDED on a small Greek island that would have been the perfect honeymoon destination for a couple who wanted to be lost in each other. It was fairly deserted. From there, they took a skiff that had been docked for them and slipped right into a Castallegnian bay with no one the wiser.

Her brother and Kulokav's men ran the docks, but there were no docks, no trade routes here. Only a small abandoned hut that reminded her of the island they'd just left.

Again, Damara found herself wishing things were different.

It was just before dawn when they finally crept

into the small hut, and Damara was exhausted. She should've slept on the plane, but she'd wanted to spend one last time with him.

She didn't understand how it was so easy for him to turn it off, to forget everything they were to each other.

But she didn't argue with him or demand they talk it out. It was what it was. Instead, she crawled into the pallet on the floor next to him.

"We'll hide out here until I get the word from Renner about the Italian navy. They should be en route."

She nodded sleepily.

"If I'm gone when you wake up, I just went down to catch a few fish. Don't worry."

"I'm not going to—" And just like the last time she was in this part of the world with her now husband, she fell asleep cradled in his arms when she expected to be awake all of the long night.

Only when she awoke, it wasn't to gunshots like on the *Circe's Storm*. It was to Grisha Kulokav and his gun pointed at her head.

She fought down panic, trying to take in the situation. Where Byron was, where she was, orient herself to her surroundings. Instead of whimpering or cowering, she said, "My husband needs to work on his aim."

"Husband? Indeed, Princess, you'd best hope that's not the case."

They were already married. There was nothing he could do about it now. "And why is that?"

"Because then I'll have to make you a widow."

"As if you could."

"He already tried to kill me once, Princess. As you can see, he's not as effective as you might think."

She didn't have any reply, so she lay there, refusing to wilt under the weight of his appraisal and the threat there.

He laughed. The bastard actually laughed with genuine mirth. "I do enjoy you, Princess. Vladimir thinks I should kill you or keep you as a mistress. But I think you are worthy." His eyes slid up her body. "A beautiful bride indeed." Grisha cocked his head to the side. "Abele, your brother, thinks the same. But I have other plans for you, *malenkaya.* Would you like to hear them?" He stroked a large meaty finger down her cheek.

"If it involves the usual threats like torture and death, probably not." She was pleased with how calm she sounded, because her insides were twisted up like barbed wire. She'd never been more terrified.

He grinned again. "For all the trouble you've caused me, you've been less of a problem than your oh-so-royal brother. I want you for my wife, and I want Castallegna. Come with me now, and I will kill your brother and we will rule Castallegna together."

"I've already told you, Grisha. There will be no ruling Castallegna. Not by us, anyway."

"Abele killed your father to keep him from making the transition. Don't you think he'd do the same to you? All of these men who want to protect you and save you, but you won't let us kill the one thing that would hurt you."

"What do you mean?" How did he know about her conversation with Byron? His promise?

A new thread of fear wound its way around her.

"I think I was pretty clear. He killed your father. It was no riding accident. Abele bashed his head in with a rock. He was very proud of this."

"And you, are you very proud of this?"

"Proud of what? The lengths I have gone to so that I may secure my woman? Of course. I'm strong. As are you." His chest puffed up with the pride he spoke of. He really didn't understand.

She had to find out if Byron was okay. Her brain processed that since they were discussing him, Grisha must not know he was on the island. So he was safe. Damara searched for her inner center, that peace that helped her forge through whatever was in her path.

"No. You haven't done anything good or noble. Nothing to be proud of." Damara felt as though she were a weed trying to stand against a hurricane. What was she? A spoiled princess who'd never lived in the world, who ran away and caused a clash of nations. Men were willing to die for her.

No, not men.

Man. One man. Her husband.

She couldn't let him. Damara had to find a way to save him.

"I haven't hurt you or sent my torturers after you like Abele."

"How did you know about that?" She cocked her head to the side.

"I know a lot of things, Princess."

"If you knew about Tunisia before I fled Castallegna, why didn't you stop me?"

He shrugged as if the answer didn't matter. "I honestly didn't think you'd get that far. Then as things progressed, you showed your true mettle. I was impressed."

Impressing the gangster had been the very last thing on her to-do list.

"Then you left with a man. I was not so well impressed with that."

"I had to do what I had to do, Grisha. I still do." Why wouldn't he understand? Worse, why did she keep trying to explain something to him he chose not to understand?

"Leave with me now and all will be well, Damara."

"I can't. I've made commitments. I can't break my word."

"Then your ranger will die, and so might you. Your brother has something planned for you. He knows you're here. A statement to the world about what defying him means. He's not too pleased to have been placed on a red notice, Interpol's wanted list. He's a king and above such things, you know."

"What's he going to do?" Damara swallowed her bile.

He tsked. "Either you will have me or you will not, Princess. You don't get this information out of the goodness of my heart. Say yes. Say yes and save your ranger. Your new friends. It's never just the target that gets hurt. It would be a shame if some little girl hoping to see a princess was blinded or crippled by shrapnel."

"Save my ranger? Have you seen him?" Damara dared ask. Grisha seemed to get some sick pleasure out of telling her the truth.

"He let you escape him. He must be done with you."

"You're horrible." She kept her expression neutral, but his words were ripping out her guts.

"And yet you will come to see things my way. Or have you forgotten all of what your father taught you?"

"Don't you dare speak of my father. You didn't know him."

"Oh, but I did. He despised me, but I knew him. He would be so disappointed in you for putting any of your needs above the people. Do they deserve to suffer for what you want? Abele's plans are already in place. No matter where you go, or who you're with, he'll be able to get to you. Just like I did."

He yanked her up off the floor and kissed her hard.

She didn't fight, because she knew it was useless, and she realized he'd want her to fight. He liked that she was rebellious and defiant. The fact that Byron had shot him only made Grisha want her more. She thought about biting his lips, but, again, he'd like that.

So instead she showed him what it would be like if he forced this on her. She held her lips hard and dry; there was no feminine softness to her mouth or in the way he held her. She was stiff and cold, carved out of ice.

She displayed no reaction either way, not fear, no revulsion and certainly not pleasure. In her head, she'd retreated to that place she went when people treated her like a princess doll instead of a person. The hours of hair and makeup, fittings, grooming, pinching and pulling on her body as though it were something that belonged to the world at large and not her.

Because she knew Grisha was right.

Would she really risk all of these people? She should've stayed on Castallegna and done whatever

Abele instructed while pretending to be the perfect vacuous doll. Then she could've started a rebellion and led her people to freedom that way.

Or she could've just slipped something into Abele's soup. Because then only he would die. No one else would ever be hurt by him again.

But that was pain and rage talking. No matter what Abele had done, Damara wasn't capable of murder.

Even knowing that Abele had killed their father. It was possible Grisha was lying, but it had given voice to what Damara had suspected for a long time. After her conversation with Abele, hearing the venom and hatred in his voice, she knew he was capable of anything.

"Fine, I'll go with you. But no one else gets hurt."

"I knew you'd see it my way."

Then she stepped out into the chilly predawn and headed toward the end of all good things.

Damara tried not to think about Byron as she slid into the backseat, but she couldn't help it. He filled her thoughts. She wondered if he was hurting, if he'd understood her message.

Though she supposed it didn't matter. This was the way things had to be.

She shifted in her seat, sore from the previous day, but she enjoyed the discomfort. Pain made memories brighter, more real. She'd need it to remember everything as clearly as she wished.

Her husband had made her feel this way, the man she'd fallen in love with. Not some crown or bank account she was supposed to give herself to for God and country.

She looked at Grisha sitting next to her in the backseat and she wondered just how she was going to escape him. It seemed an impossible task. He'd knit a rather neat little trap around her, she realized as the driver started the car.

She wished her father was there. He'd know what to do.

Except he wasn't, and wishing he was there didn't make it so. It didn't give her any answers or guidance. She had to rely on herself.

"Already plotting your escape, Princess?" His voice slashed through the silence.

"No."

"Don't lie to me." His voice was soft, but the threat there was not.

"I'm not plotting my escape. I was thinking about all of my options." Escape. Options. Same thing to her.

"Which are?"

"None."

"That's not necessarily true. This doesn't have to be a bad thing, Damara," Grisha said softly.

Damara stilled the shudder before it rolled through her. "You say this like you're the one who has to marry someone he doesn't want."

"You will want me in time." He said it as if she were just a little girl who didn't quite understand the birds and the bees.

Damara shook her head. "No, Grisha. I will not."

No, no matter what Grisha did to her, it would never be anything like Byron.

The car was big, lush. Everything had been designed with an eye of opulence and comfort, but none of that mattered to Damara. In fact, she wondered how many people's lives had paid for everything he'd tried to give her.

His wealth was dirty.

"Your father indulged you too much, Princess. You will see. It is always better to have money. Even in your precious democracies, money is what eases your way."

Damara was filled with fire. She wanted to blurt out that she didn't care about money. That all she wanted was Byron, but Grisha laughed.

"The passionate fire of first love burns in your eyes. It is the love that would let nations fall if only to be together." He laughed again. "You may think whatever you like, and, in private, you may say whatever you like. In front of my brother, or in front of my men, you will be respectful or you will be punished. Do you understand?"

There was nothing he could do to her. Nothing.

"Or perhaps I should say your whipping girl will be punished. In the days of old, royalty would have peasants who would endure their punishments for them. I would never want to mar a face as beautiful as yours. So your whipping girl shall be punished every time you disobey or embarrass me."

She was going to be sick.

Instead of showing him any reaction, she nodded coolly. "I understand."

"Good." He took a drink of his whiskey. "Tell me, Damara, what was it that made you love him?"

"Does it matter?" She shrugged and looked out the window.

"Perhaps. Perhaps not. Indulge me."

"Or you'll whip someone?" She forced herself to look at him.

"No, Damara. I told you that you may speak as you like when we're in private. But what would it hurt to let me know you?"

"You don't want to know me. You want me to be your windup Princess Barbie to Gangster Ken."

He laughed. "In public, yes. That is what I want. Although I know there is another you beneath the doll. The you that knows Krav Maga. The you that likes American pop culture."

"That me is the one who thinks privilege by blood is wrong. You have nothing in common with her." Damara turned her head and looked out the window.

When he offered her a whiskey of her own, she didn't turn it down. She downed it in one gulp. It burned like hellfire all the way down, but then it was warm, languid and sweet.

"Better?"

She studied him again. He wasn't ugly. He might have been handsome to some women if he wasn't a murdering psychopath.

"Why me?" She sighed.

"Because you're not afraid of me."

She was most certainly afraid of him, but she wasn't going to let that control her actions. Damara had more people to worry about in this scenario than herself.

"So if I start being afraid of you, will you get bored and let me go?"

"I may get bored, but I will never let you go. You belong to me, Damara." His laughter chilled her blood.

"See, all I have to do is say something you don't like and your eyes flash with rebellion."

Damara turned away from him and looked out the window again, staring blankly out onto the landscape that had once offered her succor. She could smell jasmine, and that made her doubly heartsick.

It was both wonderful and terrible to be home.

She swallowed her grief like so much bile and exited the car. Damara half expected a pack of paparazzi to meet them, but there was no one.

"There is no one to meet us?" she asked.

"No. I don't want your brother to know we're on the island."

"He has to already know. He has spies everywhere."

"No, Kulokav interests now have control of the docks, the airport and the spies he has planted. We're already running Castallegna right under his nose, Princess."

Her stomach twisted on itself. "So did you have a hand in killing those Council members?"

"Those were your brother's orders, Highness. But I would not have hesitated to do so if it would give me you."

She'd stopped trying to argue with him about what did and what did not belong to him. He'd made up his mind, and no amount of correction from her was going to change that. There was no reason to set herself a harder course than what she already had—meaning she had to pick her battles. Nomenclature wasn't worth fighting over.

"Do you think your ranger will come?" Grisha asked.

"No. I was just a mission to him."

"You put on a very convincing show for the world. You're going to have to top it if you want to convince people you left of your own free will."

Why he thought she'd ever do that was beyond her. "It wasn't a show on my part, Grisha. I love him."

He suddenly grabbed her. "Say that again and I will kill him."

She didn't need to say it. It was already tattooed on her heart. But she didn't defy Grisha; she'd already pushed him as far as she'd be able to.

Grisha must've seen the surrender in her eyes because he released her. "Glad we understand each other. We'll go to our beach house."

As the car drove down the winding cobbled roads of Castallegna City, Damara realized the route was familiar.

He was taking her to what had once been her mother's retreat house. It was where she went with the children when the Council was in session or she'd just had enough of the pomp of court.

How could Abele have given it to him?

Some of their best memories were there.

When the car took the last turn, those memories came rushing back to her. The happy days spent on the sand and in the water, her mother's large, floppy hat that was supposed to shield her from the sun but blew away on the island breezes more often than not.

She and Abele in the lagoon while he taught her to swim and showed her various fish.

That was all gone.

Now there was some gangster living in her mother's house. The house where she'd fallen in love with Damara's father, the house where she'd given birth to Abele and to Damara. The house where she'd taken her last breath trying to bring another son into the world.

She wanted to burn it down.

Damara would rather see it and everything in it disappear to ash along with the love and life that had happened in there than see it sullied by Kulokav.

"It was your mother's, yes?"

She nodded silently.

Damara didn't speak until they went inside the house. It was completely empty. Everything was gone. From the pictures of her grandmother, to her mother's favorite chair, it was all gone.

Empty. Just like Abele.

"Where are all my mother's things? Tell me they've been put into storage." She turned to face him. "Tell me."

For once the big man had nothing to say.

"Did you do this? Did you have her things removed?"

"That would have been unnecessarily cruel," Grisha acknowledged.

"One day, I will cry for the boy that my brother was. Today is not that day."

CHAPTER TWENTY-ONE

DAMARA KNEW THAT Byron would come for her.

She couldn't see him, but she knew he was out there watching, waiting for the right time to make his move. Castallegna wasn't very big. She was torn between wanting him to hurry and wanting him to flee.

If he fled, she knew that he and Abele would both live.

It wasn't long before Grisha announced it was time to go to the palace and speak with Abele.

"Are you going to kill him?" she asked.

"Do you want me to?"

"No. I don't want anyone to die." She meant that from the bottom of her heart.

"What if he tries to kill you?"

She exhaled heavily. Part of her wanted to say that, yes, he should defend her life. But she knew he'd use it as an excuse to kill her brother whether her life was in danger or not.

"Even then."

"You know that in the eyes of Castallegnian law, you are my wife already. Even if I still have to make you a widow to the Americans."

"Just stop, Grisha. Stop. You have me. I'm here. I've done everything you wanted." She was so tired of all this talk of death.

"You're not in my bed."

"You were so sure I'd come to want you—where is that confidence now?"

Grisha sighed. "I will give you one month. No more. I want sons."

More men like him who would murder, rape and steal? No. She'd never have his child. She'd drink the yam root tea to prevent conception until her fingers turned yellow if she had to.

"You are suspiciously quiet."

"Of course I'm quiet. You're taking me to see my brother after he threatened to kill me and crowned himself king. I'd be stupid not to be worried."

Her brain had been set to spin since they'd arrived on the island. Part of her kept hoping that Byron would show up with some elite commando force and fix everything. It was just a spoiled little-girl princess thing for her to think, and yet she couldn't dismiss it.

When they got to the palace—a sprawling, whitewashed, hacienda-style estate—they were met by guards she'd never seen before. In the time she'd been gone, he'd changed everything.

She inhaled the scent of jasmine, and it fortified her. All her fears and doubts didn't disappear, but they were caged and quieted.

They were led into the formal receiving room as if they were guests instead of royals.

She thought it would be terrible to face her brother, and seeing him there on the throne, wearing her father's sash and driving their country to ruin, it was terrible.

But not for the reasons she thought it would be.

He was not better than she was. He was not stronger. He was not *more.*

Damara realized that she had her own power, her own worth, and it had nothing to do with her blood, her birthright or the crown everyone wanted to keep on her head.

She finally understood what Byron had been talking about when he called her the Jewel.

She was as kind as Abele was cruel. She was as gentle as he was ruthless. She tried to find some empathy for each person she met, and all Abele had was greed.

Damara had always been loved for herself. The people loved her; her father loved her. And Byron loved her not because of her name, or her crown, but because of herself.

That realization changed something in her, made it solid and whole. There was nothing Abele could do to take it away from her now.

"The prodigal daughter returns," he sneered.

"Where are my mother's things?"

"Destroyed."

She pursed her lips. "I see."

"I don't think you do." He leaped from the throne to his feet. "I don't think you do at all, sister."

Damara didn't flinch away. She stared him down.

"Do you think that I won't punish you for what you've done?"

"I'm already punished, Abele. But I think I'm finished with that. For a long time I thought I was the spoiled and coddled princess who didn't know much of the world. It turns out I was wrong. You've been so spoiled that you don't really understand what a weight that crown should be on your head. You've been talking about what a disgrace I am? How I've shamed you? Well, Abele, I say the same about you."

He raised his hand to strike her, but when she didn't cower, his conviction wavered.

"You are an embarrassment to Castallegna, to our mother, to our father, to me. You shame the very throne you sit on." She motioned to Grisha. "You've given control of our country to gangsters because you were so afraid someone was going to take your power away. So instead, you gave it away with both hands."

A guttural sound was torn from him. "Watch how you speak to me."

"No, I won't. That hand that you've raised to strike me? It's the one that taught me how to swim, that helped teach me to read. It was with that hand I learned to love you, Abele. Now I'm just sorry that boy is dead."

"I'm right in front of you. I live. I breathe." He patted his chest.

"And still I say you're dead. You're dead to Castallegna and to me." She leaned in toward him. "Worst of all, and deep down inside you know it's true, you're dead to yourself."

"That doesn't even make sense, Damara." He snorted and returned to sit on the throne.

Abele tried to act as if he wasn't affected, but he was. This was his way of retreat.

"Control your woman, Grisha."

Grisha shrugged.

"What will you do? Hit me? Kill me? That doesn't change who you are or what you've done. You're still the same inside whether I'm breathing or not."

"Keep a civil tongue in your head. If you don't, I can still blow that town to bits. My operatives are still in place."

"You're such a coward," she spat. "Hurting innocent people and children because you didn't get what you wanted. You disgust me."

"Yet, you are still at my mercy. Guards!" he called.

Except no one came.

"Guards!" he yelled again.

"There is no one coming for you, princeling." Grisha smiled coldly. "And you are sitting in my chair."

Abele didn't know what to do; the smug expression on his face melted like wax in the summer sun. All his hopes and dreams had just shattered around him.

"This is treason."

"As are most regime changes." Grisha shrugged. "There is no one who will stand up for you. No one who will hear you. You are not a beloved leader. You have no army."

Army? The way he said that, it was if he were saying that he did have an army. She didn't want troops on Castallegna. They'd be nothing but mercenaries and thugs. Even if there were never any battles, Castallegna would be a war zone.

She had to stop this, but she had to do it without bloodshed.

WHEN HE HEARD GRISHA call for a guard, Byron took a deep breath and reported. He'd been able to snatch a guard's uniform when he found the central command post in the palace.

The room he entered was obviously the throne

room, and Grisha had faced off with Abele, with Damara watching.

"See, they do not answer to you any longer," Grisha said. Then he looked at Byron. "Escort my wife to her new chambers."

His wife? Byron imagined twenty ways he could kill him with various objects around the room.

"Grisha, no. You promised."

"I am not a man of promises, *malenkaya.* I promised no such thing. Go with the guard, unless you want to watch."

Damara stood there, anguish on her beautiful face.

"More to life," Byron said in a low voice.

Damara's eyes grew round, and she dropped her head in faux subservience. He allowed her to walk in front of him because she was the one who knew where they were going.

As soon as they were out of earshot, she shoved him into an alcove and threw her arms around him.

"Are you crazy?"

He ripped off the mask. "Me? What's wrong with you?"

"You don't hate me?" she asked softly.

"I'm pissed that to find you I had to steal an inferior bike, camp out in a field and I haven't had a shower. But why would I hate you?"

He tried to make light of the situation they were in by being blasé, although he was anything but. It felt so good to have her in his arms again, so good to know that she did love him. He was sure she did, but that validation of her embrace made everything better—made it worth it.

"Because I was gone. I left, I didn't tell you… You told me to stay there."

"Survival is the only promise I want from you, Princess. You didn't have a choice."

"Oh, God, Byron. I don't know what to do. Grisha has declared himself king because the Council validated the proxy marriage. He's inserted all of his own people in the palace guard and he has some kind of army of mercenaries. He's going to kill my brother. Please don't let him." She buried her face in his neck. "Please."

When she looked up at him, he knew he was going to save her damned brother. Against his better judgment, and against what every instinct in his body was telling him. Every instinct but the one to please her.

There wasn't a curse word invented that could describe his feelings about this development. She'd been right about him, right that when it came down to it, he wouldn't hurt her. Even if it was the best way to keep her safe.

"Would it be too much to hope for that you'd go wait somewhere safe?"

She arched a brow.

"Fine. Get to a phone and call the Interpol office in Greece." He shoved a piece of paper in her hand with the number written on it. "Tell them who you are, that the Kulokav brothers are on the island and, as princess, you give them authority in Castallegna."

"I love you."

"I love you, too, Damara. More than you could ever know." He turned away from her and headed back into the throne room.

His mouth wasn't usually in the habit of writing

checks that his ass couldn't cash, but with Abele holding a gun on Grisha and Grisha standing like a bull about to charge, it was going to be ugly.

They both turned to look at the intruder, and Grisha smiled that cold grin of his.

"It is the real cowboy motherfucker." He quoted Miklos's words about him. "I'm so glad I get to kill you."

He was out of options.

And he decided since Grisha thought he was a cowboy, he might as well live up to his reputation. He drew his guns and fired.

But he aimed low and blew out both men's left knees. A great shot, if he did say so himself. Then he hit the deck, because they fired back as they fell.

Abele was softer, not as used to pain. He dropped his weapon immediately, howling and clutching at his leg.

Grisha, however, was made of sterner stuff. He fired a good shot, and it grazed Byron's shoulder. It was like being burned with a hot pan, a sizzle and an unpleasant surprise, but it wasn't debilitating.

He launched himself at Grisha and went for the already injured knee to bring him to submission. Grisha would have kept fighting if Byron hadn't knocked his head into the marble floor a dozen times.

Byron rummaged through his utility belt and found a pouch of zip ties. They were harder to get out of than traditional handcuffs, but that didn't stop him from putting three on Grisha and two on Abele.

Abele was still moaning about his leg. When he opened his mouth to speak, Byron stopped him.

"I promised her I wouldn't kill you. Don't make me

break that promise." Yet as he looked into the man's eyes, he knew killing him would be a trial on his soul he didn't want to bear. Not only would it have hurt Damara but the bastard had her eyes. He couldn't put a bullet in a man who looked at him with his wife's eyes.

For as happy as he thought he'd be when he got to end these two, he realized this was better. He'd saved Damara. He'd saved her country, and it was a good thing.

He'd done a good thing.

And he didn't have to destroy or kill to do it.

That knowledge gave him hope that he could build something when this was over. Byron didn't know how he'd do it, but he knew he could never be parted from her forever.

Renner had promised him retirement with full benefits if he did this thing, and he'd accepted. He wasn't going to let the man go back on his word. He'd take it and come here and…and what? What would he do?

Serve the princess?

His brain wandered to all the ways he could serve her, but that was only fantasy. Reality was he was still a weapon, and here he'd be a weapon without a purpose.

And yet that was secondary to his need to be with Damara.

CHAPTER TWENTY-TWO

DAMARA HAD BEEN terrified when she'd heard the gunshots. She didn't know who to worry for most, Abele or Byron. Abele won, but only because she knew that if anyone could figure a way out, it was Byron.

She never thought she'd see him again, let alone be in his arms.

She loved him so much it hurt, and she thought her heart would explode out of her chest and fly away.

It was Byron who emerged from the room, blood on his arm.

"Have you been shot? Again?" She called for some of the old guards still loyal to her to come assist.

"Just a graze. It's nothing."

"I forbid you to get shot," she cried and flung her arms around him again. "Are they—"

"They're awaiting justice and removal."

She squeezed him tighter. "Interpol said they could have agents here in an hour and the Italian navy has Castallegna surrounded. Did we really do this?"

"Yeah, baby. We did." He squeezed her back. "Now you have a country to run."

"No, I— This wasn't what I wanted."

"It's what you got. Did you think you could just get rid of these men and then what? You have to guide the process."

"We're still going to have to be apart, aren't we?" All the joy she'd felt earlier crashed and burned.

"I don't want to leave you. But I belong to the U.S. government, at least for a little while longer."

"No. You'll just stay here." Even as she said it, she knew it was wrong. Damara couldn't ask him to give up his honor.

He pulled away from her embrace and met her eyes. "If that's what you want."

She shook her head. "No. I mean, I do. But I won't ask you to sacrifice your honor and your country for me. Not after you helped me save mine." She worried her lip with her teeth. "You know, since we're married, if you want to speak technically, you're the crown prince of Castallegna."

"No more kings, no princes. Right?" he asked her.

She'd thought before that he might be the only man who'd give up a crown just because it was the right thing to do. "Right. Come with me. I want to show you something."

"We shouldn't—"

"Baka and Kon are both loyal to me. They helped me escape the palace in the first place. They're more than capable and happy to sit on Abele and Grisha until Interpol arrives. Come." She pulled his hand. "This is important."

She took him to her father's office. It was in the process of being packed up, but his desk was still as he'd left it. Probably because of the painting of him hanging on the back wall. It seemed as if he were watching all who entered the room and would know if you were up to something he didn't like.

He had a stern demeanor, but beneath that, he was kind and fair. He was a good leader.

His bookshelves were largely untouched. *The Art of War* by Sun Tzu, *A Summary View of the Rights of British America* by Thomas Jefferson, *Beyond Good and Evil* by Frederick Nietzsche, Plato's *Theory of Knowledge*… And she'd read them all. Or he'd read them to her.

This was the place where she'd felt closest to her father. Surrounded by his books, the scent of good cigars and fine whiskey.

Her nose prickled and her eyes burned as tears welled. She wished her father were there in person to meet him instead of just sharing with Byron the remnants of his life.

"Grisha told me that Abele killed my father. I don't want to believe him, but I do."

Byron looked around the room slowly, taking it all in. "Then you should tell that to the agents."

"That's the problem. My father was an educated man. A teacher, a philosopher. An idealist. I don't think he'd want me to. Abele will already be punished for those other things he's done."

"Damara, I think you should do what you can best live with. They say that justice is for the victims, but it's a lot like funerals. They're grief rituals for the living. But I think that you would rather honor him and his wishes than see Abele punished any more than he already is. You wouldn't let me kill him, after all."

"My father would have liked you, Byron."

"Do you really think so?" He flashed her a cocky grin. "I know if I were him, I wouldn't approve of me."

"I know it's going to sound silly, but that's kind

of why I brought you here. I wanted him to meet you." She rushed on. "It's weird, but it feels like part of him is still here in this room and these things, I know they're just things. But they were *his* things—he touched them and loved them."

Byron nodded. "It's not silly."

"Oh, Byron." She leaned against him. "I don't want to do any of this without you."

"And I don't want you to. I want to spend our lives together. You're my wife, and I want to be your husband. I'm just not sure how to do that."

"Do you mean it?" Hope surged in her chest. Was this possible? Did she get to be a fairy-tale princess after all?

"I won't lie. I'm afraid. Terrified."

She cupped his face. "Of what?"

"Of failing you. Of hurting you."

"Your team, Byron..."

"And damn it, I'm selfish. I'm afraid I'm doing this because I want you so badly that the only thing worse than failing you is living without you. If I was a good man, I'd tell you that it was over and I'd go home and drown in the bottom of a bottle while I tried to forget you. But I'm not. I'm selfish and I can't give you up."

"Then I'm selfish, too, because I don't want to do any of this without you. I could do it. Thanks to you, I know I can do anything. But I don't want to. I want you with me. I'm asking you to give up your country, your home, to come here and stay with me while I fix what my brother has broken."

"Anywhere with you is paradise, Damara. But there's something I have to do first."

She nodded. "You need to go to Texas." Damara knew he needed that closure.

"I need to tell Belinda I'm sorry. I need to see her and know she's okay. And maybe leave that last piece of him with her."

"I want to go with you. You faced Abele with me. I want to be with you to do this."

He pulled her close, and she just marveled at the feel of his arms around her. She'd thought this wasn't possible.

"Highness, the agents are here," a guard interrupted them.

"Are you okay if I check in with Renner?" he asked.

Damara realized that she was okay. She could do this. "Yes. See if you can get him started on that paperwork for the retirement he promised you." She smiled and headed toward the throne room.

Damara held her head high as she walked. She was proud of herself. Proud of Byron. And even if things were hard because they'd have to be separated for a while, it wouldn't be forever.

Byron's job was part of who he was. She'd been so worried about being something besides a princess, she hadn't realized that it wasn't just a mask she pulled on and off. Her duty was to serve her people. And it was more than a duty—it was a calling.

She faced the agents with a practiced calm she'd perfected.

"They don't have the right," Abele choked out. "We're a sovereign nation. There's no Interpol office on Castallegna. They can't—"

She turned away from the men.

"They can. I've authorized their presence, their

authority. And Castallegna will soon be joining their ranks. I've decided the offices here will concentrate on human trafficking and war crimes."

Abele didn't say anything else.

"Please go on, gentlemen." Damara turned her attention back to the men in front of her.

"Is that true?" the blond agent asked her.

"Yes, it is."

"They've been trying to finalize plans for a long time. Since right before your father died."

She nodded. "I know. Castallegna is about to go through some serious changes. My father wanted to transition away from a monarchy to a democracy. But we have a commitment to upholding the law, regardless of the power structure."

"Would you like to make a statement?"

"Not at this time. Grisha Kulokav and my brother are both wanted for crimes in other countries? Castallegna will cede to their charges."

"That's very generous."

"Not so much. I really just want them out of my home." Damara laughed. "We can't reform with anchors and old hurts hanging around our necks—and if anything, my brother is still an open wound for a lot of the people here. Especially me."

"What about Vladimir? He's wanted, as well."

"By the United States, too," Byron said from the door. "I have some intel that he's trying to leave the island via plane. One of our agents slashed the tires on the plane, but that's only going to stop them so long. If he gets in the air, we may not get another chance at him. He has unlimited resources."

"If Castallegna handed over its king, we'll let you

keep the older Russian," the other agent said, as if they were playing a game of Go Fish rather than dealing with international crime bosses.

Damara headed toward the door.

"Where are you going?" Byron asked her.

"With you of course." She eyed him. "If you tell me to stay here, it's not going to go well for you."

"She's power mad," Byron teased.

"Princesses can be that," the agent answered.

"Yes, yes I can." Damara grinned. "What are we waiting for? Let's go take out the trash."

DAMARA HAD BLOOMED rather than wilted when faced with her demons. Not that Byron had expected she'd do otherwise, but he knew she'd doubted herself.

He hadn't been kidding. He really did want her to stay safely ensconced where nothing could hurt her, but he decided if she couldn't ask him to give up his job, he couldn't do any less than support her in this.

Even if that meant chasing down an evil bastard like Vladimir Kulokav.

Byron didn't enjoy being this enlightened. It'd be much more comforting if he could just be a knuckle-dragging caveman and lock her up at home—preferably in the bedroom.

He sighed.

Byron was trying desperately not to look for trouble where there was none, but he had a bad feeling. A gnawing in his gut that something awful was going to happen. He hoped it was just that part of himself that still thought he didn't deserve Damara.

They sped toward the airfield and saw the mechanic was in the process of changing the tire with a gun to his head.

When he got out of the car, he recognized the mechanic as being part of Renner's crew.

Never shall I fail my comrades.

Byron knew what he had to do.

And so did Damara.

"You can talk to him—"

"He has nothing to lose and everything to gain by killing that man. Do you recognize him? He met us on the tarmac in D.C."

"Then let me help."

"You are helping. I couldn't make you stay at the palace and I wouldn't, but I need you to stay in the car. My head won't be in the game if I'm worried about you." When she would've spoken again, he said, "I have to let you do your job, so you have to let me do mine, right? Trust me. It'll be okay."

It was the first time he'd lied to her.

He couldn't swear it was going to be okay. There was a very real possibility that he'd die.

Recognizing that I volunteered as a Ranger, fully knowing the hazards of my chosen profession... Yet, there was a part of him that did believe it would be okay. He believed that he'd kept her safe this long; he could finish this job. His team, this team, would all go home.

"I love you, Damara." He wanted her to hear it, just in case.

"You better tell me that again when you get back."

"As many times as you want." He turned to the driver. "Keep the princess safe."

"Always," he answered.

Byron walked out toward the tarmac as there was nowhere for him to hide. No way to sneak up on him. His only chance was to go head-to-head with this guy.

"Stop where you are, Hawkins. Or I'll kill your snitch," Vladimir Kulokav said in perfect, unaccented English.

"You're going to kill him anyway." He put on a mask of indifference; it might be what saved the man's life.

"That's true." He nodded. "The *Bratva* doesn't tolerate snitches or bitches amongst its ranks."

"They tolerated your brother fine."

The 9 mm was trained on his chest. "Say that again."

Byron gambled that the man's grief for his brother would temporarily outweigh his need for revenge. At least long enough to give them a window in which to operate. He smiled. "I only had to shoot him once this time. Bigger gun."

While Vladimir was frozen at the mention of his brother, Byron drew his gun from his waist and fired in a single smooth motion. He dropped Vladimir before he could get off a round.

A MILLION THINGS RUSHED through Damara's mind as she watched the scene unfold before her and the other man crumpled. It hurt her heart to see anyone lose their life, but she knew Vladimir wouldn't have had the same qualms.

As he fell, the tarmac burst into action and suddenly there were Italian helicopters landing and Damara could see several Italian navy ships anchored in the bay.

She couldn't help but think that everything really would be okay.

Damara burst from the car and flung herself into his arms, holding him so tightly that she'd never let go.

"I thought I told you to stay in the car," he said softly, his own embrace no less fierce.

"I told you not to get shot and you didn't listen."

"Oh, God, Damara." He buried his face in her hair. "What happens now?"

"We keep doing what we've been doing, just together. I need to hold an emergency election. Do you think Renner will let you stay as my personal protection?"

"Is that what I'll be to you?"

"You'll be my husband. You're the prince of Castallegna. If I'm the Jewel, you're the Heart. Because you're my heart."

"How easily you speak of these things."

"With the same ease with which you speak of death, I speak of life." She pulled away from him. "Are you saying that you've changed your mind?"

Her heart would shatter in a million pieces if he did.

"No, Damara. I just… I'm a mercenary."

"You're a ranger."

"And I can be neither as your husband. What will I do as a dethroned prince?"

"Mostly whatever you like. Are you sure you're not having second thoughts?"

"About you? Never. About me? I just… Remember how I told you I break things?"

She laughed. "You're not going to break me. Haven't you learned that by now?"

"I'm still afraid that all this darkness inside me is going to hurt you."

"All it's done is protect me, brought us to the here and now. I love everything about you, Hawkins. Not just the shiny things."

"Yeah, but you've got more heart than common sense," he teased her.

"I don't think that's a bad thing."

"No, Princess, it's not. You're absolutely perfect." He kissed the top of her head.

The helicopters landed and men in black tactical suits swarmed the area, surrounding them.

Byron was suddenly in his element, taking charge of the commandos and directing the flow of people.

He was so much more than he believed himself to be.

CHAPTER TWENTY-THREE

IT TOOK A DAY to organize the special election, and Damara waited until the news outlets that had so faithfully covered their love story arrived. She wanted all the world to see who and what Castallegna had become.

This transition wasn't meant to be some small, quiet affair. It was a rebirth, and it deserved all the accolades and celebration that came with that.

Once again, she found herself facing the press with Byron Hawkins by her side and Sonja fielding questions.

As much as she'd disliked the woman upon first meeting her, that had all changed. She was very good at what she did, and Damara liked to think she'd convinced her to use her powers for good—at least when she was working for Damara. Together, they could push and pull at the flow and feel of a room until they got exactly the reactions and the questions they wanted. That was no small feat.

One of the first questions: "Italy wants to know what happens now."

She smiled. "Right now? We wait." Her answer was met with some low-key laughter. "That's most of governing, I think. Waiting. The ballots are being counted and tallied. Soon we'll know who our new prime minister is going to be and we've replaced key positions on the Council." Damara took a deep breath. "At this time, I'd also like to thank those who took such an active role in our struggles. Italy, the United States and the hardworking officers of Interpol."

"Are you on the ballot, Princess Damara?"

"No. I'll continue to serve my country and work for social change and equality, but prime minister is a job for someone who is not a Petrakis."

"We've heard some of the people on the street have been writing your name into the ballots."

"When my father first told me of his dream to bring Castallegna to democracy, he said that having a royal in any government position would be no true democracy at all. I believe he's right," she answered.

"What about the ranger?" was the next question.

"Was it all just a sham to get the world to look at Castallegna?"

"I won't deny that I needed the world to see what was happening in my country. But as you can see, my husband is next to me. If it were a sham, I'd be addressing you alone."

"This is for Lt. Hawkins—Prince Byron. How does it feel to have a hollow crown?"

Byron flashed an easy grin. "It was never my crown to start with. As a ranger, I fought for freedom. How could I do any less for my wife?"

She melted and smiled. "He doesn't need a crown to be a prince."

"I'm sure you both know the story of the princess and the marine. That ended poorly. What do you see for yourselves in the future?"

Damara didn't know how to answer that. Thus far,

she'd fielded most of the questions and she wanted to know the answer to this one, as well. She knew he wanted to be with her, but what was that going to be like?

"Happily ever after. That's how this stuff works, right? I got the princess." His mouth curled into that sexy grin.

"All due respect, that's not a real answer. It's romantic, but it doesn't address where you'll live, or how long until you get out of the service..."

The room was suddenly heavy with tension and expectation. Damara thought it was strange they'd been talking about the evolution of a government, a great day in history, and all they cared about was the love story.

"I think that's the best part about it, ma'am," Byron supplied. "We don't know how that's going to work out, but believe me when I say it will."

And she did. Damara utterly believed that it would.

Cameras started flashing fast and furious and she knew it was because of the way she was looking at her husband—as if he set the sun in the sky. For Damara, he did.

He took her hand and kissed it, eyes meeting like the slow draw of mercury. Everything she felt for him flared and burned. The lust, the instant slam of need that ricocheted through her every time he touched her, the joy of knowing that he was hers and the love that was so deep it was part of her on a cellular level. She didn't care who saw it.

There was a tap on her shoulder, and someone handed her an envelope.

"This is the moment we've all been waiting for,"

she said into the microphones. "Before I open this envelope that tells us who our new prime minister shall be, I wanted to share with you my first and last act as ruler of Castallegna. Before me is the bill ratified by the Council that will make us a democratic nation. All that's left is for me to sign it into law. This was my father's dream. This is my dream. Thank you for sharing it with me."

Byron's hand was firm on the small of her back, almost as if he were holding her up. And maybe he was. It was his solid presence and only him that kept her from crying as, with only her signature, she changed the future of her country.

In that moment, she felt her father's presence as keenly as her husband's. He'd be so proud.

She looked around at the members of the Council and the press as she smiled. "It is my great honor to turn this government and sovereignty over to those who will do it best, the people of Castallegna." With that, she scrawled her name on the documents, signing away her royalty and her privilege.

A cheer went up and the cameras were still rolling. All around the world, people saw the princess and the ranger give a country back to the public.

She'd done what she'd set out to do.

"Thank you, Byron. I couldn't have done this without you."

"It's what you were born to do. You would have found another way." He quoted several of their earlier discussions back to her. Damara kept insisting that no matter what, she would have found another way.

"But another way wouldn't have put us here."

The press was still recording everything, but she didn't care.

"Open the envelope, Princess," Sonja encouraged.

Damara wondered who the people had chosen and when she read the name, she smiled. "It is my pleasure to introduce to you the new prime minister of Castallegna, Hamdi Naserdine." He'd been her father's right-hand man, an advocate for human rights. She'd spent many evenings in her youth sharpening her political skills on his.

He was a distinguished gentleman, and had sharp eyes that seemed to see everything. When he came forward, she didn't hesitate to kiss both of his cheeks.

"I know Castallegna is safe in your hands."

"Our hands, Princess Damara. Our hands." He accentuated the point by taking her hands and holding them tight. "But after your honeymoon."

She wanted to say that she couldn't possibly leave, but he was right. From the questions they'd gotten today, the world was still very much interested in the love story.

It would be easy for another faction to move in and try to break this fragile freedom. If the Russians and Americans wanted their ports, others would, too. She wanted to be there, to start programs and education, but Hamdi would make a place for her. And taking a week or two with Byron wouldn't be any great torture.

She could go with him to Texas and help him bury his ghosts the same way he'd helped her bury hers.

And in doing so, she could secure future media interest and keep the world eye on Castallegna as she grew and prospered in relative safety. Then the Americans would have their base and their safe houses, and she'd have an ally, as well.

Her suspicion was proved correct when the next question posed was, "Where are you going on your honeymoon, Princess?"

"Byron hasn't told me."

"Some parts of a marriage shouldn't be open to the public, and that's one of them." He winked and took Damara's hand.

She wanted this to be about Castallegna, not her marriage. So she said, "Without further ado, the prime minister would like address the press."

Hamdi took the microphone.

"IT STILL FEELS WRONG to be leaving at this stage, but I know logically it's what I need to do. Even if it's only for two weeks," Damara said as they were boarding the plane.

"Damara, if you want to, you could hide out at your mother's house for two weeks. You don't have to come with me."

"Yes, I do have to come with you to Texas. There's no way I'd let you do this on your own. After all you've done for me? All you've given up for me?"

"I haven't given up anything for you but my fear, Damara. You changed me, helped me start to heal. Before I met you, I never could've faced Belinda."

"You know that for her, this isn't facing some demon. She's getting another piece of her husband by meeting you."

"I know, and I'm still not sure how I feel about that." Speaking with Belinda Foxworth seemed pointless—

it would just be an experience in pain and learning to rip old wounds open with new weapons.

Byron was sure her invitation to visit wasn't one he was supposed to accept. Not that Belinda would be insincere, but it might have sounded good at the time and she was probably wishing she could take it back, pluck it out of the air like a fly ball and put it back down in the dirt and dust where it belonged.

"I'm sure you're afraid, hopeful, aching and maybe a little excited."

"I'm all of those things and more. How do I tell a woman I'm sorry that it's my fault her husband is dead? I'm sorry that I got to live the life he was denied? I'm sorry that her children don't have a father? I'm sorry that she doesn't have a husband?" he questioned quietly.

"Maybe just like that, if those are the things you need to say to her. But if she felt that way, I don't think she would've invited you to visit the ranch."

"But I want her to. I need her to be angry with me."

"Haven't you punished yourself enough?"

"It doesn't seem right that I get this life. I get to be with you and he's gone. Dust and dirt."

"He's not gone. He lives in her. In his children." Damara paused for a long moment. "He lives in you. Not just in your nightmares, but in the piece of you that wants to do good in the world, the piece of you that wants to honor what he sacrificed."

Byron was uncomfortable with that. It sounded too much like praise. He owed the man a debt of honor, and he had no idea how to repay it.

So he changed the subject. "What's the first thing you want to work on when we get back?"

Her face brightened. "Education for women."

"Do you have a plan?"

"Not yet, but I might have brought some reading materials." She pulled out an overstuffed attaché case.

"Only you would bring work on your honeymoon," he teased.

"And only you would understand." She smiled.

"That's because I know I'll get what I want later."

"You think so?" She flushed.

He reached out and traced a finger down her cheek. "I know so."

"It's a good thing I don't have to be a princess anymore." She nipped at his finger. "I'd never get anything done."

"We seemed to get plenty done."

"But it was hard. So very *hard,*" Damara teased him back.

"You're as bad as I am. You know that, right?"

She laughed, and the sound was music to him. He didn't think Damara would ever be his. He didn't think retirement would suit him. And yet here he was, utterly content with overseeing Damara's security detail personally.

He couldn't help but think about Austin Foxworth again and the life he hadn't been able to live. Damara seemed to sense his retreat into his own head and was content to let him be while she worked.

He liked that she understood that about him and the peaceful silence they could share together. Each moment didn't have to be filled with inane chatter. They could just be.

The flight was interminably long, and Damara was her usual self. She swore she wasn't tired but fell asleep with her papers still in her lap. Byron spent the rest of the flight thinking.

Thinking about what had transpired, what he would say to Belinda.

When the pilot announced they were landing, he had a moment of sudden panic. He couldn't do this. More important, he shouldn't be doing this. He should let sleeping ghosts lie.

Only he supposed Austin wasn't a sleeping ghost. He was a very real presence, and the weight of Byron's guilt was still drowning him. He owed it to Damara to try to put this to rest.

He was glad they'd kept this part of their trip a secret. He didn't want this pain, the remnants of Austin's life, on display like some poor pinned insect under glass.

Damara's hand was tucked into his, and he didn't realize how much strength was in her little hand. He'd thought it before, but the point was driven home over and over again. She kept surprising him. This time it wasn't because of how much she'd done—it was what she didn't do. She was just there, and somehow that shored him up, filled in the holes where the darkness would have been.

Part of him wanted to believe it was some higher power telling him that she could survive him. It was okay to want her, to need her, because she was made of sterner stuff.

When the car turned down a long winding drive and finally pulled up in front of a large house, there was a woman standing outside waiting to greet him.

She was petite, like Damara, but blonde. She was

wearing frayed jeans and cowboy boots, with two little girls clinging to her legs.

Damara released his hand slowly. "Go on. You can do this."

When he got out of the car, he didn't know what to feel first. Everything crashed into him at once.

As did Belinda Foxworth. She flung her arms around him and hugged him tight.

He would've stood on ceremony, he would have kept his distance, but she wouldn't allow it. Her embrace was scalding and soothing at the same time.

"It is so good to meet you, Hawkins."

If not for Damara's warm presence at his back, he might have sobbed like a child. "I'm glad to meet you, too, Belinda. He talked about you all the time. You look just like your picture."

"I know which one you mean. He took it. That was senior skip day back in high school. We went to the lake." She looked wistful but then pursed her lips, as if she was trying to hold something back. "And this must be your lovely princess."

Damara smiled and held out her hand, but Belinda hugged her, too. "Thank you so much for bringing him. I know if he was anything like Austin, he probably didn't want to come."

"It's not that I didn't want to come—"

"But you thought you shouldn't. Now you're here anyway, and I'm glad. I don't know who that guy was who called in, but you needed to know. I don't blame you, and neither would Austin." She was fierce, again so much like Damara.

He wanted to say so much, but he wanted to keep silent at the same time. He didn't want to give her more darkness than what she already had, but something in him demanded he speak. Demanded he do his duty and tell her how her husband died—that even though it was a horrible death, Austin was honorable and strong until the end.

"Are you a real princess? Momma says I shouldn't bother you or ask too many questions," the little girl with blond pigtails and a tiny voice said to Damara.

"Well, you must always listen to your mother. But if it's okay with her, maybe you could show me around and we can ask each other questions. How does that sound?"

Leave it to Damara to know exactly what he needed and how to get him there.

Belinda nodded. *Thank you,* she mouthed to Damara.

The princess walked away with two excited, chattering little girls.

He didn't know where to start. He wished he had Austin's voice in his head now telling him what to say to the woman he'd left behind. The woman that Byron himself had taken him from. He didn't know if he should tell her that he was a good man, because Belinda already knew that. She wouldn't have married him, had his children or grieved for him when he was gone if he hadn't been.

"I dream about him," he confessed.

"Me, too." Belinda nodded. "At first, when the grief was so heavy I thought it was going to crush me, I'd bawl myself to sleep and he'd always tell me, 'There's more to life than this, hoss.'"

A wrecking ball crashed through him. He must've

paled, because Belinda gave a fey smile. "He said that all the time. I take it he's said it to you, too."

"He says it in my dreams." Byron didn't add that it was with his face blown off or carrion eaters picking at his bones.

"Because I wasn't living. And I get the feeling that neither are you." Belinda looked down at her boots. "Shit. I'm sorry. I shouldn't have said that. I really don't know anything about you."

"You can tell me anything you want to tell me, Belinda." He wanted to look down at his feet, at the wide-open landscape behind her, anywhere but in her eyes. There was where his pain lay, his failure. But he forced himself to meet her gaze head-on. "I'd hoped that when I came here, you'd throw things at me. Hit me. Scream at me. Hate me."

"It's not your fault. You did what you thought was best. I knew who and what Austin was when I married him. I knew he could die. He knew it, too. He chose to follow you. He was a ranger."

The itchy feeling he'd had before was nothing like this new sensation. Everything was exposed, raw. It was like walking around without skin.

"I invited you because there's something I think you need to see. It's a memorial to Austin. It's something that he wanted. He had a letter on file that he wanted sent to me if for some reason he didn't come home." Her voice was quiet and almost choked with tears but not quite. Determination laced her words.

Byron was rooted to the spot. If he took a step forward, he knew it would change everything. He realized that he was more comfortable with being born bad than he was with seeing a way to his redemption.

His misery was an armor, and if he moved forward, he might have to shed it. Pick it out of his skin like so much broken glass. Yet, he'd already shed part of it when he'd told Damara he'd stay with her. He'd find a way. He was living his life, loving his life, even though there was some part of him that still thought it was a crime that a man like him could walk away and Austin was left with nothing. His family was left with nothing.

Morbidly, he imagined what it would be like for Damara if the situation were reversed. He'd want whoever had come to speak with her to do anything she asked—even if she asked for the moon.

"You came all this way, and I know Austin would want you to see it."

"I—"

"Come." She took his hand and led him toward the side of the house.

There beneath a tree was a headstone that marked a grave without a body. Yet somehow he knew that Austin Foxworth was more present here than he'd been in his own bones.

"He wanted this here so the girls could come talk to him whenever they needed him. So I wouldn't feel so alone. Even if his body isn't there, I know he is. I know he hears me." Belinda put her hand on his shoulder. "I'll be in the house. Just come on in when you're ready."

Byron sank down on his knees, gripping the headstone with such force his knuckles had gone white.

He choked on his emotion, his body taut and his muscles bulging as if he were going to explode. Byron had nowhere to put his sorrow, his regret—his rage.

His vision blurred and he said it again. "I'm sorry. So fucking sorry."

Recognizing that I volunteered as a Ranger, fully knowing the hazards of my chosen profession, I will always endeavor to uphold the prestige, honor and high esprit de corps of the Rangers. He heard Foxworth's voice reciting the creed in his head, and he focused on the granite stone.

The creed was etched in the stone. This was what he'd wanted. This was his legacy. And this was what he had to say to those who loved him after his death.

Fully knowing the hazards of my profession.

He felt as though Foxworth was there with him. Maybe it was because he'd met the man's wife, because he'd seen his children. He'd been invited into their sacred sanctuary and invited to mourn at their table. In the place where the man had laughed, loved and lived. Whether it was some passing fancy of a burdened soul or a grief-clouded mind, he found comfort in it, and, while he didn't feel peace, he could see it.

Much like hope.

He recited the stanza again and it was as if they were speaking it together, as they had in his nightmare, but this time he wasn't ashamed of his words. This time, he could speak them all.

"Never shall I fail my comrades. I will always keep myself mentally alert, physically strong and morally straight, and I will shoulder more than my share of the task whatever it may be, one hundred percent and then some.

"Gallantly will I show the world that I am a specially selected and well-trained soldier. My courtesy to superior officers, neatness of dress and care of equipment shall set the example for others to follow.

"Energetically will I meet the enemies of my country. I shall defeat them on the field of battle for I am better trained and will fight with all my might. Surrender is not a Ranger word. I will never leave a fallen comrade to fall into the hands of the enemy and under no circumstances will I ever embarrass my country.

"Readily will I display the intestinal fortitude required to fight on to the Ranger objective and complete the mission though I be the lone survivor."

A heavy weight was lifted from his chest and he could breathe again. His surroundings became supernaturally bright, the sun in the sky, the rolling expanse of Texas plains, the scents of the place. He'd not even realized it was a working ranch until that moment.

"Rangers lead the way," he whispered.

Byron thought he'd have so much more to say, but he didn't. He'd said it all. It was all there in the creed. There in the hug he'd shared with Belinda. There in his secret hopes. And there in the world around him.

He patted the back of the stone like he would've the man's back, had he been there. This moment hadn't been an eraser, it didn't change everything, but it changed enough.

Byron reined in his emotions and walked around to the back door, where Belinda was talking with Damara and the girls had changed into their Disney princess costumes and were currently playing with Damara's hair as she chatted.

It was such a simple scene, something that a lot of people would take for granted. Two women talking, children playing. Drinking iced tea. It wasn't anything special. It happened a million times a day in a billion households around the world.

Yet it was special to him.

He couldn't articulate why, and he wanted to. So he was content to watch them for a moment.

"Hey, you ready to come in? A glass of sweet tea?" Belinda offered.

Damara started to turn to him, but one of the girls stopped her. "I'm not done with your braid. Hair first. Boys later."

Damara laughed and said, "As you wish."

"Oooh, Momma. She said it. She said it!"

Belinda looked embarrassed.

"What did I say?" Damara asked.

"*The Princess Bride.* It's a movie. In it, the farm boy tells the girl he loves her by saying 'as you wish.' It's the best thing ever," the older girl said.

"Last month it was *Pretty in Pink* and now it's *The Princess Bride,*" Belinda explained.

"I see. I think we'll have to watch that when we get home," Damara said.

"You have to," the youngest girl said. "Because you're a princess and you're a bride. Byron is your Wesley."

"He is? Is Wesley a prince?"

"No, silly. He's a farm boy pirate."

"I'm glad you came, even if it was just for an hour. You're welcome back anytime," Belinda said. "Even if it's just to talk to Austin."

"Thank you, Belinda. You take care of those girls."

"I try." She smiled.

Marie stopped fussing with Damara's hair and

walked over to him. "You're the man who knew my daddy?"

"Yes." He didn't know if he could take any more of this today. His battered heart was already full again and ready to break. He'd kept it sealed off for so long.

"Did you like him?"

"I liked your daddy very much. I called him my brother." He didn't know if she could understand what he meant.

"That's what Momma said. I was just checking. If you're daddy's brother, then you're my family, too." She hugged him.

And he thought he was going to die. That her little arms would smash him into a million pieces.

"You need anything, Belinda, anything at all, you call us," he said when Austin's daughter released him.

"Thank you." She looked at the girls. "I have to talk in private for a minute. Our friends have to leave. So you run on upstairs."

The girls did as they were told without fussing, although they did turn around and wave.

"I want you to know that the same applies to you. If you need anything, you come straight here."

As if he'd ever do anything to put Belinda in danger. Not a chance.

"I see that look on your face, Ranger. It was the same one that Austin got when he was just going to humor me. I mean it. He would've wanted you to be safe. I miss him every day, but I know he died for something bigger. He was trying to help people. And if Uganda hadn't happened, you might not have been in a position to help the princess. You've brought democracy to a whole country. Austin would've been so proud of you. Hell, I'm sure he is watching over you and I'm sure he is proud."

"You're welcome to come visit us anytime. Your girls are beautiful," Damara said. "I had a good time with them."

"I'm sorry they invited themselves to Castallegna." She looked slightly embarrassed.

"We'd be so happy to have them as long as you'd like to stay." Damara sighed, looking up the stairs after the girls.

"I think you're amazing. I'm glad there are women like you in the world that my girls can look up to."

Damara blushed. "I don't know about that. I just do what I can."

"That's all any of us can do," Belinda said. "Are you sure you can't stay longer?"

"No. The paparazzi seem too interested in where we're going. I wouldn't want to bring that down on you. I'm sure by now, they've figured out we'll be here sooner or later."

"We know how to deal with trespassers in Texas." Belinda grinned. "Austin didn't marry a fool."

"I can certainly see that." Byron nodded.

Damara hugged her and kissed both of her cheeks. "Thank you."

"Take care of yourself, Belinda."

"I will."

When they were in the car again, Damara asked him, "Are you sure you didn't want to stay longer?"

"I couldn't."

She seemed to understand.

Byron knew he wouldn't hear Austin's voice ever again, and that was how it should be. He'd put him to rest in his head along with most of his other demons. He still had a few doubts, a few shadows, but what man didn't? He'd already started moving forward, he'd promised Damara a good life, and he was determined to give it to her.

"This doesn't look like the way back to the airport," she said.

"No, it sure doesn't, does it?"

"What did you do?"

"It was on a ship that I first reached out for what I wanted, and it was on a tiny boat that we talked about hopes and dreams and stars. And all the other things I thought were bullshit. So it's on a ship that we're going home to Castallegna. That's our honeymoon."

EPILOGUE

ONCE ON BOARD the ship in Galveston and settled in a state room, Byron wasted no time pulling Damara into his arms.

"What are you doing?"

"Honeymoon was supposed to start when we left the reception. We're late. I'm just catching up."

She flitted out of his embrace. "I thought you said once we left the reception it was all over."

"I lied. Come here."

"You'll have to catch me." She twisted away from him, but he plucked her back easily and she laughed.

Byron had no words for how he felt about her. So he kissed her. He brushed his lips across hers softly at first—reverently. Her lips tasted like sweet wine, and he wanted to drink her in. Byron threaded his hands through her hair and enjoyed the silky texture as it curled around his fingers.

Byron kissed her until her lips were swollen and bee-stung, and she rubbed her body against his with wanton abandon.

He moved down to her throat, where he suckled at the pulse and kneaded that tender bit of flesh lightly between his teeth until it was just a little sensitive; then he laved his tongue over that bit of skin.

It drew the first moan from her, her nails scoring his shoulders. It would be the first of many.

He peeled her clothes from her body, and each time was still like the first. Each time was still like unwrapping a gift that he couldn't believe was his. His hands moved over her, fingertips skimming flesh ever so lightly. She responded to every brush of skin on skin.

Byron rose above her and just looked, drank in the sight of her as he had the taste. She lay with her hair a dark halo around her head, those lips still so swollen and ripe. And then she smiled.

"What are you looking at?"

"The most beautiful woman in the world."

She looked away, seeming almost embarrassed by the praise.

He dipped his head to her throat again, and, before long, she'd lost all sense of self-consciousness. Or so it seemed as evidenced by the naughty things she whispered in his ear, but he continued with his planned strategy. He wanted her strung so tight that all it would take would be for him to play the right note and she'd come undone.

Byron moved down to her breasts, taking one taut nipple gently between his teeth as he'd done with that tender bit of skin at her throat. He worked it softly until she was clawing at his back again and arching up to his caress, demanding more—always more. Then he moved to the other, his fingers replacing his mouth and plucking at the bud damp from his tongue.

By the time Byron finally moved to between her thighs she was right on the edge and begging. He touched his tongue to her in the most decadent of kisses, and she was so damn sweet, he just couldn't get enough of her.

She unraveled around his caress, shuddering and spasming as the jolts of pleasure rocked her. He'd missed this so much, not only the physical release but the physical connection. The mark of his touch on her skin, the taste of her, of knowing she was meant for him.

He slid into her while she was still trembling with her release, her sweet heat contracting around him. Byron pushed them both higher, hips rocking, hands still teasing her flesh until she was clinging to him like a life raft in a hurricane and screaming his name all over again.

Indeed, there was nothing more to life than this: his wife safe in his arms, and all the years of their life spread before them in the best mission he'd ever taken on. To give his princess happily ever after.

* * * * *

JULIE PLEC

From the creator of *The Originals*, the hit spin-off television show of *The Vampire Diaries*, come three never-before-released prequel stories featuring the Original vampire family, set in 18th century New Orleans.

Available now!

Coming March 31!

Coming May 26!

Family is power. The Original vampire family swore it to each other a thousand years ago. They pledged to remain together always and forever. But even when you're immortal, promises are hard to keep.

Pick up your copies and visit
www.TheOriginalsBooks.com
to discover more!

www.HQNBooks.com

PHTOS0215R2

***New York Times* bestselling author**

KAT MARTIN

brings you the irresistible story of one unlikely couple's fight for their future

Real estate agent Julie Ferris is enjoying a day at the beach with her sister when a strange charge fills thc air, and under the hot Malibu sun, time stops altogether. Neither sister can explain their "lost day"—nor the headaches and horrific nightmares that follow—but Julie chalks it up to the stress she's been under since her boss's son took over Donovan Real Estate.

Patrick Donovan would be a real catch, if not for his notorious playboy lifestyle. But when a cocaine-fueled heart attack nearly kills him, Patrick makes an astonishingly fast—and peculiar—recovery. Julie barely recognizes the newly sober Patrick and she can't help sensing something just isn't…right.

As Julie's feelings for Patrick intensify, she's about to discover how that day at the beach links her newfound happiness with all her suspicions…

Available now, wherever books are sold!

Be sure to connect with us at:

Harlequin.com/Newsletters

Facebook.com/HarlequinBooks

Twitter.com/HarlequinBooks

www.MIRABooks.com

MKM1734